A Deadly Clue

Also available by Victoria Gilbert

The Hunter and Clewe Mysteries

A Killer Clue
A Cryptic Clue

The Campus Sleuth Mysteries

Schooled in Murder

The Book Lover's B&B Mysteries

A Fatal Booking
Reserved for Murder
Booked for Death

The Blue Ridge Library Mysteries

Death and the Librarian
Murder Checks Out
Death in the Margins
Renewed for Murder
A Deadly Edition
Bound for Murder
Past Due for Murder
Shelved Under Murder
A Murder for the Books

The Mirror of Immortality Series

Scepter of Fire
Crown of Ice

A Deadly Clue

A HUNTER AND CLEWE MYSTERY

Victoria Gilbert

NEW YORK

Books should be disposed of and recycled according to local requirements.
All paper materials used are FSC compliant.

Published in the United States by Crooked Lane Books, an imprint of
The Quick Brown Fox & Company LLC.

Crooked Lane Books and its logo are trademarks of The Quick Brown Fox & Company LLC.

Library of Congress Catalog-in-Publication data available upon request.

ISBN (hardcover): 979-8-89242-215-4
ISBN (ebook): 979-8-89242-216-1

Cover design by Alan Ayers

Printed in the United States.

www.crookedlanebooks.com

Crooked Lane Books
34 West 27th St., 10th Floor
New York, NY 10001

First Edition: January 2026

The authorized representative in the EU for product safety and compliance is eucomply OÜPärnu mnt 139b-14, 11317 Tallinn, Estonia,
hello@eucompliancepartner.com, +33757690241

10 9 8 7 6 5 4 3 2 1

Dedicated to everyone
who still believes
in love, hope, kindness,
and dreams.

Keep believing - our world
needs you!

Chapter One

A garden in winter is like a closed book—all its wonders are concealed.

From my walks through the extensive gardens at Aircroft, the estate owned by my employer, wealthy businessman Cameron Clewe, I could picture the herbs and flowers hidden under the cover of bare branches and brown mulch. But on a cold January day, only a few evergreens provided a splash of color.

Maintaining a fast pace, I reached the steps leading up to a marble-columned, open-sided pavilion with a timber roof. I paused at a koi pond. In warmer seasons, a waterfall tumbled down a stepped water feature that was flanked by the marble stairs. But in winter the fountain at the top of the steps was drained and the pond covered with a domed greenhouse structure to prevent the water from freezing. I couldn't see the fish through the green plastic panels but knew they were fine, as they were checked regularly by an expert.

I turned to face the back façade of the sprawling Aircroft mansion. A long flagstone path, bordered on one side by the now sleeping beds and on the other by a rectangle of faded grass, was mirrored by a matching path on the other side of the garden.

Striding down one of the paths was a tall, slender figure in a knee-length black wool coat. Open over a cream fisherman's cable-knit sweater and turquoise turtleneck, the coat's unbuttoned front edges flapped in the sharp wind. The man wore gloves but no hat, and the winter sunlight lit the tips of his shaggy auburn hair with flame.

"Jane," he called out as he approached me. "You're finally here."

I pushed back the hood of my navy down coat. "On the second Monday in January, as promised."

"Yes, yes, I know." Cam stopped in front of me, his sea-green gaze focused on my face. "Did you have a good trip?"

"Of course. New York is always magical during the holidays, and I got to spend time with my daughter. What could be better?"

Cam thrust his hands into the pockets of his coat. "How is Bailey? I assume you saw her show?"

"Twice, actually. And she's doing great." I smiled as the image of my thirty-two-year-old actress daughter flashed through my mind. "They have hopes that the musical can make the leap from off- to on-Broadway."

"I wish I could see that," Cam said

I studied him for a moment. "You can, anytime you want. I'll even get you a free ticket."

"Navigating New York might be a little beyond my capability. I know you think I should continue to push my boundaries . . ."

I nodded. "Absolutely."

"But a city like New York can intimidate the average person, much less someone who has trouble dealing with even small crowds."

"Somebody could accompany you. Me, for instance, or"—I offered him a sly smile—"Lauren. The way you make her work twenty-four-seven, I'm sure she'd enjoy an all-expenses-paid getaway."

Cam slid his hands from his pockets and waved this suggestion aside. "She just had a break. After you left, she decided to join her family for the holidays, leaving me alone."

"That's not entirely true, is it?" I tipped my head to one side. "Fess up. I bet you didn't allow either Jenna or Mateo more than a day or two off."

Cam's lips thinned. "They didn't ask for more than that. Besides, I gave them both a bonus."

"Glad to hear it." I reached out to lay my gloved fingers on his arm. "Sorry, I shouldn't tease you right after getting back. I know Aircroft can feel empty when there aren't many visitors, much less with limited staff. Speaking of which," I added, lifting my hand, "how was Christmas dinner? Mateo told me he was cooking a feast for your grandmother and great-uncle."

Cam's face paled, throwing the smattering of freckles over his high cheekbones into high relief. "I'd rather not discuss that fiasco."

I studied him with narrowed eyes. It had been less than six months since Cam had learned that his biological father, Rafe Glenn, had gone missing. *And that he has a living grandmother and great-uncle,* I thought. *Neither of whom ever disclosed their existence until last summer. Far too late in Cam's opinion, and mine. Long past the time when a lonely, motherless child could've used their love and support.*

Which was why I empathized with Cam's reluctance to welcome them into his life. Lily Glenn and her younger brother Gordy had made several attempts to meet with Cam after they'd revealed their family connection, all of which he'd refused. He'd only contacted them by phone and email, and then simply in relation to the ongoing search for his missing father. I also knew he'd been convinced to invite Lily and Gordy for Christmas dinner because I, the librarian he'd hired to catalog his extensive book collections, and his personal assistant, Lauren Walker, had talked him into it.

"I'm guessing it didn't go well." I offered him a sympathetic smile.

"Chekhov would've taken notes. That's all I'm going to say."

I shook my head. "That bad, huh?" Since my daughter was an actress, I'd seen several Chekhov plays, all of which had depicted highly dysfunctional families.

"I tried my best, but I'm afraid my resentment got the better of me." Cam tapped his foot against the flagstones in a waltz beat. He often felt compelled to do things in threes, a symptom of his untreated obsessive-compulsive disorder. That, combined with his anxiety and a slight case of agoraphobia, meant he rarely ventured off the estate.

It was a shame. He'd been doing better, visiting me at my garage apartment from time to time as well as enjoying a few meals out with friends. *Until the news of his father's disappearance and his realization of the abandonment of his grandmother and great-uncle,* I thought, with a frown. *That's set him back.*

I pulled my hood back over my short salt-and-pepper hair. "Well, I think I'm going to go inside. Cold and my old bones don't get along these days."

"You're always telling me that sixty-two isn't that old," Cam said.

"Okay, then let's say I'm going in because I have a stack of books to catalog," I headed toward the house at a brisk walk.

Cam kept pace with me. "Speaking of which, I have a mission for you."

"Related to the search for your birth father?" I cast him a sidelong glance.

"No, something else." Cam cleared his throat. "I need you to pick up some books I bought from an estate sale."

I wiped away the dampness the cold wind had drawn from my eyes. "You can't have them shipped here? What's so valuable?"

"That isn't the reason. Anyway, it's a small collection of books, so it shouldn't be an issue transporting it by car." Cam's long stride had taken him a few paces in front of me. He paused to allow me to catch up. "Do you remember me talking about Macnamara Stewart?"

"The man who liked to best your stepfather at auctions for rare books and paintings and such?"

Cam grimaced. "Right, and often did, much to Al's chagrin."

"You said Mac Stewart was even richer than Albert Clewe, which must have contributed to the rivalry."

"He was. Mac also outlived Al by quite a few years. He passed away about four months ago, age ninety-something." Cam stopped at the entrance to the kitchen garden, where his chef, Mateo Marin, grew herbs and vegetables. "Mac sold me a few items from his book collection not long before he died, but fell ill before he could have them shipped to Aircroft."

I lifted my head to meet Cam's gaze. "You're afraid the family doesn't know which books you bought?"

"I'm sure they don't. It was a private deal between us." Cam clasped his gloved hands in front of his chest. "The family seems to have little interest in books, even though Mac was a connoisseur. As I mentioned, he often competed with Al when valuable books or antiques went on the market. That's actually how they became acquainted in the first place."

I pulled open the door to the mudroom attached to Aircroft's expansive kitchen. "Were they friends?"

"Not really." Cam grabbed the upper edge of the door to follow me inside. "Although they did socialize. We hosted various members of the Stewart clan here from time to time."

"Which means you've met some of them." I sat down on a bench to pull off my boots and slip on the loafers I'd left in the mudroom.

Cam remained standing, balancing himself by pressing a palm against the plaster wall as he changed his shoes. "Just in passing. It was Al entertaining them, not me. But back to the mission—I need you to take the bill of sale Mac sent me and find the actual volumes in his personal library."

"In other words, you want to make sure the editions and copyright dates match what you bought." I tugged up my wool socks. "Are you afraid no one in the Stewart clan is capable of doing that?"

Cam shot me a sardonic smile. "Let's just say I'd rather not have any books shipped here, only to have to send some volumes back. Not to mention the possibility of someone in the family selling off Mac's personal property without the knowledge that a few items already belong to me."

"You could call them, or do a video chat."

"I don't believe that would suffice. I will have Lauren call to alert the Stewarts to the business transaction, and tell them exactly which volumes are involved, but I'd like you, as a professional, to verify anything they pull from the shelves." Cam shrugged off his coat and hung it on one of the wooden pegs lining one wall of the mud room. "Mac told me none of his descendants had any clue about the value of his library, which is how he wanted to keep things. He said if they knew, books might disappear before he could sell them to reputable collectors." Cam shrugged. "Apparently he didn't trust everyone in his family."

"Or anyone, it seems." I stood up to face him. "Okay, so I need to go in person to make sure you get what you paid for. When do you want me to undertake this mission?"

Cam laid a hand on my shoulder. "Tomorrow. Before any member of the Stewart family realizes the actual value of the books and changes their mind."

Chapter Two

If there was one person who might be able to help me understand what den of society elites I'd be walking into the next day, it was my landlord and neighbor, Vincent Fisher. Retired as a reporter for a local newspaper, Vince still had numerous connections in the field of journalism. It was also likely he'd covered the Stewart family in the past.

I parked my compact car in the small gravel lot in front of Vince's 1920s brick bungalow, next to a vehicle belonging to Vince's girlfriend, Donna Valenti. The garage where Vince had parked his car was off to one side, with the steep wooden stairs that led to my upstairs apartment still draped in dried-out climbing rose vines. It was a convenient rental—relatively inexpensive and only a short walk to downtown Bradfordville, the small town not far from both Winston-Salem and Greensboro. I crossed to the covered porch and rang the doorbell, which was answered immediately by a stocky man of medium height.

"Hello, so nice to see you," Vince said, his hazel eyes sparkling behind the lenses of his wire-framed glasses. "You haven't been by since you got back from New York. Please, come in and share all the details."

"Glad to, but I do have an ulterior motive for this visit," I said, as I followed him into the house.

Although I'd visited Vince's home many times before, the interior always surprised me. Vince hadn't changed the exterior of his vintage home, but he'd adopted a totally different style inside. It was sleek Scandinavian modern, with blonde wood floors and trim, low-backed ivory sofas, and sculptural wooden chairs. Everything was simple, but stylish.

"Jane, long time no see." Relaxing in one of the wooden chairs, Donna Valenti waved and cast me a bright smile. A plump woman who always looked put-together, she was wearing a long-sleeved crimson wool dress with a hem that fell below her knees. Unlike Vince's thatch of gray hair, the pewter-colored ponytail that draped over Donna's shoulder was threaded with numerous black strands. Laugh lines crinkled the corners of her dark brown eyes, while her smooth skin and flushed cheeks exuded youthful energy.

I answered Donna's greeting with a nod as I sat down on the sofa facing her chair. "I just got back over the weekend, and, before you ask, New York was a blast."

"How's Bailey? She must be busy." Vince headed into the kitchen, which was separated from the living room by a quartz-topped island.

"Very. She has a performance every day except Monday, and two on Saturday." I crossed my legs and rested one elbow on the sofa's armrest. "But she loves it, so she never complains."

Donna scooted closer to the front edge of her chair. "Is she still keeping in touch with that young man? You know, the chauffer who's actually a writer. What's his name?"

"Taylor Iverson, and yes, they're still chatting over texts and video calls at least twice a week."

Donna clapped her hands. "I knew those two were meant for each other!"

"I don't know about that, but they do seem to get along well. I mean, it's clear they're friends. As for anything else . . ." I shrugged. "Anyway, I dropped by this evening because Cam asked me to drive to the Stewart estate tomorrow to pick up some books. I'd like to know a little more about the family before my visit, just so I don't commit a faux-pas or two."

"I'd imagine, being the librarian you are, you've already done some research." Vince held up a wine glass. "Red or white?"

I leaned back into the sturdy sofa cushions. "White, please, and actually, I haven't done much. I know the basics; that's it. Of course, everyone in North Carolina has at least heard of the family, but I don't know any details."

Donna tapped her short fingernails against the arm of the chair. "You're probably aware they made their fortune in tobacco, back when that was the state's main crop."

"Yes, that's common knowledge," I said. "But they left that business behind a decade or so ago, didn't they?"

"They did." Vince crossed the room and handed me a glass of wine before sitting down next to me. "Just like Cam, they divested their holdings in problematic ventures. Well, obvious ones." Vince took a sip of his own wine. "I'm sure they still have money in other investments that aren't exactly prohealth or environmentally friendly, but the tobacco trade was far too visible. When Macnamara Stewart stepped down, the first thing his oldest son Duff did as the new CEO was to exit the tobacco business."

"Duff must be my age," I said, setting my wineglass on a coaster on the sleek side table.

"A little older. He's sixty-eight." Donna leaned forward, flipping her braid behind her shoulder. "Three years older than me. Not that I ever met him, but I often saw his photo on the society pages of the newspaper. Always with a different girl."

"I suppose he was considered quite a catch back then," I said.

Donna lifted her own wine glass from the glass-topped table next to her chair. "Most definitely. He had those all-American looks and well"—she winked and took a sip—"he was rich. Really rich, not like the sons of doctors and lawyers who thought they were all that when I was a girl."

"Duff hasn't actually been CEO as long as you'd think," Vince said, swirling the wine in his glass. "Mac Stewart refused to hand over the reins until he was in his eighties, so Duff didn't get promoted until he was fifty."

Donna nodded. "And I'd take bets that Duff's going to follow in his father's footsteps and keep working beyond normal retirement age."

"Probably, even though he certainly wouldn't need to. His wife, Sharon, is focused on charity work, and his youngest child, Malcolm, is an artist and teacher at the Sawtooth Center in downtown Winston-Salem. Neither of them are involved in the business, but his oldest, Ainsley, is forty and the director of marketing for the family holdings. There's also an older son—Finlay, called Finn. He's thirty-eight and is the chief financial officer. Normally, you'd expect Duff Stewart to step aside for one of them to become CEO, but from what I've heard, he has no intention of doing so anytime soon." Vince glanced at Donna. "More wine, dear?"

"No, I'd better stop at this." Donna set her empty glass back down. "I need to stay sensible enough to help make dinner," she added with a grin.

"Good point." Vince smiled at her before turning to me. "Speaking of which, would you like to join us? We're just having spaghetti and a salad, but you're welcome to stay."

"Thanks, but I think I want to head home after I collect more intel for tomorrow. I have a few leftovers in the fridge I need to eat and, honestly, tonight I just want to put on pajamas and watch mindless TV before bed."

"Totally understand." Donna leaned back in her chair. "I think lounging about at home is an underrated pleasure."

"Anway, speaking of all that information, I suppose you've heard that the Stewart family has had to deal with a few tragedies in the past," Vince said.

"I seem to recall something about one of Mac Stewart's children dying young." I cast Vince a questioning glance. "It was a suicide, wasn't it?"

"Sadly, yes. That was Kimberly Stewart, or I should say, Kimberly Stewart Ward." Vince frowned. "I had to cover that story for my college paper, and it was a shocker. Kimberly was barely twenty-six and had only been married for a year when she took her life."

A shiver vibrated through my shoulders as the image of my daughter flashed through my mind. "How terrible. I can't imagine losing Bailey like that."

"It was dreadfully sad. There were pictures and news footage from the funeral, and it all seemed so tragic." Donna pressed one hand to her heart. "The reports didn't go into a lot of detail, but I did read it was an overdose of some kind. Such a loss."

Vince nodded. "In more ways than one. From what I heard, Mac's wife, Leonora, never really recovered and passed away from cancer a few years later. There were rumors she simply gave up rather than pursuing the more rigorous treatments Mac urged her to undergo."

"It's the same old story—money doesn't mean you don't have problems," I said.

Donna shook her head. "It certainly doesn't. In fact, I think it sometimes makes things worse." She shifted her gaze to Vince. "There was something else, wasn't there? Some sort of accident involving members of the Stewart family?"

"That was definitely before Kimberly died, but yes, there was a bad car crash. I don't remember many details because it happened when I was at college and hadn't yet joined the school paper," Vince said.

Donna's dark eyelashes fluttered. "I vaguely remember it. There was a flurry of coverage that died down surprisingly quickly."

"Probably due to the Stewart family influence. I believe it involved Duff and his cousins, Lucas and Gabriel Neri. I think Lucas is around Duff's age and Gabriel is several years younger, but like I said, I don't recall all the specifics." Vince tapped his chin. "I assume you have a library card, Jane? The county system offers digitized copies of local and major state newspapers you can search online. You might be able to find out more that way, if you're interested."

"I've used those resources before, but thanks for reminding me. It's one of the benefits of having a library card that's easy to overlook." I finished off my wine and set down my glass. "Anyway, I suppose I'll only be meeting Duff and his wife tomorrow, unless other members of the family live with them."

Vince sat forward, gripping his knees. "Ainsley does still live on the estate. She was married briefly but came back home after her divorce. Mainly to indulge her passion for horses, I think."

"Yeah, she's won numerous jumping and dressage championships. I've also heard that her niece, Ara, is an excellent junior rider. That's Finn and his wife, Soo Jin's, thirteen-year-old daughter," Donna said. "They live in Clemmons, not far from the Stewart estate. One of those exclusive developments. But Ara has the use of the Stewart family stables." Donna shot me a conspiratorial look. "I only know this because my friend's granddaughter also rides and has competed against Ara. Honestly, I've heard way too much about the girl."

"Well, I shouldn't take up more of your time," I said as I stood up. "Thanks for the wine, and the information. I now feel less like I'll be diving into unknown waters tomorrow."

"Happy to help." Vince rose to his feet to face me. "Let me know if you need any more background on the Stewarts. I still have friends working in the news business."

"I know, and it does come in handy," I said, with a smile. "Not to mention your rather encyclopedic knowledge of people here and throughout the state, Donna."

"Oh, my dear, call it what it is," Donna said, with another grin. "Gossip."

"Gossip or not, it can be very useful." I crossed the room but paused at the door to add, "I'll let you know what happens after my little excursion tomorrow."

As I opened the door and stepped onto the porch, Donna called out, "You'd better."

Chapter Three

Fortunately, despite it being January, the weather was clear for my trip to the Stewart estate. Most of the drive was on the busy interstate where I had to drive ten miles over the posted speed limit just to avoid being run over by other vehicles, so I breathed a sigh of relief as I took the exit off the highway. Following the directions from my GPS, I turned onto rustic roads until I reached the estate.

The entrance was marked by white brick columns topped with black metal pedestals and spires. There was no sign to designate the estate, and surprisingly, no gate. I drove down a winding blacktopped driveway. It was bordered on both sides by oak trees planted so close together that their bare branches interlaced overhead, drawing a dark filagree against the clear sky.

Spying two large barns and a paddock at the edge of one of the fields adjacent to the driveway, I remembered Vince and Donna's information about Ainsley Stewart and her niece. Behind the row of trees lining the drive, white wooden fencing proclaimed wealth as loudly as the barns and acres of rolling fields.

I slowed the car as it crested a hill to catch a panoramic view of the Stewart mansion. Unlike Aircroft, which had a taller central section and two long wings bent at slight angles like open arms, this house was much less welcoming. While Aircroft's natural stone façade and loam brown trim gave off an earthy quality, this home's white-painted brick and contrasting forest green shutters and trim gleamed like fine porcelain under the bright winter sun. Everything was perfectly manicured and maintained, from the formal landscaping to the copper-roofed portico that allowed visitors to be dropped off at the main entrance without suffering any effects from the weather. Massive stone urns holding evergreens trimmed into spires flanked the tall double doors.

It looks like a hotel, or a country club, I thought as I drove closer. *I feel like I should be arriving with luggage.*

I pulled up under the portico and parked in one of several designated spots off to the left side. After yanking off my gloves and shoving them into the pocket of my coat, I climbed out of my car and surveyed the house's façade, immediately realizing it wasn't a true vintage home.

Not that Aircroft was ancient, having been constructed in the 1920s, but this house looked like something built in the 1980s. I stared at the net of tiny white lights that covered the evergreens, wondering whether the decoration was a leftover from the holiday season or was used year-round.

I stepped forward, but before I could press the bell, the massive front doors—dark mahogany crisscrossed with bands of metal—swung open. A solitary figure appeared, outlined by the light spilling from the entry hall.

"Welcome," said the woman, whose simple black pantsuit, crisp white blouse, and sensible shoes marked her as a maid or housekeeper. "You must be Mr. Stewart's visitor from Aircroft."

I removed my sunglasses and tucked them into my purse. "Yes, I'm Jane Hunter, and as Mr. Clewe's assistant must've informed you, I've been sent to personally pick up the books purchased by Cameron Clewe."

"Of course." The woman's smile was more practiced than welcoming. "I'm Ms. Warner, the housekeeper. Please come in. I'm afraid Mr. Stewart is still tied up on a business call, but he asked me to direct you to the library."

Trailing her into the mansion's front hall, I was momentarily dazzled by the enormous crystal chandelier hanging above the parquet floor. It wasn't antique or even vintage, but rather an aggressively modern piece that featured icicle-shaped crystals of various lengths dangling from a metal grid.

Like so many knives or swords poised to rain down on an unsuspecting victim, I thought, lowering my gaze to take in the staircase that began at an open balcony over the foyer and swept down in a wide curve of white wood and elaborate black wrought-iron railings.

"This way, please. Since Mr. Clewe's assistant said you were bringing the bill of sale, Mr. Stewart informed me that you should feel free to check over the books before he arrives," Ms. Warner said, leading me through one of several arches enclosing the foyer.

Walking into the library, which had floor-to-ceiling white bookcases on two walls as well as a shorter dual-sided bookcase dividing the room in two, I immediately noticed a large oil painting of a young woman hanging above the white marble fireplace.

Ms. Warner registered my interest. "That's Mr. Stewart's sister, Kimberly," she said in a hushed tone. "She tragically passed away many years ago." She examined the painting, frown lines wrinkling her brow. "I've been told the artist caught her likeness, but not her gentle spirit."

A shaft of light from the room's front window fell onto the marble hearth like a pool of gold. I looked up, fixing my gaze on the painting. *Gentle?* I thought, observing the set of Kimberly's lips and the hint of fire in her dark brown eyes. *No, the painter didn't capture that, if that truly was her nature.*

The painter had placed Kinberly in front of a sky-blue drape that brought out the gold highlights in her light brown hair. Standing beside a small table decorated with a vase holding sunflowers, Kimberly stared straight out at the viewer with disinterest. Only her hands, clasped tightly at the waist of her simple sapphire-blue dress, betrayed any emotion.

She's holding herself together, I thought. *Fighting to keep from flying apart. She appears still and calm, but that isn't what she was feeling.*

I was certain I was right, because I'd seen that look and posture before.

It seemed Kimberly had been just as nervy as Cam, and just as determined to keep her anxiety hidden.

Chapter Four

Ms. Warner directed my attention to a pile of books stacked on top of the short bookcase. "Mr. Stewart had his secretary pull the books from Mr. Cameron's list, but I know you need to double-check them. Please feel free to start that process. I must take care of something in the kitchen, but Mr. Stewart will join you shortly."

"Thanks so much," I called out as Ms. Warner left hastily. Strolling over to the bookcase, I pulled the bill of sale from my purse and began checking the inventory list against the stack of books. Cam had only purchased ten volumes, so it didn't take long to determine that the books matched his bill of sale. When I completed my examination and stepped back, I caught the heel of my loafer on the edge of a rug covering a portion of the light oak flooring.

A swear word escaped my lips as I stumbled forward and grabbed the top edge of the bookcase to keep from falling. Unfortunately, my action disturbed the stack of books, sending one of them sailing to the floor on the opposite side of the bookcase.

Obviously alerted by the noise, a man's voice called out, "Excuse me, who are you and what are you doing here?"

I straightened and surveyed the other half of the room. "I'm sorry, I didn't realize someone was here."

An older man sat slumped in an armchair upholstered in fawn-colored leather, a closed book clutched in his bony hands. Thin to the point of gauntness, his deep-set onyx eyes provided the only life to his hollow-cheeked face. At first glance I assumed he was older than me by at least a decade, but as I looked closer, I noticed that his thinning chestnut-brown hair showed no signs of gray.

This isn't Duff Stewart, I realized, remembering Donna's mention of Duff's all-American-boy looks as well as images from family pictures I'd skimmed online. I didn't recall seeing this man, but was certain I'd seen someone with his angular features in a few of the photos.

I squared up the book stack. "I'm Jane Hunter, a librarian. I work for Cameron Clewe, cataloging his book collections."

Fixing me with a hooded-eye stare, the man examined me for a moment, then smiled. "Ah, right. Duff told me someone was coming to pick up a few of Mac's books today. I'm Gabe Neri."

Leonora Neri Stewart, I thought. *Duff's mom. He looks like photos of his mother I found in my online research on the family.*

Gabe rose to his feet, gripping his book in one hand. He wavered for a second before he found his balance. "Nice to meet you." Reaching the bookcase, he bent down to retrieve the book that had tumbled to the floor. "Thankfully, this doesn't appear to be damaged."

"That's good. I'd hate to have to explain a broken spine to Cam." Facing him, I noticed that his skin, while pale, wasn't crisscrossed with many lines. *Perhaps he's ill, rather than elderly.* "I'm guessing you're a cousin."

Gabe's eyes narrowed as he looked me over. "It seems you've heard of my family."

I opened my mouth and snapped it shut again before I blurted out a question about his involvement in a long-ago car accident. "I think most people in the state have, considering your connection to the Stewarts. I believe your father was Leonora Stewart's brother?"

Gabe pressed the two books he held to his chest. "Correct. He and his sister were very close, so the two families have always remained in touch, even after the older generation passed. But to be clear, I don't actually live here, or even nearby. I have a condo in Asheville. I just drove in today because of tonight's family gathering to celebrate Finn's birthday. That's Duff's son," he added. "I usually don't join these things, but I like Finn and decided to make an exception."

"I see. I suppose your brother is coming as well?"

"Lucas? Yes, he'll be here. He lives in Winston, but still seems to finagle an overnight stay out of Duff whenever he visits." Gabe cast me a wry smile. "It's so he doesn't have to drive after the party. He likes his cocktails, you see."

I forced a smile. "It's nice for a family to be close. I'm afraid I've never experienced much of that. I was an only child, and both my parents died rather young. They were only children as well, which really made the family tree wither."

"So just a nuclear family?" Gabe's thin lips twitched. "Or perhaps you live alone, like me?"

"I do, but I have a daughter. Kicked out the ex-husband years ago." I flippantly tossed this off, despite the punch in the stomach memories of my marriage always evoked. "Bailey doesn't live with me, though. She's thirty-two and out on her own."

"You don't look old enough to have a child in their thirties," Gabe said, with a smile.

"Thank you, but since I'm sixty-two, it's easily possible," I said. "Anyway, I finished checking over these books, so if you'll excuse me . . ."

Gabe's gaze remained fixed on my face. "You're taking the books to Aircroft, I assume?"

"Yes. I'll be cataloging them and adding them to Cam's library. Which reminds me—I need that book that fell."

Gabe's gaze shifted to the stacked books. "I heard Cameron Clewe has a new hobby. Something about investigating cold cases, Miss Marple-style?"

"If you mean as an amateur detective, yes. Although I'm not sure Cam is a good stand-in for Christie's elderly sleuth." I smiled. "I assist him in those endeavors, so maybe that would be my role."

"Still not old enough. At least, not looks-wise." Gabe swiftly slid the book he'd picked up into the middle of the stack. "Wait a moment, I believe there's a canvas tote stuffed into one of the shelves on my side. Let me grab that so you can use it to carry these to your car."

"That would be great," I said as he bent down again.

Gabe stood up, flourishing the tote bag. "I remembered Sharon kept this here so she could easily carry books to her room." He offered me a wry smile. "She likes to stash things around the house, just in case she needs them. I think there's a flashlight kept on one of the shelves on your side."

He was right, there was a flashlight acting as a bookend. "I don't know, perhaps I shouldn't walk off with Ms. Stewart's bag."

"Nonsense, I'm sure she has others." Gabe gave me a wink. "Or if not, she can certainly afford to buy more."

"Buy more of what?"

I turned to face the man who'd just walked into the library. Of average height with a stocky build, he had white hair that gleamed against his ruddy complexion.

He spends a lot of time outdoors, sailing, fishing, or golfing, I bet, I thought as I examined him. The man wore a simple but elegant houndstooth jacket and brown wool pants. His hazel eyes were narrow and overshadowed by bushy brows currently drawn together over his bumpy nose.

"Ms. Hunter, I assume?" he said, striding across the room to meet me." I'm Duff Stewart. Very nice to meet you. Sorry to make you wait." His words were clipped as short as his hair.

"No problem at all. I was able to check over the books already so you didn't waste my time." I extended my hand. "Jane Hunter, Cameron Clewe's personal librarian. I'm currently cataloging his collection of books and ephemera."

Duff's eyebrows shot up as he shook my hand. "My, my, he must have accumulated quite a lot of books to require a professional cataloger. That seems rather . . . excessive." He offered me a toothy smile.

I felt myself bristling. "It's primarily because he wants to eventually share his collection with scholars. Cam isn't a hoarder; he actually plans to allow researchers to discover his holdings through an international online catalog. Of course, researchers would have to travel to Aircroft to make use of the materials, but Cam is fine with that as well."

"How benevolent of him," Duff said. The amusement glinting in his eyes faded as he looked beyond me and caught sight of Gabe.

"I see my cousin has been keeping you company. I wondered where you'd gotten to, Gabe. Did you forget our upcoming conference call with the family lawyer?"

"I haven't forgotten," Gabe snapped.

I turned my head at Gabe's words, curious about the anger dripping from his words. His expression shifted as soon as he caught my eye.

"And voila," he said, motioning toward the tote bag, which he'd apparently filled with the books. "I told Ms. Hunter she could borrow this tote, Duff. It would be difficult to handle the books otherwise."

"Borrow?" Duff's gaze remained fixed on his cousin. "No need for that. Just take it, Ms. Hunter. My wife has duplicates scattered all over the house."

"Thanks," I said, but before I could add anything more, Gabe circled around the bookshelf to stand next to me.

"Anyway, as for locating me, you should know this is my favorite room," he said. "Especially since Kim's portrait is here."

Duff's gaze shifted to the painting. "Ah yes, you and Kimberly were always close, weren't you?"

"More so than you ever were, anyway," Gabe said, his tone barbed with spite.

I glanced from Duff to Gabe, observing the animosity enlivening the faces of both men. "She was beautiful," I interjected. "My condolences to you both."

"Thank you, but it's been quite some time. One adjusts, you know." Duff crossed his muscular arms over his broad chest.

I bit back a comment, startled by how nonchalant he appeared. I didn't think I'd remain so unaffected by a sibling's death, even after a decade or two. At least, I hoped I wouldn't have.

Gabe appeared similarly taken aback. "Excuse me, cousin. *Adjusting* may be easy for you, but it's certainly not something I've been able to do."

"Sorry, Ms. Hunter," Duff said, obviously ignoring his cousin's words. "I'm sure you simply want to complete your assignment and head back to Aircroft. We shouldn't hold you up with our little family squabbles. Besides"—he glared at Gabe—"we have that conference call."

Gabe thrust his hands into the pockets of his trousers. "Go ahead. I'm going to help Ms. Hunter carry the books to her car first. I'll join you in the office after that."

"That really isn't necessary." I lifted the tote bag and slid the strap over my shoulder. "Thanks for offering, Mr. Neri, but I'm fine carrying this much along with my purse." I cast him a bright smile. "I'm used to hauling books around."

"I'm sure that's true, Ms. Hunter. You do look rather sturdy. Now, come along, Gabe, leave the professional to do her job." Duff bobbed his head in a truncated bow. "Thank you for coming here to collect the books, Ms. Hunter. We could've made other arrangements, but honestly, I had no idea my father was selling off parts of his library before his death. It was a surprise to get a call from Mr. Clewe's assistant yesterday, but once I thought it over, I was glad a respected collector like your employer purchased them. Hopefully they aren't worth substantially more than he paid for them, but that was my father's business, so . . ." He shrugged.

Gabe tapped my arm. Looking over at him, I was surprised by the intensity of his gaze. *Almost as if he's trying to tell me something,* I thought. *Something he doesn't want to say aloud.*

"I'm glad to have met you," he said. "I'm sure you and Mr. Clewe will handle things well. Let me know if you discover anything . . . unexpected."

"OK," I said, still not sure what he was trying to convey. I watched him follow Duff out of the library, his narrow shoulders hunched and his feet shuffling. It was clear he was suffering in some way, but whether from illness or an old injury, I couldn't tell.

Chapter Five

I pulled the front edges of my oversized sweater together with one hand while rolling a metal book cart closer to my desk. The zipper had broken earlier in the day, a victim of my frustration over its lack of cooperation with my cold, fumbling fingers.

I flexed those chilly appendages in my thin white cotton gloves. As a cataloging librarian, I used to wear the gloves to protect older, archival quality materials, but even though practices had changed I still kept them around for cold days. Although beautiful, Aircroft's size made heating specific rooms difficult, and the library where I did the bulk of my cataloging work was no exception.

Due to the typical interstate traffic, worsened by an accident near the mall in Winston-Salem, I'd returned to Aircroft much later than I'd expected the previous day. Lauren, greeting me after I'd secured the new books in the library, suggested that I head home for the day, especially since Cam was busy with videoconferences.

"I'm sure you're tired from driving, and there's nothing urgent you need to handle," she'd told me. "I'll let Cam know you'll check in with him tomorrow."

Happy to follow this suggestion, I'd simply transferred the books from the tote bag to a rolling metal book cart before leaving for the day. I'd also sent a text to Vince, asking him to share it with Donna. Wanting to keep my promise and let them know what had transpired during my trip to the Stewart estate, I mentioned meeting Gabe Neri as well as Duff Stewart.

It wasn't until I checked the books the next morning that I discovered an anomaly. Cam's bill of sale had listed ten books, but when I looked over the volumes, I realized there were eleven. One of the books Gabe Neri had placed in the tote bag wasn't actually part of the purchase. The volume was a copy of Daphne du Maurier's *My Cousin Rachel.* Although it was a first edition from 1951, it was definitely not in pristine condition. With the top corners of certain pages turned down and some underlining of passages, it appeared to have been well used. It was a wonderful novel, but not the sort of item Cam would typically add to his collection.

After deciding to return the book to the Stewart family, I indulged my curiosity and took a quick look at it. Opening the cover, I examined the finely etched signature that had been inscribed across the flyleaf. I was expecting it to read *Macnamara Stewart*, but that was not the name that graced the inside of this volume.

"Kimberly Stewart Ward," I read aloud. Studying the signature, I frowned. Not only was this book absent from the inventory list Cam had given me, it might not have even been Macnamara Stewart's property. If it was a personal item that had once belonged to Kimberly Ward, perhaps I should send it to her widower, the author Kaden Ward, rather than Duff Stewart.

Especially given how distant he seemed from his sister, I thought. *I'd better check with Cam on this.* Rolling back my task chair, I picked up the novel and left the library, striding down Aircroft's maze of hallways to reach Cam's office.

Aircroft had been built in the 1920s, but its design features were more in keeping with a grand nineteenth century British estate. Of course, that was what the original owners had intended. Having risen from poverty, Samuel and Bridget Airley wanted to let the world know they were part of America's new aristocracy, the one made up of wealthy industrialists. Ivory plaster walls decorated with paintings that depicted a variety of landscapes rose above the ebony wood wainscotting, and the hall light fixtures were pewter and glass sconces that had been converted from gas to electricity.

I used one of the hallways that connected the two sides of the house to reach Cam's office. When I'd first arrived at Aircroft, the numerous rooms and corridors had confused me, but I'd quickly developed a clear mental floorplan of the mansion, including the halls that bisected the main floor.

Cam's office was located at a far corner of the main wing, away from public spaces like the library, dining rooms, and ballroom. It had also been renovated to reflect my boss's aesthetic, with the landed gentry style of the rest of the house exchanged for minimalism. Other than an L-shaped glass desk set on sleek chrome legs, a brushed metal storage cabinet, and several legal-sized, silver-toned, metal file cabinets, furniture was sparse. Picture windows filled two walls of the room, with the window on the back wall providing an unobstructed view into Aircroft's extensive gardens.

Even though the door was slightly ajar, I gave it a couple of raps and announced myself. "It's Jane. Sorry to interrupt. I just have a quick question."

"It's fine. Please come in," Cam replied.

As I stepped into the room, he closed his laptop and rolled his chair back from his desk. "What's the issue?"

"Nothing crucial. I just discovered something I wanted to bring to your attention." My rubber-soled loafers squeaked as I crossed the wood plank floor.

Cam's eyes narrowed. "Is there a problem?"

"Maybe. It seems an extra volume was added to the books I brought back from the Stewart estate." I held up the du Maurier. "It's odd, because it was actually Gabriel Neri, Duff Stewart's cousin, who packed the books in a tote bag for me."

Cam arched his eyebrows. "You think he deliberately included this particular book?"

"I don't know. It could've been a mistake. He was holding a book when I first saw him, so perhaps he automatically packed that one in with the rest without thinking about it, but . . ."

"Was there anything unusual in your interactions?" Cam thin lips twitched. "Don't dismiss it. You can trust that sixth sense of yours, Jane. It's served you well in the past."

"It did seem like he wanted to tell me something, but wouldn't, or couldn't, in front of Duff." I opened the book. "There's one other thing—the signature in this book indicates it was owned by someone other than Mac Stewart."

Cam rose to his feet. In his ice-blue cashmere sweater and crisp white shirt he looked like a model for an upscale menswear magazine rather than a businessman who managed several major companies and foundations. "Oh? That's odd. I was told the items I purchased were Mac's personal property."

"And maybe it was. He could've added this volume after . . ." I cleared my throat. "This book contains Kimberly Stewart Ward's signature. I realize she died some time ago, but her husband is still alive. I didn't know if we should check with him before we mail it back." I held out the book. "Take a look."

Cam reached over the desk and took the book from my hand. "A first edition, but not exceedingly rare, and rather worn," he said, setting the book down after a cursory glance. "I doubt Kaden Ward would care, but you're right, we should probably contact him, just in case." Cam's fingers beat a tattoo against the cloth-bound surface of the novel.

"It was probably something Kimberly left in her bedroom at the Stewart home," I said. "However, since she was married . . ."

"And her widower is not particularly fond of the Stewarts." Cam flashed a humorless smile. "Kaden Ward's been known to speak ill of Kimberly's family publicly, so it would be wise to doublecheck and make sure he doesn't want to claim this book as part of his wife's inheritance."

Cam curled his fingers around the book and lifted it by the spine. As the pages fanned open, a folded square of lavender paper slipped out from between the pages and fluttered to the desktop. He frowned. "Don't people know better than to leave things in books?"

"Sadly, they never do," I said, leaning over to pick up the paper. "While cataloging older books I've uncovered all sorts of things—receipts, airplane tickets, pressed flowers, feathers, gum wrappers, and so on. You name it, I've found it." I unfolded the note, my fingers sensing the weight of the paper. "This is fine stationary and has the initials KSW embossed as a letterhead."

"Kimberly Stewart Ward," Cam said thoughtfully. "Is it signed?"

I nodded. "And dated. May 1982, which was the month she died. The signature also matches the one in the book." I peered at the curlicue handwriting used in the body of the note. "It's a little hard to read, but I'll try to make it out."

"A secret message?" Cam's lips twitched, indicating either tension or amusement.

Or maybe both, I thought. *Sometimes it's difficult to tell.*

Slowly deciphering the note, I swallowed back a swear word. "This is quite disturbing. Read it, and you'll see what I mean."

Cam took the paper from my outstretched fingers and stared at it for a moment. "Please, I beg you," he read aloud, the slight tremor in his voice matching the trembling of the note in his hand. "If you receive this, alert the authorities. I've tried, but they've been poisoned against me. Everyone thinks I'm simply depressed, or even insane. The lies have worked. Whoever is behind these attempts is determined to silence me." He looked up, blinking rapidly. "As you said, the signatures match, so it must've been written by Kimberly Ward, but it doesn't make sense. Her death has always been unequivocally accepted as a suicide. But in this note she's claiming someone wanted to harm her." Cam lowered his rose-gold lashes, shadowing his eyes. "Or maybe it's more than that. Forget simple harm; Kimberly obviously believed someone was trying to kill her. And maybe . . ."

"They did," I said.

Chapter Six

"We shouldn't jump to conclusions," Cam said, after a long pause. "If the stories are true, Kimberly Stewart struggled with anxiety and depression from childhood. This note could simply be a manifestation of her descent into paranoia."

"True, but still—why was she so afraid? No smoke without fire." I crossed my arms over my chest. "We could always poke around a little and see what turns up. We don't have any other cases right now . . ."

"Except for the ongoing search for my missing father." Cam slipped the note back into the book and glanced at his watch. "Speaking of which, someone who claims to have some clues about his disappearance should have arrived by now."

"Here?" I asked, lifting my eyebrows. "You didn't tell me your latest source was traveling to Aircroft."

Cam grimaced. "Sorry, I should've alerted you, but it slipped my mind." Tapping his temple with one finger, he added, "Too much noise up here these days."

Studying my boss for a moment, I realized he seemed to have lost weight, despite the recent holiday season and its typical indulgences. *He's still processing the sudden reappearance of family members,* I reminded myself, struggling to wipe any evidence of concern from my face. "Is this one of the people your private investigators found? Back in early December you told me they provided you with some information and names."

"No." Cam swept his shaggy hair away from his forehead. "She contacted me after we posted that request for information regarding Rafe Glenn on social media."

"You think this one might actually be legit?" I pursed my lips. Cam had received an avalanche of tips when he'd offered a reward for information, but so far most of the respondents had turned out to be frauds.

"Possibly, but just in case, I had her thoroughly investigated. Her name is Vanessa Gale, and she has a solid track record as a journalist. She's written for several publications that featured my father's photographic work, including *National Geographic.*" Cam circled around the desk to stand in front of me. "Since you're already on a cataloging break, why don't you join us? I asked Lauren to show Ms. Gale into the sitting room. We were supposed to meet thirty minutes ago, so I imagine she's there now." He flashed a humorless smile. "It doesn't hurt to make her wait. If she is trying to pull some sort of con, a little time cooling her heels may bring out the nerves."

"Smart," I said, following him out of the office and down another hall that led to the sitting room.

"I have my moments," he called out over his shoulder.

I snorted. Cam was one of the most intelligent people I'd ever met. *And one of the most troubled,* I reminded myself. Not that he didn't have reason to be—after losing his mother when he was a toddler, he'd been raised by a series of nannies hired by his wealthy but often absent stepfather. The fact that Albert

Clewe always knew he was not Cam's biological father certainly didn't help their relationship, especially since, until he was much older, Cam had no idea why Al was so distant with him. By then the damage was done. Even though Al Clewe had provided Cam with everything he needed in terms of education and material goods, his obvious lack of love for the cuckoo in his nest had caused Cam significant pain.

Still mulling over these thoughts, I walked into the sitting room right behind Cam, almost stepping on his heels. "Sorry," I said, taking a step to the side as I searched for the visitor. I didn't see her at first. The moss green plaster walls rising above the wood wainscotting made the room dark, even with the brocade drapes thrown back from the windows. The January sky, dull and gray as lead, provided little illumination.

Cam strolled over to a maroon leather armchair that faced a matching black leather chair and turned on a pewter floor lamp. It cast a pool of light across the space between the chairs. As if drawn like a moth, a tall, thin figure emerged from the shadows behind one of the room's glass and wood display cases.

"Hello, I'm Vanessa Gale. You must be Cam." The speaker was a woman who appeared to be in her late thirties or early forties. She'd artfully dressed down in designer jeans, boots, and a plaid flannel shirt over a tank top. Her short, feathery hair looked white in the dim light, but as she stepped closer to the lamp, I realized she was a very fair blonde. Her pale blue eyes studied me with interest. "I wasn't expecting anyone else."

"This is my personal librarian," Cam said, shooting me a glance, "and friend, Jane Hunter."

"The one who works with you on cold cases?" Amusement laced Vanessa's tone. "That's your hobby, isn't it?" She smiled at Cam. "I've read up on you, as I'm sure you have on me."

Cam examined Vanessa with that cool detachment I knew he adopted when he was on edge. "Of course. I don't allow just anyone in my home."

"It's quite a place," Vanessa said, her gaze sweeping the room. "Do you mind?" she added, motioning toward the maroon armchair.

"Please, have a seat." Cam strode over to a smaller chair upholstered in green velvet and placed it between the two leather armchairs. "I think we should all sit down before we hear your information, Ms. Gale."

"Vanessa," she corrected, eyeing him as he settled into the black leather armchair.

I hurried over to the green chair and perched on the front edge of the seat cushion. "You said you had information on Rafe Glenn?"

"Right to the point. I like that," Vanessa said.

I fixed her with a steady stare. "That's why you're here, isn't it?" I didn't say what I was thinking, which was that Vanessa might have an ulterior motive, but from her searching gaze I could tell she'd picked up on my suspicion.

"Of course." Vanessa shifted her focus to Cam. "I worked with your father a few times. Once in China, after one of the bad earthquakes, once in India, and twice in South America. My connections in that part of the world were actually the ones who informed me that Rafe was pursuing a project in Peru right before he went dark."

Cam straightened in his chair. "Peru? Was he working in the mountains or along the Amazon, or somewhere in between?"

"I'm not sure about the details," Vanessa said. "I know he was deeply concerned about rainforests and wanted to travel the world to create a photographic record of them, but whether this trip was for that purpose"—she lifted her hands—"I really can't say."

"It would be a good place to start, though, don't you think?" I swiveled to face Cam.

His expression was unreadable. "I suppose. But I'd like to have a little more information before I hire anyone to look for him in a foreign country, especially one with a lot of remote territories to search."

"Well, here's the thing." Vanessa leaned forward, gripping her knees with both hands. "I'd be willing to travel to Peru to conduct a more detailed investigation, if you'd like. As I said, I still have contacts there, and I speak fluent Spanish. Of course, as a journalist, I also possess excellent investigative skills. I'm even between contracted projects right now. All I'd need . . ."

"Is money?" I asked dryly.

Vanessa side-eyed me. "I would need travel and living expenses, but I'm not asking for a finder's fee or reward or anything like that. I like Rafe and would be happy to facilitate his safe return."

Resting his elbows on the chair arm and intertwining his fingers in front of his chest, Cam examined Vanessa for a moment. "Do you have any idea why my father might have been in Peru, other than perhaps photographing the rainforest? Because I've heard rumors that there may have been something else going on."

"Really? It's my understanding that no one has more information than I do." Vanessa settled against the chair's tall back.

Cam raised his eyebrows. "Not even about my father helping teams attempting to repatriate stolen art and antiquities? One of my private investigators turned up evidence that he may have been photographing locations to match them to stolen objects."

"That was in India," Vanessa said, meeting Cam's intense stare without flinching.

"Isn't it possible he was doing the same thing in Peru? Work that may have put him in peril from organized groups of thieves and brokers?" Cam dropped his hands into his lap and leaned forward, his gaze fixed on Vanessa.

"What do you mean, matching location and objects?" I interjected, hoping to break the intensity of their staring contest.

Vanessa waved a hand through the air. "Oh, it's things like finding the intact base for a sculpture that's been looted and sold to collectors or museums. Rafe was able to take detailed photos so that groups like India Pride or the New York's District Attorney's Antiquities Trafficking Unit could help return a piece to the country of its origin."

"I see." I glanced at Cam, noting his clenched jaw. "I imagine that could make someone a target for kidnappers or other criminals, especially if theft rings were still operating in the country where he was working."

"Which could turn any search for my father into a dangerous proposition," Cam said. "Are you sure you're equipped to undertake such a mission, Ms. Gale?"

"Vanessa, please, and yes, I can gather the proper support to ensure the safety of my team and myself."

Cam's foot tapped the floor. "But it will be expensive."

"That shouldn't be an issue for you," Vanessa said, with a smug smile. "I know your worth, Cam."

"Do you? And I'd prefer Mr. Clewe if you don't mind." Cam rose to his feet. "At any rate, I'm not prepared to decide on your proposition today, Ms. Gale. I'd like a few days to think it over."

When Vanessa stood up, I realized she and Cam were the same height, but despite Cam's slender frame, Vanessa appeared waifish beside him. "Of course. I've booked an extended-stay hotel in Winston-Salem, and can easily hang out in the area until you make up your mind." Vanessa ran her fingers through her feathered hair. "I don't mind playing tourist. There are places I'd like to check out anyway, like Old Salem and Reynolda House."

"I have your number. I'll call you when I've decided whether or not to move forward with your plan." Cam glanced at his watch and turned to me. "Do you mind showing Ms. Gale out, Jane? I have a video conference starting soon."

"No problem." I stood up to face the two of them.

Cam left the room first. As I headed for the door, I noticed that Vanessa had paused beside one of the display cases and was examining the objects inside.

"Some of these items are quite rare, you know," she said.

"I don't doubt it. But if you'll just come this way . . ." I gestured toward the door.

"Sure thing." Vanessa strolled over. Looking me over, she smiled. "You aren't convinced I'm legit, are you, Jane?"

"It's a little too soon to decide. Now, please follow me. Aircroft has a lot of halls and passageways. It's easy to get lost if you don't have a guide."

Vanessa trailed me out the door, but her longer stride soon put us side-by-side as we headed for the main entry hall.

"Your boss is an interesting man," she said, after a few moments of silence. "All that money and good looks, but his social skills are a bit lacking, don't you think?"

I shot her a sharp look. "That isn't really relevant to your interests, is it?"

"Whoa." Vanessa raised her hands, palms out. "Don't get defensive. I was just voicing an observation."

"Here we are," I said, as we crossed into the grand entry hall. "Just head out those double doors and you'll be able to access the driveway. I assume you parked somewhere along the circle?"

"I did." Vanessa's gaze swept over me. "I can tell you're loyal to Mr. Clewe. That's great. I hope I can prove my loyalty as well."

"I hope so too," I said. As I watched her stride toward her car, my phone vibrated in my pocket. I slid it out, immediately noticing the icon for texts indicated a new message.

It was from Vince. I stared at the screen and blinked before the words made any sense.

Thought you should know, it said. *News just broke. Gabriel Neri is dead.*

Chapter Seven

I stared at my screen for a moment before turning on my heel and hurrying back across the front hall. Walking briskly, I reached Cam's office in record time, but just as I was about to rap on the half-opened door, I heard raised voices and took a step back.

"Which is exactly why you need to try to understand Lily and Gordy." Frustration shimmered in Lauren Walker's voice.

"I have tried."

"Then try harder."

"I don't think this is exactly any of your business," Cam said, his words staccato sharp.

"It's my business because I have to work closely with you, and your attitude over these last months is fraying my last nerve."

"You *have to*? No, you don't have to. You can leave at any time."

Lauren didn't reply, but the brisk tapping of her heels told me to move away from the door. Sure enough, it flew open, the pewter doorknob banging into the wall as Lauren strode out of the office.

She shot me a warning glance. “Might want to come back later. He’s is a foul mood, as I’m sure you heard.”

“Yes, well, there’s something important . . .”

Anger flared in Lauren’s dark eyes. “Give it a try, then. Just don’t say I didn’t warn you.”

I waited until she’d stalked off down the hall, then gave the door one knock and slipped into the office. “Hello,” I called out. “Sorry to intrude, but there’s news I feel you’d want to know.”

“It’s fine, it’s fine.” All the fire in Cam’s tone had crumbled to ash.

Pausing just inside the doorway, I stared at him. He was rocking back and forth in his chair, his arms crossed over his chest and his hands gripping his upper arms. “I can return later.”

“Just come in.” Cam leaned forward until his forehead was pressed against the glass surface of his desk. “I suppose you heard that,” he mumbled after a moment of silence.

I crossed to the desk. “I’m afraid so. I also witnessed Lauren’s rather dramatic exit.”

“I shouldn’t have lost my temper. It’s just . . .” Cam lifted his head and met my sympathetic gaze squarely. “She was urging me to give my grandmother and great-uncle another chance.”

“So I gathered. And perhaps she was a little too insistent, but you know she’s only pushing you on this point because she cares about you.”

Cam lowered his hands to grip the padded arms of his chair. “Yes, I know.”

“She thinks you shouldn’t reject this chance to have a real family, and I have to agree with her to a certain extent. You’ve never really had the chance before, so it would be a shame to miss it now. But"—I held up my forefinger to silence him—"I also understand your point of view. Lily and Gordon Glenn didn't get in touch with you for years, even after they knew about your stepfather's lies. Sure, he told your real father that you had died not long after your mother, but that was easily proven false once you were old enough for word to get around about Albert Clewe's son. Even if Lily lived elsewhere and Rafe was out-of-touch due to his globetrotting work schedule, Gordy still lived in the area. He had to have realized the truth fairly early on."

"Exactly. He would've told his sister, who would've told my father, so there's no excuse. They knew, and abandoned me." Cam's fingers drummed against the chair arms.

"I suppose they did, in a way." I strolled over to the side window and stared out over a rolling lawn bordered by a stand of pine trees. "The thing is, as Lily's told me, they didn't want to disrupt your life. Let's face it—Albert Clewe could give you every advantage. They couldn't, and felt they shouldn't rip you away from all this." I turned and swept one hand through the air. "Lily wanted you to inherit Aircroft. She's always believed it's your proper legacy, since Calvin Airley was your grandfather."

"Such an old-fashioned attitude. The rightful heir must be crowned king." Cam tightened his lips. "Logically, I understand their reasoning. I can even comprehend why Rafe Glenn wouldn't want to take me away from Aircroft. With his career, he probably thought he couldn't give me what Albert Clewe could—wealth, and a proper, stable home. But"—Cam rolled back his chair and rose to his feet—"they made no effort. None. They could've worked out a deal with Al. He wasn't warm or loving, but he also wasn't unreasonable. If they had kept things quiet, he probably would've allowed some contact with all three of them. A visit here or there. I mean, Al knew from the beginning that I wasn't his biological son, and he was still willing to raise me."

"Absolutely valid points," I said. "But as you said, they were hobbled by many old-fashioned attitudes. I truly believe Lily was affected by the Airley family's scorn for someone of her station in life. They would've said she was definitely *lower class*, and would've treated her as such. Then she was traumatized when your grandfather Calvin died before your father was even born. Don't forget that she had to flee the area to prevent the Airleys from discovering she was pregnant and ultimately taking her child away."

Cam thrust his hands into the pockets of his slacks and rocked back on his heels. "It sounds like you and Lauren have been discussing this subject, because she just said basically the same things."

"We may have talked about it a few times," I said, with a wry smile. "Because, shocker—we both really care about you."

"That doesn't give you the right to tell me what to do or how to feel." Cam's green eyes narrowed.

"Heaven forbid," I said, lifting my hands. "Who would dare instruct a man who knows everything?"

As Cam stared at me, obviously processing my jibe, his stony expression softened. "Sorry. I don't mean to give that impression. It's simply . . . well, I never feel anyone can truly understand me."

"I certainly don't claim to be able to do that," I said. "Not completely, anyway. But I do know that you crave the human connection you never received when you were young. Which is perfectly normal and why I have to agree with Lauren about not pushing your family away. I don't mean you should forget and forgive everything, but surely there's a way to keep them in your life. Face it—Lily and Gordy are both in their nineties. They may not be around much longer. Don't you want to learn a few things about your family heritage from them, for your own benefit, if nothing else?"

Cam cast me an ironic smile. "Using common sense and facts to circumvent my defenses?"

"As always. Now"—I brushed my hands together, as if dusting away the previous topic—"as for the news I wanted to share, which I assure you is strictly factual, are you ready to hear it?"

"Clever segue." Cam settled back in his office chair. "Very well, what is it?"

I walked over to the chair facing his desk and sat down. "It has to do with Gabriel Neri, Duff Stewart's first cousin, whom I met yesterday."

Cam met my gaze, curiosity lighting up his pale face. "What about him?"

"Apparently he just died," I said, pulling out my cell phone. "Or maybe it was overnight. At any rate, it may have happened at the Stewart estate, since Gabe told me he was staying there for Finlay Stewart's birthday party."

"Wait, the same Gabe Neri who packed up the books, including the du Maurier with the note inside?" Cam reached for his laptop, pulling it closer and flipping it open.

"That's the one. A little odd, isn't it?" I pulled up the search engine on my phone and tapped in *Gabriel Neri* and *death*.

Cam had obviously done the same. "They suspect an overdose since he's struggled with addiction issues in the past."

"Pills," I said, reading through the article on my screen. "He had an off-and-on problem with opioids." An image of Gabe's unhealthy appearance and unsteady stride surfaced in my mind. "He didn't look well. He was fragile and gaunt."

"Did he seem to be in pain?" Cam tapped the edge of his keyboard.

"Maybe. He was my age but looked ten years older. Or at least, I hope so," I said with a twitch of my lips.

Cam raised his eyebrows. "Fishing for compliments again? But you're right. Judging by this photo, I'd have said the man was in his seventies rather than his sixties."

"If he was an addict, that probably took a toll."

"No doubt." Cam stared at his computer screen. "He wasn't involved in the family business, except for a few foundations set up on the Neri side."

The reference to opioids made me wonder if Gabe had been introduced to the pills after a serious injury. *The car accident,* I thought, although there was no mention of that incident in any of the news reports. "Do you think it's possible Gabe wanted us to find the note? He slipped Kimberly's book in with the others, and also mentioned something about our amateur sleuthing efforts. Maybe he was trying to send a message."

"Perhaps." Cam closed his laptop. "We can certainly do a little digging into his background, just in case, see if there's anything that would connect him to the note."

"He said he was close to Kimberly, and there was that car accident . . ." Seeing Cam's puzzled expression, I added, "Duff and his cousins were involved in a wreck when they were in their twenties. Well, Gabe was probably still a teenager, since he was eight years younger than Duff and Lucas. Anway, I can research that; see if it's possible that's what kicked off his addiction," I said, thinking of Vince's reminder about digitized newspapers. "Not sure how that would connect to his cousin Kimberly, but you never know."

"Good idea. This sudden death does make me suspicious, especially after the victim may have slipped us a clue." Cam's right foot beat a tattoo against the plank floor. "I'll have one of my investigators on retainer do some background work as well."

I examined him for a moment. The possibility of a new case had replaced his anger and anxiety with excitement. "Before you do that, perhaps you should go find Lauren and apologize. I mean, you did tell her she could leave, so she might be taking you at your word and packing up her personal items right now . . ."

Before I could say anything else, Cam bolted from his chair and dashed out of the room.

Chapter Eight

As soon as I got home after work and changed into a loose sweatshirt and sweatpants, I embarked on an in-depth search of the online newspapers provided by my local library system. I had to guess at the timeframe, but a few calculations allowed me to narrow it down to a span between 1977 and early 1982. Vince had mentioned being away at college when the wreck occurred, and since he was approximately the same age as Duff Stewart and Lucas Neri, I estimated they'd have been in their early twenties during that time period. Vince had also said he was sure the accident happened before Kimberly's death in May 1982, so that gave me a solid cut-off point.

Scouring the databases once again made me glad to have attended library school when online research was in its infancy. We hadn't had search engines that would return a laundry list of results if you simply typed in a word or random phrase—we had to learn how to construct SQL string queries, logical equations that looked like algebra problems. But having to boil a research question down to its essential parts, and place those pieces into the appropriate query arrangement, had trained me to think about digital resources in a way that allowed for more nuanced searches and precise results.

Armed with a glass of wine, it didn't take long for me to discover a bevy of articles, most of which were relatively short and lacking in detail. But they were reports on a vehicular accident that had involved Duff Stewart and his cousins. Donna was right—the coverage stopped rather abruptly after the original flurry of articles, but I was able to pull together enough facts to provide a clear picture of what had happened.

The wreck had occurred in December 1981. Lucas Neri, then twenty-four, had been driving, with Duff Stewart riding shotgun and sixteen-year-old Gabe Neri in the back seat. The articles stated that they'd been on their way home from a holiday party and that conditions were not great—it was dark and there were still patches of ice from a storm a few days before. The authorities determined that those conditions had undoubtedly contributed to the severity of the accident. However, despite the mention of a party, they found no alcohol in Lucas's system, ruling out a DUI.

In fact, the accident was determined to have been the fault of the other driver, Joseph Carson, a twenty-year-old construction worker. The official police statement claimed that he'd crossed over the middle line of the two-lane road, slamming into Lucas's car head-on. Duff, Lucas, and Gabe had all sustained injuries. Gabe, who was not wearing a seatbelt, was the most severely hurt. Joseph Carson had also been seriously injured and, more tragically, his twenty-year-old wife, Leslie, and two-year-old daughter, Tiffany, had died at the scene.

I emailed links to a few of the articles to Cam before closing out my search. It seemed likely that Gabe could have become hooked on painkillers after this event, creating a lifelong addiction to opioids. *One that eventually killed him,* I thought, as I slid my laptop to one side of my kitchen table. It was time for some food, so I stood and crossed to my kitchenette. My refrigerator held a tempting assortment of salad ingredients, but I reached for a container of leftover Chinese takeout. I just didn't feel like chopping vegetables and rinsing lettuce.

Lazy bones, I told myself as I plopped shrimp Lo Mein onto a plate and popped the plate in the microwave. *Bailey would be ashamed.*

As if conjured by my thoughts, my cell phone vibrated in the pocket of my sweatpants. Pulling it out, I saw Bailey's number.

"What are you eating, Mom?" she asked after a quick *hello.*

"Is that why you always call at dinner time? To keep tabs on my diet?" I placed my heated plate of leftovers on the table and sat down.

"You bet your life I do. And you're betting your life if you're living off take-out and all those prepared foods." Bailey's voice, while warm, held a hint of disapproval.

"How do you know that's what I'm having?" I asked, stirring the noodles with my fork.

"I heard the ding of the microwave, clear as a bell, so I can make a good guess." Bailey sighed. "Really, Mom, we've talked about this so many times."

"Indeed. *So* many times," I replied. "And yet I continue to do as I please. Which should've taught you something by now."

"That you're stubborn and don't like to be told what to do?" Bailey's bright laugh dissolved the slight frisson of tension between us. "OK, I give up. Eat what you want. I'm just concerned for your health."

"I know, and you're right. I should eat fresh food and prepare meals from scratch. I know you've had more energy since you started doing the same. But I don't always want to go to all that trouble for something I'm going to sit and eat by myself." I took a bite of my Lo Mein. "Besides, sometimes I just crave takeout."

Bailey sighed. "You and Taylor should set up some dinner dates. He says the same thing about eating alone."

I adopted my best seductive tone which, to be honest, wasn't too convincing. "Aren't you afraid I might steal him away from you?"

"If you can, go for it," Bailey said with a laugh. "But seriously, Mom, I do worry about you overextending yourself. You basically work two jobs for Cam. I know he pays well, but I think you need a little more time off."

"I just visited you for two weeks." I lifted another forkful of noodles. "Besides, I like to keep busy. You know that."

"I sure do. You were dragging me to museums on my one day off when you were here."

"As if you aren't always on the go. Performing, practicing, voice lessons, dance lessons, acting lessons, sourcing organic ingredients and preparing all your own food . . ." I took a deep breath. "Have I left anything out?"

"Texting and video-chatting with Taylor, and spending time with him whenever he can get up here, but that's about it."

"Right. Just that." I smiled. I was actually glad that Bailey had so many positive things in her life now. That hadn't always been the case when she was a child and I was a struggling single mother. "Is your show still selling out?"

"Pretty much. I just hope if they take it to Broadway, I'll be able to go with it. That doesn't always happen, you know."

"They'd be fools not to keep you," I said firmly. Of course I was biased, but I thought Bailey's depiction of the unicorn-turned-woman in a musical adaption of *The Last Unicorn* was too perfect to be matched by anyone else.

"But you know *what fools these mortals be*," Bailey said, quoting Puck from *A Midsummer Night's Dream,* a role she'd played in college.

"Too true, unfortunately. Anyway, sharing a little gossip, Cam and Lauren had a fight today. Well, more like a shouting match, but still pretty heated. She keeps trying to help him deal with the long-lost family situation, and he continues to resist her efforts."

Bailey sighed. "You should just lock those two in a room together until they figure things out."

"That could take a while," I said. "I might have to provide a stash of food and water so they don't expire before realizing how much they like each other."

"I think Lauren already knows. It's just Cam who's clueless."

"As ever." I shifted in my chair. "Oh, before you go, I should also let you know about the new mystery I'm researching. Perhaps you can offer me some more of your brilliant insights." I launched into a description of my encounter with Gabe Neri, his possible intention to involve Cam and me in a private investigation, and his sudden death.

"Intriguing," Bailey said after I concluded my overview. "I don't know if I have anything to offer in terms of advice, but based on what I've learned about motives and human nature in my acting studies, I'd put money on your theory that Gabe Neri included his cousin's book and note on purpose. He knew about your sleuthing work with Cam and decided to take the opportunity to pique your interest in what really happened to Kimberly."

"That's my conclusion as well. From the note it sounds like she feared for her life, so why would she kill herself not long after? It doesn't add up."

"What about Gabe Neri? Could his death be suspicious as well?" Bailey asked in a thoughtful tone.

"It does make me wonder. Supposedly, he was an addict, but he appeared clean and sober when I met him."

"He was staying at the Stewart estate that night because there was a family event?"

"Yes, a birthday party for Finlay Stewart, who's in his late thirties. He's currently the CFO for the Stewart family's various businesses."

"So the entire family, as well as some friends, could've been there." Bailey chuckled. "Right up your alley, Mom. Lots of suspects means lots of motives."

"I hadn't thought about it quite like that, but you're right," I said, my thoughts spinning around this idea. "See, I knew you'd help. How'd you get to be so smart, anyway?"

Bailey clucked her tongue. "Really, Mom. I inherited it from you, of course."

Chapter Nine

The next morning, I ran into Lauren while grabbing a mug of coffee from the kitchen.

Like Cam's office, the style of this space contrasted with Aircroft's other rooms. White marble countertops and subway tiles, brushed metal racks, and modern appliances gleamed in the sunlight falling from tall, mullioned windows. It looked more like a modern commercial kitchen than anything from the 1920s.

As I entered, I greeted Mateo Marin, who was standing behind the massive central work island. A man of average height whose muscular arms were at odds with the rest of his wiry build, he was rolling out dough on the marble countertop. His lips were tightened in concentration, and one lock of his slicked-back dark hair fell over his broad forehead.

"Good morning, Jane," he said, without looking up. "The coffee's fresh and there are some pastries on the counter. Please help yourself."

Glancing over his shoulder to one of the counters lining the kitchen, I noticed Lauren filling her white ceramic mug from the expensive coffee-maker that could do everything except roast the beans.

"Hi there," I said, my rubber-soled loafers scuffing against the smooth slate floor as I crossed to join her. After I filled my own mug and stirred in cream, I leaned against the edge of the counter and looked her up and down. "How are you this morning, Lauren?"

"I'm fine. Just a little tired." Lauren held up her mug. "This helps."

I focused on the spoon I was casually swirling in my coffee. "Sorry I barged in yesterday,"

"Don't be silly. I should be the one to apologize. I had no business losing my temper like that."

I looked up, observing the signs of strain etched onto her lovely face. "Well, Cam can drive you to it sometimes."

We both turned our heads at the loud bark of laughter from Mateo. He held up one flour-dusted hand. "I know that was out of line, but I couldn't help it."

"See, Mateo knows the score," I said. "As do I. You'd have to be a saint to maintain a calm composure around our boss at all times."

Lauren tapped the rim of her mug with one pink-polished fingernail. "I suppose. It wasn't very professional, though."

"He wasn't exactly being the picture of politeness either," I said.

"That's true. But I knew I was pushing him a little too hard." Lauren took another sip of coffee.

"Never poke the bear," Mateo said. "I learned that the hard way."

I glanced over at him. "The thing is, Lauren was only trying to help Cam."

"Especially then." Mateo laid down his rolling pin and turned to face us. "You should've seen what happened at Christmas dinner. That would cure you of any desire to intervene in Cam's personal affairs."

"I heard it didn't go well," I said

Mateo wiped his hands on his white apron. "Understatement of the year. We never even made it to dessert. Well, the older folks stayed, but Cam left the table after the main course and didn't return. It was awkward, to say the least."

"Sorry to hear that. But see, Lauren"—I set down my half-empty mug—"Cam does need some prodding to make nice with his family. You weren't really out of line. Like I told him, we only do these things because we care."

Lauren's eyes widened. "You said that?"

"Why not? It's true, isn't it?" I asked.

Mateo laughed again, but this time it was an amused chuckle. "Don't worry, Lauren. I'm sure it sailed right over his head."

"Perhaps, although he rushed off when I said something about you packing up your personal belongings," I said.

Lauren stared down into the oily surface of the coffee in her mug as if trying to read an omen there. "He did profusely apologize, which was odd. But now that I know you urged him to do so, it makes a little more sense, Jane. He listens to you better than anyone else, it seems."

"True. You seem to possess a special talent for handling him." Mateo turned back to the work island and picked up his rolling pin. "Without resorting to anger," he added, giving the dough a firm smack.

"I don't know about that. Maybe it's just because I'm older and remind him of his former nannies or something." I picked up my mug and took a long swallow of the now tepid coffee. "As for spurring him into a profuse apology, Lauren, I simply reminded him that you might actually take him up on his offer to leave your job here at Aircroft."

"I'm sure that would galvanize him," Mateo said, casting Lauren a smile. "He seemed pretty lost when you were gone over the holidays. Imagining you gone forever must've been terrifying."

Lauren set down her mug so hard I was afraid it might crack. "Oh, for heaven's sake. Cam isn't a child. I'm sure he'd be fine if he hired someone else as an assistant."

Mateo and I stole a glance at one another and shook our heads.

"You handle so much for him, Lauren. I don't think there's another assistant or secretary who'd take all that on," Mateo said.

Before I could chime in with my agreement, my cell vibrated in my pocket. Setting down my now-empty mug, I pulled out the phone and noticed I had a new text message.

"That's odd," I said.

"What is it?" Lauren refilled her coffee mug. "Anything serious?"

"I don't think so, but it's from Malcolm Stewart, Duff and Sharon's younger son. I didn't meet him the other day so I have no idea why he'd be contacting me, or even where he got my number." I tapped to open the message.

"Didn't someone just die in that family?" Mateo rolled the dough into a thin rectangle. "I heard something on the news about that."

"It was a cousin, Gabriel Neri. The authorities think it was an overdose," I said absently, my gaze fixed on my phone.

The text Malcolm had sent was a request to meet with him later in the day.

"He wants to meet with me at his loft condo in Winston-Salem to talk about his cousin's death," I said in a bemused tone. "I can't imagine why, unless . . ." I thought about my conversation with Cam, and our speculation over whether Gabe had deliberately given us Kimberly's book and the note inside. I typed in my reply.

"Are you going to meet with him?" Lauren asked.

"Yes. I'd like to learn more about Gabriel Neri from someone who really knew him. Or at least I assume that's the case, even though Malcolm must be three decades younger than Gabe. I'm just curious, you know?" I met Lauren's questioning gaze with a smile. "Don't worry. This isn't a situation that's going to turn dangerous. Just a chat."

Concern clouded Lauren's eyes. "I've heard that before, from both you and Cam, and it doesn't always turn out to be true."

Mateo lifted the rolling pin above his head. "You can always borrow this if you want."

Chapter Ten

When I informed Cam about the meeting with Malcolm Stewart, he was pleased that I'd decided to go, but also slightly wary.

"Mateo did offer me his rolling pin," I said.

Cam tugged down the sleeves of his cashmere sweater. "I doubt that will be necessary, but you should text me when you arrive and leave the condo."

"No problem, boss." I gave him a mock salute, which earned me a sigh.

"I wish we knew more about Malcolm's relationship with Gabe, but I doubt he killed his older cousin and then immediately decided to confess to a complete stranger, so I think you'll be fine." Cam shuffled some papers on his desk. "By the way, I did clear things up with Lauren."

"She told me you apologized. Smart move," I said.

Cam looked up at me. "It would be difficult to replace her."

"No doubt. Not to mention . . ." I closed my lips over what I'd almost said. I was certainly willing to be a cheerleader for any relationship between Lauren and Cam, but I had to allow them to realize their feelings on their own. *It isn't exactly altruistic,* I admitted to myself. *You just don't want to push them together only to have the relationship implode later. Not only would they both be terribly hurt; you might lose two friends and your job.*

Fortunately, Cam was too distracted to notice. "I wouldn't tell Malcolm about the book or the note. If he brings it up, you could pursue that angle, but if he doesn't, there's no point in showing our hand so soon."

"Agreed. I'm going to let him do most of the talking," I said.

"That's the best way to approach it, I think." Cam frowned as he stared at a document he'd lifted from the pile of papers. "Sorry, Jane, but I need to make a phone call. Something on this report looks odd."

"Of course. I'll contact you later, then," I said, before wishing him a good day and exiting the office.

Later, I left work a little early, hoping to miss some of the afternoon traffic. Malcolm had texted his address as well as a suggestion that I park in one of the downtown parking garages. I didn't drive into Winston-Salem that often and remained on alert until I reached the garage. From previous experience I knew that the city's transit authority made frequent changes—roads turning from dual direction to one-way and street closures were not uncommon, not to mention there always seemed to be some type of construction project underway.

After parking, I sent Cam a brief text confirming my arrival and walked two blocks to a five-story brick building that appeared to have been constructed in the 1940s or 50s. Restaurants and shops filled the lower level, so it took me a moment to locate the discreetly marked door leading to the residences above. I entered into a small vestibule with an intercom system on one wall labeled with apartment numbers but no names. It seemed the residents were fond of their privacy, which made sense. I pressed the button for the top floor apartment.

"Hello," I said. "It's Jane Hunter. You asked me to stop by today."

A scratchy version of "come on up" was followed by the buzz from the inner glass doors. I pushed the doors open and made my way to an elevator that appeared to be older than me.

The jolt when it started cemented my opinion that it was not modern equipment. I pressed one hand against the slick wall, which had the patina of old bronze.

I was startled by the bump when the elevator stopped but wasn't surprised when the doors opened directly into Malcolm Stewart's condo. He obviously owned the entire top floor, which wasn't unexpected given his family's wealth. Stepping out onto an expanse of weathered pine planks, my gaze was captured by the floor-to-ceiling windows that filled the opposite wall.

"Northern-facing," said the young man who crossed the expansive open space to greet me. "I chose this unit for that reason."

"For your artwork?" I studied him, my nerves soothed by his genuine smile.

"That's right. Northern light is best for painting." When he held out his hand, I noticed a rim of turquoise paint under a few of his fingernails. "Hi, I'm Malcolm Stewart."

"Jane Hunter." I extended my fingers, which he clasped for just a moment. "I see you take after both the Stewart and Neri families."

Malcolm's bright blue eyes provided a vivid contrast with his ebony hair and lush black lashes and brows. Certainly striking, he radiated an energy that made his presence feel much larger than his short stature and slight frame.

"Yes, I'm a mix of the two. The best of both, or so I hope." His smile swept any arrogance from his words. He looked me over. "You have an interesting face, Ms. Hunter. The kind I like to paint."

Glancing around the loft, which was sparsely furnished and had an open ceiling with the pipes and other mechanical elements painted black, I noticed a cluster of easels set up near the windows. "You use this space as your studio as well as your home?"

"I've always felt that the studio was my home." Malcolm gestured toward an arrangement of upholstered chairs anchored by a large wool rug woven with the tones of a southern desert sunset. It looked like it was handmade.

Probably is, I thought, as Malcolm directed me to sit in one of the elegant but unassuming cream-colored chairs. *I bet he buys most of his stuff from artisans.*

"You were probably surprised to get my text," Malcolm said as he sat down in a chair facing mine.

"Seeing as how we've never met, yes I was." I gazed over his shoulder at the loft's lone dividing wall. A small kitchen lined the wall, which had one door I assumed led to the bathroom. Every other space, including the bedroom, was only delineated by tall double-sided metal shelves. "But since you mentioned your cousin, Gabe, whom I met the other day, I decided I'd come and talk to you. I didn't know him, really, but he seemed like such a nice gentleman." I shifted in my chair. "My condolences, by the way. Guess I should have said that first."

"Thank you, and no worries. Gabe actually mentioned you to me when we talked later that day." Malcolm's smile faded from bright to wistful. "He thought you seemed nice as well."

"I'm glad I made a good impression," I said.

Malcolm leaned forward, pressing his palms against his upper thighs. "He was particularly interested in the amateur detective work you've done in collaboration with Cameron Clewe. Apparently, Gabe has been following news of your activities for some time. He said you focus on cold cases or on instances when an innocent suspect is being unjustly accused."

"That's true." I met Malcolm's intense gaze with a lift of my eyebrows. "But I don't think we've really been in the news that much. We usually try to avoid claiming any serious involvement in our cases, allowing the accolades go to law enforcement."

"I think Gabe meant the 'news' that circulates through various levels of society."

"Oh, gossip? OK, I'm sure we've been talked about in certain circles, especially considering Cam's wealth and position." I settled back in my chair. "And his social peculiarities, of course."

Malcolm grinned, but I was relieved to see his expression held no mockery. "Even I've heard stories, and I don't hang out in upper crust business circles. It seems your boss doesn't often leave his estate, and has been known to insult many of his former girlfriends' families, among other things."

"You've heard right. But he does have legitimate reasons for his behavior," I said.

"I'm sure he does. Most people don't really think about why someone is acting a certain way, though." Malcolm lifted his hands. "It was the same for Gabe."

"You were close?"

"Yes, even though he was thirty years older than me. He's"—Malcolm cleared his throat—"I mean, he was my first cousin once removed. I think that's how you say it."

"Your dad's first cousin," I said.

"Right. Anyway, we always got along. I actually felt closer to Gabe than to my own father." Malcolm sank back in his chair. "My dad didn't like that. To be honest, my dad doesn't like me much either."

I didn't jump in with a rebuttal of this sentiment. Despite society's insistence that family was everything, I'd often encountered situations like Malcolm's seeming estrangement from his father. It was one reason I always rolled my eyes whenever advertisements promised they treated customers "like family." That wasn't always a good thing, in my opinion.

"The official reports claim Gabe died of an overdose. Is that true?"

"No." Malcolm leapt to his feet and paced the length of the rug and back. "Here's the thing, Ms. Hunter—my cousin was an addict, but he'd been clean for ten years. He took his sobriety very seriously and attended Narcotics Anonymous meetings several times a week. I don't believe he overdosed." Malcolm stopped short in front of my chair. "I think he was murdered."

Chapter Eleven

I stared up at him. “That would mean someone in your family . . .”

“Not necessarily. There were other people at my brother’s birthday party. A few friends and a couple members of the board and some of the family’s legal team.” Malcolm turned on his heel and strode back to his chair but stood behind it instead of sitting down. “Roger Easton, who used to be the lead lawyer for our family’s business interests, was the most high-profile person, I suppose.”

“He’s running for governor this fall, isn’t he?”

Malcolm nodded. “He’s a few years younger than my dad, but they went through law school together because Duff took a couple of years off after getting his undergraduate degree and Roger didn’t.”

“That means there’s a whole list of people who could’ve harmed Gabe,” I said. “But why would they?”

“I don’t know.” Malcolm gripped the back of his chair, his expression bleak. “But Gabe was definitely afraid something might happen. He said he’d received anonymous threats.”

“Did he have copies of the messages or whatever they were?”

"No, they were phone calls, and Gabe didn't record his calls." Malcolm's eyes widened. "Oh, I'm an idiot. I haven't offered you anything to drink or eat. That's a serious crime in the South, you know."

"It's fine, I won't report you," I said with a smile.

"Good to know. I'm already on my family's blacklist as it is. Now, what can I get you?"

"Water is fine." I rose to my feet and followed him over to the kitchen. "Why talk to me about your concerns, though? Why not the police?"

Malcolm pulled a glass bottle of water from the refrigerator. It was a brand that was too pricey for me, but I supposed he was used to such things. Even if he was the black sheep of the Stewart family, it seemed he still had access to some of their wealth.

"The police are convinced it was an overdose," Malcolm said as he handed me the water. "Or, I should say, they were convinced to be convinced."

I leaned against the cool edge of the granite countertop. "You think your family had a hand in that?"

"Of course. Just like they always do." Malcolm grabbed his own bottle of water and after closing the fridge, turned to face me. "My brother and sister and I can all boast of never having received so much as a traffic ticket, but that's not because we've never broken any laws."

"The power of the Stewart name," I said, under my breath.

"The point is"—Malcolm took a swig from his bottle—"Gabe was acting anxious and jittery during Finn's party. Then he pulled me aside right after they cut the cake and asked me to meet him in the library, warning me to keep our meeting a secret. That piqued my curiosity, so I agreed. That's when he mentioned you and Cameron Clewe, and told me about passing you a book with a note inside."

"So he did want us to investigate," I said, more to myself than Malcolm.

"He hoped you would. Of course, I'm sure he meant to be in touch with you after a few days, to see what you and Mr. Clewe thought about the note."

"Did you read it?" I asked, swirling the water in my bottle.

"No. Like I said, Gabe only spoke with me about this after the birthday party that evening, and he'd already slipped you the book and note earlier." Malcolm studied me for a moment. "It involved my late Aunt Kimberly, didn't it?"

I nodded. "Did Gabe harbor suspicions about Kimberly's death? He mentioned they were close."

"He didn't believe she committed suicide, or at least he wasn't convinced that she had. She died from an overdose too, you know." Malcolm tapped his water bottle against his palm. "In her case, since she hadn't had issues with addiction prior to her death, they ruled it a deliberate suicide, while in Gabe's case . . ."

"He had conveniently dealt with drug addiction in the past, so people would easily believe he fell off the wagon."

Malcolm's lips thinned. "Exactly. It didn't help that Gabe did have lingering physical problems, from his prior drug abuse but also from an accident he was in when he was only sixteen."

"I heard about that. Your father and Gabe's older brother were also involved."

"They were, but it was Gabe who was seriously injured." Malcolm set his water bottle on the granite countertop. "That's where his addiction started. He was in really bad shape and never fully recovered. You may have noticed that he was a little unsteady on his feet. That's because his legs were broken in so many places, and they couldn't really fix them properly back then."

"I suppose he was given opioids for the pain. Which he probably needed, but then it became a double-edged sword." I took another sip of water and pondered this information. It was likely that everyone at the birthday party would have been aware of Gabe's addiction issues. Any of them could have slipped an overdose in his coffee or switched out his nonopioid pills or otherwise tampered with something that Gabe could have unknowingly ingested. Then when the drugs showed up in his system it would have been easy enough to blame it on a relapse.

"That's where the problem started, although Gabe would willingly confess that he was the one at fault for escalating his use of the painkillers rather than tapering off. But he was still in pain from time to time. It made me wish I could do something to help, but he said he just had to live with it." Malcolm pulled open one of the lower kitchen cabinets and tossed his water bottle into a recycling bin.

I did the same with my bottle, then followed Malcolm over to the wall of windows. "I take it you'd like Cam and me to do a little quiet investigating into Gabe's death?"

Twilight cast deep shadows across the canyon created by the city's eclectic mixture of tall and squat buildings. Staring out at the darkening sky, Malcolm clasped his hands together against his chest. "If you're willing, I'd be very grateful. I'd be glad to pay your expenses . . ."

"Cam never takes money for this type of thing. He doesn't need it and honestly, he pays me well, so I'd never ask for it either. However, we'd be very grateful for your help. You can connect us to people we need to speak with, as well as provide background information on Gabe and others in your family."

"I'm happy to do whatever I can," Malcolm said, his gaze still fixed on the scene framed by the windows.

I laid my hand on his arm. "For starters, I'd love to see the guest list for the birthday party."

He glanced over at me. "Mom might still have it. I'll certainly see what I can do."

"Those names will be invaluable, so let me know once you talk to your mom. Also, I think it would be extremely helpful if you'd visit Aircroft and talk directly to Cam about your impressions of everyone at the party. Things like whether there were arguments or whether anyone was acting strangely. Also, who had the opportunity to slip drugs to Gabe, and that sort of thing."

"You'll be there as well?" Malcolm asked.

"Of course. Cam and I are a team," I said, with a warm smile. "Just call or text me and I'll coordinate schedules. Well, I'll work with Lauren, Cam's assistant, to do that, but I'm sure we can set up a mutually agreeable time."

Malcolm's answering smile faded. "Not until after this weekend. The funeral is Saturday."

"Once again, I'm so sorry for your loss," I said, patting his arm.

"Thank you." A sheen of tears clouded Malcolm's bright eyes. "Like I said, Gabe was more like a father to me than my own dad. He supported my art career and never questioned my refusal to get involved with the family's business interests. He often defended me against Dad's rants, too. Which caused a rift between them, but Gabe claimed he never regretted taking my side. I believe, maybe, he thought of me, just a little, as a surrogate son."

"Then let's try to figure this out, for Gabe's sake, and yours, and maybe even for your Aunt Kimberly. I think your cousin would've wanted that too."

Malcolm clasped both of my hands. "He did, he would. So I say yes, let's join forces and reveal the truth, whatever it is."

"I have to warn you, the investigation could reveal things that might negatively affect your family and friends. Are you prepared for that?" I asked, squeezing his fingers.

"Absolutely," Malcolm replied fervently. "The truth needs to come out, no matter what skeletons spill out of the closets."

I gave him a nod of approval. "OK, I'll make sure to be ready with the broom and dustbin."

Chapter Twelve

"When I shared the conversation with Cam the following day, he readily agreed to meet Malcolm.

"Lauren can set it up, since she manages my schedule," he said. "And waiting until next week is no problem. We have another meeting before that anyway. Tomorrow, as a matter of fact."

"With Vanessa Gale?" I asked, glancing up from my laptop screen. Cam had stopped by the library to check in with me, as he typically did at least once during the workday. The visits became more frequent, of course, when we were working a case.

Cam strolled over to one of the bookshelves. "No, I haven't responded to her yet. I'm still not sure I want to fund any expedition she plans to lead. Even though neither my investigator nor I have uncovered any red flags in her past, there's something about her that feels a little . . ."

"Off?" I suggested. "I agree. But perhaps you could provide her with just enough funding for a solo trip to Peru. If she could return with some solid evidence of your father's presence in that country, you could mount a full-fledged expedition later."

"That's a good idea." Turning to face me, Cam leaned his back against the end of one shelf unit. "This is why I value you so much, Jane. You have an exceptionally logical mind."

"Not for my charm and good looks? I'm hurt." I flashed a grin to counter the downward curve of his lips. "Just kidding. Anyway, if it isn't Ms. Gale, who are we meeting?"

"Kaden Ward. When Lauren contacted him about the book Gabe Neri added to my recent acquisitions, he asked if we could bring it to his house." Cam rolled down the sleeves of his pale blue dress shirt. "I've spoken to someone about the heating situation, by the way. The best option they could offer was adding space heaters."

I surveyed the books on the shelves behind him. Many were leather-bound; all were valuable. "I think I'd prefer to just wear layers. Space heaters are notorious for causing fires."

His head down, Cam appeared focused on buttoning his cuffs, but I caught a sliver of a smile. "I assumed you'd say that."

"Librarians are understandably anxious when it comes to fire," I said. "No one wants to emulate the fate of the Library of Alexandria."

"Not the main library, anyway," Cam said, confirming the breadth of his esoteric knowledge.

"Right, the second one was destroyed by religious fervor in the fourth century." I shook my head. "An extreme example of book banning if ever there was one."

"I suppose destroying pagan texts seemed like the right thing to do at the time," Cam said absently, his attention diverted by the appearance of Lauren in the library doorway.

"A guest has arrived," she said. "I put them in the music room."

Cam squared his shoulders. "Who is it? We weren't expecting anyone today, were we?"

"No, this person just showed up on the doorstep." Lauren's dark eyes were filled with worry as she met Cam's questioning gaze. "I know you hate surprises, and visitors who drop by without warning, but I think you might want to make an exception today." She lifted her hands. "It's Ainsley Stewart, of all people."

From Cam's expression I could tell this was not welcome news. "Perhaps Malcolm talked to her?"

I straightened in my chair "I doubt it. He seemed committed to keeping our investigation a secret."

"We'll see." Cam straightened and strode to the door. "Please ask Mateo to prepare coffee and tea," he told Lauren. "Come, Jane. Let's see what Ms. Stewart has to say for herself."

He brushed past Lauren and disappeared down the hall. I rose to my feet and walked over to Lauren, who hadn't moved.

"Something you should know," she said as she stepped into the hall to allow me to pass. "Cam and Ainsley have a rather . . . turbulent past."

I met her concerned gaze with a lift of my eyebrows. "Did they date?"

"No, but not because she didn't want to. Even though she's five years older than Cam, she seemed to think they were a perfect match." Lauren rolled her eyes. "Same social standing and all that nonsense."

"She must've met him at parties held here," I said thoughtfully. "If it was a few years ago, they wouldn't have run into each other any other way."

"Ainsley was on the board of a couple of charities Cam supports, so she was on the guest list for various events. But she hasn't visited Aircroft in at least four years. Not since . . ." Lauren clamped her lips shut.

"Cam inadvertently humiliated her in some way?"

"Yes, but it wasn't inadvertent. She came on too strong at one of the charity fundraisers, and Cam publicly rejected her."

"Ah, I see. Well, perhaps I'd better hustle and join them in the music room before things get ugly." I patted Lauren's shoulder. "Maybe you should sneak a bit of brandy into my coffee."

"I'll just have the bottle ready for after the meeting," Lauren replied with a smile. "I should run too. Cam isn't going to want to wait too long for the distraction of refreshments."

Lauren took off for the kitchen at a brisk walk while I hurried down the hall in the opposite direction. The music room wasn't too far from the library, but by the time I entered, Cam and Ainsley had already squared off.

They stood at one end of the room, in front of an elaborate audio system and shelves filled with vinyl records. Although a set of armchairs anchored the elaborately-patterned Persian rug, it appeared neither was in any hurry to take a seat.

"Hello," I said, fighting to keep my voice upbeat. "You must be Ainsley Stewart. I'm Jane Hunter, Cam's personal librarian."

Although Ainsley had to be forty, she didn't look it. Her lean figure displayed the exquisite tailoring of her brown-and-blue plaid jacket and beige wool slacks to perfection and her crisp ivory blouse had a stand-up collar that reminded me of an equestrian outfit. *Of course, she's a rider,* I remined myself. Her blonde hair was cut in a sleek bob and her hazel eyes were carefully made-up to look as if they weren't.

"I've heard about you, Ms. Hunter," Ainsley said in a sultry voice that evoked old Lauren Bacall films. "It seems you not only catalog books, you also aid Cam in his little amateur detective hobby. Two jobs in one, isn't it? How industrious of you. And dedicated," she added, with a sharp glance at Cam.

"He pays me well for both," I said, calmly taking a seat in one of the armchairs.

"I'm sure." Ainsley's dark eyes flashed. "Cam has no problems with money."

Although it was clear she meant he had plenty of other problems, I offered her an innocent smile. "Yes, he's quite generous, isn't he?"

Ainsley stalked over to the chair facing mine and sat down, crossing her long legs at her ankles. Her short leather boots were worn to a sheen at the toes. "With charitable giving, you mean? Absolutely."

Cam sat in the chair beside me. "Why are you gracing us with your presence here today, Ainsley? I'm sure you must be busy, having to deal with all the preparations for a family funeral, among other things. Condolences, by the way."

The haughty gaze Ainsley fixed on Cam was tinged with another emotion. *Desire,* I realized. *The stare of a cat eyeing a mouse.*

"Oh, I have very little to do with that," Ainsley said, waving one of her slender hands through the air. "Lucas is in charge of everything. Well, my little brother Malcolm is involved as well. It seems he loved that old druggie cousin of ours for some reason." She sat forward in her chair, her eyes still on Cam.

No, not a cat, but a bird of prey. A raptor, half-starved, sighting its next meal.

"Did Malcolm ask you to meet with us?" Cam asked, a flash of anger in his green eyes.

Ainsley examined her short, unpolished fingernails. "Heavens, no. We barely speak. I simply wanted to ask for your help in shutting down some unfortunate rumors."

"How would I, or Jane, be able to assist you with that?" Cam stretched his legs out in front of him. Only the slight bounce of one heel against the rug betrayed his nerves.

"Most of our crowd are aware of your sleuthing exploits, even though you don't seem eager to broadcast them." Ainsley swept her honey-colored hair behind her ears, which were studded with large pearls. "I thought perhaps you'd be willing to share a statement, confirming that Gabriel's death was an overdose. Just say you looked into it and agree with the official reports. I know you don't get out much, but perhaps you could use Ms. Hunter as your mouthpiece?" She turned her hawk-like gaze on me. "I believe she mingles with a wide group of people, some who are quite talented at spreading gossip."

I pinned her with my coldest stare. "It seems you're more than capable of dispensing that yourself, Ms. Stewart. Why involve us?"

Ainsley stretched out both arms, her movements languid as a lioness. "People tend to think a family like mine is involved in any number of cover-ups. Comes with the territory, doesn't it, Cam? No one believes so much money can be accumulated without someone committing crimes or other atrocities."

"I haven't found that to be true, but then, as you say, I don't get out much." Cam stood and straightened to his full height. "But I admit even I've heard speculation about the Stewart family."

Rising to her feet, Ainsley took several strides forward, stopping just short of the toes of Cam's shoes. "Listen, Cam," she said, lifting her sharp chin to look up into his face. "I realize you always think you're better than everyone else in the room, but don't you dare speak ill about my family. I suspect the Clewe family harbors plenty of secrets too."

That hit a little too close to home. Cam stared over her shoulder, refusing to meet her eyes. "At any rate, I have no interest in helping you draw a veil over your family's questionable behavior, no matter how innocuous it is. I can't imagine why you'd think I would."

"Your father and my grandfather were friends. Doesn't that count for anything?" Ainsley's low voice took on a plaintive tone.

"Actually, no they weren't, and no it doesn't." Cam turned aside and strolled over to the built-in shelves housing the audio system. "Jane and I have already started looking into a cold case right now," he said, keeping his back to us. "One that was declared a suicide but perhaps was something else entirely."

Ainsley's sharp intake of breath was muted by the sound of Lauren's heels tapping across the hardwood floor.

"I have coffee or hot tea. Just let me know what you prefer," she said, placing a pewter tray laden with cups and saucers on the console table behind the sofa.

"Nothing, please. I've learned to expect that when I visit Aircroft," Ainsley said, breezing past me. She exited the room without a goodbye or a backward glance.

Chapter Thirteen

"Do you two want anything to drink or should I carry it back to the kitchen?" Lauren asked.

"Just take it away," Cam said, with a dismissive wave of his hand. But as Lauren picked up the tray and the cups rattled, he spun around. "Thank you, Lauren. Sorry for making you go to all that trouble for nothing."

He's learning, I thought.

Lauren's pressed lips curved upward. "It's no problem. You couldn't anticipate how rude our guest would be." She offered Cam and me a warm smile before leaving the room.

Cam glanced over at me. "As you may have guessed, Ainsley Stewart and I aren't on great terms."

"Don't worry, Lauren warned me, so I wasn't shocked."

"Then you know about my public rejection of Ainsley's advances? I promise I tried other methods, but she refused to accept defeat without humiliation." Cam lifted his hands in a *what-can-you-do gesture*. "Then she decided to spread some interesting speculation about me."

"Because, how could any man turn her down?"

My sarcastic tone wasn't lost on Cam, who shrugged. "Not that I care, but the sheer pettiness of it soured any friendship we might've had. I really don't have much tolerance for narcissistic behavior. Had enough of that in the past."

With his stepfather, I realized. But I knew better than to broach that topic. "Even though I don't believe Malcolm told her anything, it seems she knew we were looking into Gabe's death. Otherwise, why show up in person hoping to convince us to corroborate the official story?"

"Which begs the question—why is Ainsley, or anyone from the Stewart family, keeping tabs on us?" Cam crossed to chair facing mine and sat down.

I shook my head. "I don't think it's us. They're watching Malcolm."

"You're probably right," Cam said, casting me an approving glance. "The wolves are circling the black sheep."

"Because they don't want him to bleat out any of their secrets." I examined Cam's thoughtful expression. "You're aware Malcolm is *persona non grata* in the Stewart family?"

"Of course. It's common knowledge in business circles that he refuses to participate in the Stewart empire." Cam leaned one elbow into the padded chair arm and rested his chin on his hand. "He's an artist, I believe. I'm sure that's not the life Duff had in mind for his youngest child. Hobby, perhaps, but not a career."

"Well, compared to Ainsley, Malcolm is definitely a more pleasant individual."

"That wouldn't be difficult to achieve." Cam dropped his arm and leaned back in his chair. "It will be interesting to see what Kaden Ward has to say tomorrow, especially in terms of Gabe's and Kimberly's deaths."

"Whether he has any suspicions, you mean?"

"Yes, but of course we should also be careful." Cam drummed his fingers against the chair arm. "Ward could turn out to be the killer, at least in Kimberly's case. The spouse is the most likely suspect when someone dies under suspicious circumstances."

"True, and believe me, I can understand the impulse," I said, with a frown.

Cam's gaze swept over me. "You had a bad marriage, right? You've never really talked about it in detail, but I've gleaned that much."

"It was a huge mistake. Except for Bailey. It was awful, but I can't totally regret it because of her." I tipped my head to one side and studied Cam for a second. "I'm sure Lily felt the same about your grandfather Calvin. It wasn't a similar situation, of course, but she did have to raise your father as a single mom, just like I had to raise Bailey alone. It was tough, but I never regretted having my daughter, just like I bet Lily never regretted raising Rafe."

Cam frowned. "You think I should cut Lily a little slack because she had a challenging life?"

"Not just that, but yes, I think you should. I know you're upset that she, Rafe, and Gordy didn't choose to be a part of your life when you were young, but if I've learned anything in sixty-plus years, it's that it's best to leave the past in the past. You have a chance to connect with them now; why waste it?"

Cam's right leg was shaking despite the pressure he appeared to be placing on his foot. "To be fair, thanks to Al, my father thought I died in childhood, so it was really up to Gordy, and then later, Lily, to tell him otherwise. But they didn't do that."

"You could ask them why, but you'd probably have to develop a better relationship before they'll tell you," I said.

Cam jumped to his feet. "Point taken. Now, I'm going to get back to work and urge you to do so as well. You'll have to take time off tomorrow to meet with Kaden Ward."

"Are you planning to join me for that, or am I going solo?" I stood up slowly, my thoughts focused on Cam's family issues and his refusal to deal with them. I knew I couldn't push too hard or he would shut down completely, but I also felt I had to keep trying, for his sake, if no one else's.

"I thought you could handle it." Cam tossed this comment off without a hint of apology.

"Are you busy or just trying to avoid leaving Aircroft?" I asked, with equal nonchalance.

Cam shot me a sharp look. "Busy. Anyway, Ward's house is in Winston-Salem, not too far from downtown. I'll make sure Lauren gives you the address and his number."

Another drive into the city. Great. "Are you planning for me to return the book?"

"The book, yes. The note, no." Cam crossed his arms over his chest. "He wasn't told about the note."

"OK." I made a zipper motion across my lips. "I won't say anything unless he mentions it first."

"I doubt he will. Lauren said he seemed surprised to hear about the book, and he didn't mention anything special about it. Unless he's a good actor, he doesn't appear to have been aware of his wife's plea for help."

"Perhaps because he was the cause of it," I said. "How much do you know about Kaden Ward or his marriage?"

"Not a great deal. I've heard he dislikes the Stewart family and hasn't socialized with them since Kimberly died, but apparently, he isn't particularly interested in social events no matter who's involved. He does some appearances to promote his books, but tends to avoid society parties or anything of that nature."

Like someone else I know, I thought, eyeing Cam. He'd shoved his hands into his pockets, a sure sign that he was trying to hide the shakes. "I find it interesting that he writes thrillers and mysteries. That could point to a mind capable of creating a fool-proof murder."

"I'm not sure we should equate an author's books with their personal actions," Cam said over his shoulder as he headed for the door. "To play devil's advocate—a mystery writer would also be aware of how difficult it is to kill someone and not leave a trace, especially with the forensic tools the authorities have these days."

I followed him out of the music room and into the hall. "Yes, but people do get away with murder. We've seen that in the cold cases we've investigated. Or at least, they can get away with it for long periods of time."

"But not forever." Cam stopped and turned to look at me. "That's why our *sleuthing exploits*, as Ainsley put it, are so valuable. Even if all we can do is provide the police or other legal entities with enough information to reopen an old case, it's still worth the effort, don't you think?"

"Absolutely. I wouldn't be willing to help you, otherwise." I wrinkled my nose at him. "Except for the extra salary, of course. That is an attractive inducement."

"Honest, as always," Cam said dryly. "Don't you ever consider stroking people's egos?"

I strolled closer to him. "Nope. I've always said cats and dogs should be stroked while human egos should be challenged."

Cam flashed me a sardonic smile. "And it seems you do your best to live by that philosophy."

Chapter Fourteen

Kaden Ward's house wasn't as difficult to find as I'd feared—he lived in an older residential neighborhood not far from Donna Valenti's home. Since I'd visited Donna several times, I knew a couple of backroad routes to avoid city traffic.

The street Ward lived on was lined with trees that arched over the sidewalks and included several larger vintage homes as well as Craftsman-style cottages. I parked on the street in front of the house—a charming bungalow with a front yard that sloped steeply down to the sidewalk. Walking up the cracked concrete driveway, I admired the plantings of small shrubs and ornamental grasses that filled the landscape. From the piles of desiccated stalks and scattered leaves, it looked like the yard would be a riot of color and fragrance during the spring, summer, and early fall, but right now it was as dull as the leaden winter sky.

The covered wooden front porch, painted a creamy vanilla, ran the full width of the house. Its trim was painted jade green to match the window frames and shutters, creating an elegant contrast with the ivory-painted brick of the body of the home. Checking my watch to make sure I wasn't too early, I pressed the brass doorbell on one side of the natural-wood door.

The man who opened the door took me aback. Due to a little online research, I knew that author Kaden Ward was seventy, but any expectation of a bookish, professorial individual was instantly shattered. Ward was tall and robust, resembling a prize fighter rather than the stereotypical writer. His sparse gray hair encircled a gleaming bald spot that gave him the look of a medieval monk, albeit one who did the heavy labor at the monastery rather than a scribe.

"Good afternoon. I assume you're Jane Hunter?" Kaden Ward's voice was deep and rich, complimenting his commanding presence.

"Yes, that's right." I shifted the du Maurier book from my right hand to my left so I could accept Ward's proffered handshake. His fingers swallowed up mine in a hearty grip. "I work for Cameron Clewe."

"You're the librarian?" Ward looked me up and down, his light brown eyes expressing surprise. "You don't have the look."

"Is there really such a thing?" I asked, fighting to keep irritation from sharpening my tone. "In my experience we come in all shapes, sizes, and colors. Rather like cats—or authors."

Ward released my hand. "Touché. Please come in, Ms. Hunter," he added, gesturing inside.

"You can call me Jane," I said as I crossed to a wood-framed sofa with deep umber cushions. Since this was the style of home that didn't have a foyer, I wasn't sure what to do with my coat and decided to simply set it on the sofa cushion beside me, placing the book on top of the coat folds.

"Then please, call me Kaden," he said, closing the front door without locking it. "And, if you'd like, I can hang that coat on the hall tree for you."

"It's fine here, if that's all right with you," I said, pushing up the sleeves of my loose crimson sweater. The room, stuffed with American Primitive antiques as well as a few Victorian pieces, felt more compact than its actual size. The flames leaping up from the gas logs in the tile-framed fireplace added to the oppressive heat. I wished I'd worn lighter-weight slacks rather than my black jeans, but obviously I'd dressed for Aircroft and outdoors, not this overheated house.

"Of course. Now, what can I get you to drink? I have wine or beer as well as water and some sparkling juices."

"Water is fine," I said, watching as he disappeared through a narrow archway into the home's small kitchen. He was so tall his head almost bumped the inside of the arch and broad enough that one shoulder brushed the side.

I'd expect a large man like him to get hot easily, but judging by the temperature in the house, that doesn't seem to be the case, I mused. *I wonder if he has some sort of medical condition, like poor circulation.*

Kaden returned with two glasses of water. He handed me one before sitting in an oversized armchair across from me. "I was surprised when Mr. Clewe's secretary called," he said, after taking a gulp of water. "It seems there was some confusion over a book that may have belonged to my late wife?"

"It definitely did." I lifted the du Maurier off my coat and held it up. "There's a signature inside that marks it as the property of Kimberly Stewart Ward."

Squinting, Kaden stared at the book cover for a moment. "*My Cousin Rachel.*" His mobile face stilled to stone. "Was it Gabriel Neri who packed up the books? If so, it's . . . unsettling."

"How so?" I asked.

"Because Gabe gave Kim that book for her twenty-fifth birthday. After she passed away, I looked all over for it. I wanted to give it back to him, as a sort of memento. But I couldn't find it among her things."

Because it was probably hidden in Mac Stewart's library, I thought, laying the book across my knees. "You were living with the Stewart family when Kimberly died?"

Kaden shifted in his chair. "Yes. My first book was published right before our wedding, so I hadn't earned much yet, even a year later. Kim thought . . ." He squeezed his fingers into fists. "Well, she wanted me to concentrate on my writing. She convinced me to live with her family. Lord knows the house was big enough."

I decided to change my approach. "How did you and Kimberly meet?"

"At work. It was when she was a graduate student." Kaden fell silent, as if lost in thought. "Of course I knew who she was, but she never flaunted her wealth, even though she had money in her own name that she'd inherited from her grandmother. But she didn't admit that until after I'd known her for some time. In fact, she went out of her way to pretend to be the typical poor student—sharing a rather dingy apartment with two other girls and working part-time at a local café. That's where we actually met. We were both servers and often ended up on the same shifts."

"It sounds like you enjoyed a typical college romance," I said.

"We did. Everything was great until"—the lines bracketing Kaden's lips deepened—"we became more serious, and Kim felt she should introduce me to her family."

"They didn't welcome you?"

"What do you think? Here I was, a wannabe author still trying to get a book deal. My only income at that point was the pittance I earned as a newly minted English instructor at a community college." Kaden cast me a self-deprecating glance. "Not exactly a catch, in their eyes."

"But from the things I've heard, I bet Kimberly didn't care about that," I said, watching Kaden's expression closely. He seemed to remember his wife fondly, but there was still something guarded about his responses, like he was carefully picking and choosing his words.

"She didn't." Kaden stood and crossed to me. "May I see the book?"

"Of course." I handed it to him. "Cam and I thought you might wish to keep it, since it has your wife's signature."

Opening the cover, Kaden stared at the flyleaf. "She had to add the Stewart," he said under his breath. "Never could escape it."

Unsure whether he was referencing Kimberly or himself, I crossed my hands in my lap and remained silent as he flipped through the pages.

"It's ironic," he said at last. "Gabriel Neri just died, but somehow he managed to send this book to Aircroft." He looked down at me, his eyes hooded. "Do you have any idea why?"

My mind raced as I considered my next words, which would have to include a lie. Since Kaden hadn't mentioned the note, I wasn't about to bring it up. "Not really sure. Perhaps he hoped Cam or I would return it to you. Maybe he didn't trust any of the Stewarts to do that?"

"Trusting the Stewarts about anything . . ." Kaden's brief burst of laughter was laden with anger. "Anyway, I'm glad you thought of me, Jane. It's better for me to have this than that lot, that's for sure."

Why? I thought, as he strolled back to his chair, clutching the book to his chest. *Because you suspected there was a message hidden in the book? Perhaps not a note, but maybe in some underlined passages or even in the theme of the book itself?*

"It seems Kimberly was fond of that novel, based on how well-worn it is," I said.

"I guess so. She didn't share her thoughts about it with me, but I know she and Gabe had some deep discussions about it. I think they felt a connection to the unreliable narrator aspect, since both of them were often accused of making up stories by the family. And the gaslighting the narrator may or may not have experienced from the woman he loved probably echoed their problems with differentiating imagination from reality." Kaden laid the book on a small table next to his chair. "Funny, now that I think about it, Kim and I rarely discussed literature. Maybe because I was so focused on my own work that I really didn't give her much of an opportunity."

I studied him for a moment, wondering if I could ask him about Kimberly's mental state before her death. "She was apparently a very sensitive young woman."

Kaden's eyebrows drew together over his crooked nose. "If you mean she suffered from depression and anxiety, that's certainly true. She was honest about her problems with me as soon as we started dating. It wasn't a dealbreaker for me, but she did go downhill after we moved into the Stewart home. Kim was never delusional or paranoid before that, but she changed." He rubbed his jaw with one hand. "It was almost like it happened with the flip of a switch. I tried to help her, but . . ." He inhaled a deep breath.

I wanted to believe him but reminded myself that someone who'd murdered their wife and framed it as a suicide would naturally want people to believe their spouse was mentally unraveling. "Did she ever say why? I mean, I understand how depression can overwhelm you, but usually there's a trigger for a real break with reality."

"She never told me a reason, if there was one. But I know there must've been something, because one day she was herself and then the next day she basically fell apart." Kaden appeared to unconsciously press his palm against the du Maurier novel on the table.

"And nothing happened that could've caused such a reaction? That must've been hard on you," I said, infusing my words with as much sympathy as I could muster.

"I can't recall observing any trigger. It happened after a family dinner celebrating her cousin Lucas's birthday, but I don't remember anything happening that evening that could've caused such a dramatic change."

I scooted to the front edge of the sofa. "Lucas Neri? Gabe's older brother?"

"Yes. I mean, Gabe was high on something, which created some tension, but I never saw any real traumatic incidents. Nothing that should've affected Kim so much, anyway. Gabe and Kim did have a private conversation when she met him in the library after dinner, but she never told me what they talked about. If it had been something important, I'm certain she would've let me know." Kaden frowned. "Or at least I hope so."

"I'm sure you tried your best to help her." I was not at all sure, but it seemed better to remain an ally rather than turn into an antagonist, especially if we needed more information from Kaden in the future. I rose to my feet, throwing my coat over my arm. "Well, I should go. Thanks so much for chatting with me today. I must confess I haven't read any of your books, but I plan to remedy that oversight soon."

"I can help you with that." Kaden stood and crossed to a low bookshelf. He pulled out a brightly colored paperback with an abstract gun and female figure on the cover. "Here you go—my latest. More of a noir than most of my work, but it seems to be doing well." Picking up a pen from the top of the bookcase, he flipped open the book and scrawled a hasty signature on the title page. "Here you go. Signed and everything."

Thanking him as he handed the book to me, I promised to add it to the top of my "to-be-read" pile.

"Oh, don't worry, get to it when you can," Kaden said, ushering me out onto the porch. "It's not the Great American Novel or anything, but I hope it's entertaining."

When I reached the bottom of the porch steps and turned to offer him a goodbye, he fixed me with a dark look and added, "By the way, I know about Cameron Clewe's amateur detective exploits, and that you've acted as his assistant in the past. Next time, when you want to know something, you can be a bit more direct."

I opened my mouth to formulate a response, but he'd already stepped back into the house and closed the door before I could reply.

Chapter Fifteen

On Sunday I joined Vince and Donna at a local café. We had started a tradition of meeting for brunch at least once a month after the harrowing events of the last major case Cam and I had been involved in.

Occasionally Cam joined us, but since he'd been absent for several months, I was surprised to see him seated in the booth across from Vince and Donna.

"Well, hello," I said as I slid into the booth beside him. "Glad to see you here, even if you're going incognito."

Cam, dressed more casually than I'd ever seen him, in faded jeans and a navy sweatshirt, cast me a sidelong glance. "Vince called and suggested we meet to discuss the Stewart case."

"I've collected a little new information," Vince said, after greeting me. "Some courtesy of Donna's network of connections."

Donna, who'd pulled her braided hair up to wrap around her head like a crown, shifted forward in her seat and laid one arm on the table. "It's amazing what you hear when you're wandering around the farmer's market."

"It's open this time of year?" I asked with a lift of my eyebrows.

"Oh sure. They have those covered spaces and an inside building, so some vendors are there all year long. I head there every couple of weeks, even in January. I prefer the market's jams and winter vegetables and such over the grocery store's," Donna said. "Anyway, I sometimes overhear interesting conversations and often run into people I know."

"Not surprising when you seem to be acquainted with half the local population," Vince said, with a smile.

Donna grinned. "I'm a friendly person."

"That's true," I said. "And you have a cheerful nature that draws people in. More so than me, for sure."

"Certainly more so than me," Cam said under his breath.

At that moment the waiter appeared. While we placed our orders, I leaned closer to Cam and said, "You got my text about my meeting with Ward, I assume?"

Cam nodded. "We can talk more later."

Vince, placing his napkin in his lap, looked up. "Kaden Ward? That's funny—he's tied to one of the rumors Donna heard recently."

"Yes, I was quite surprised," Donna said. "There I was, buying some honey and winter squash, and I overheard the vendor chatting with another customer about Gabriel Neri's death. Of course, I inched a little closer . . ."

"Naturally," Vince said, patting her arm.

Donna wrinkled her nose at him. "Do you want me to share this with Cam and Jane or not?"

"Sorry, please continue," he replied, but then held up his hand when the waiter approached with our coffee.

"Alright, here's the gist," Donna said after the waiter disappeared. "Apparently, the customer knew Kaden Ward because she took a writing course from him at one of the local community colleges. She said he was a good teacher but a bit intimidating."

"He is a big man." I stirred cream into my mug. "And rather brusque."

Donna took a sip of her coffee before responding. "Yes, but that wasn't it. She claimed that during one session, a strange man came to the partially open classroom door. He lingered out in the hall long enough that Ward went to check it out, and when he saw who it was, he stormed out of the room, slamming the door behind him"

"The stranger was Gabe Neri?" Noticing he was tapping his spoon against the edge of his plate, I reached over and touched the back of Cam's hand. He shot me a look but laid down the spoon.

"That's right. One of her classmates recognized him. The customer said he and Ward argued in the hallway. She could only pick out a few words, but she was sure they were discussing Kaden Ward's late wife, Kimberly."

Cam pressed his hand against his right leg, which had been bouncing up and down, slightly shaking our bench seat. "It seems there was bad blood between Gabe Neri and Kaden Ward." He glanced over at me. "Jane met with Ward yesterday and reported that he was aware of our investigations into both Kimberly's and Gabe's deaths."

"An interesting coincidence. When Donna told me what she heard at the market, I remembered some research I'd done on Kaden Ward for an article." Vince waved his fork at Donna. "This is why I don't throw out all those papers I keep boxed up in the basement. They can come in handy."

"Sure, sure," Donna said, rolling her eyes.

The waiter returned with our food—a jazzed-up avocado toast and fruit for me, eggs benedict for Cam, and pancakes and sausage for both Vince and Donna.

"What did you find?' Cam asked, poking his eggs to allow the runny yolks to drench the Canadian bacon and English muffin.

Vince poured maple syrup over his plate before handing the bottle to Donna. "Years ago, Kaden Ward brought a lawsuit against Mac Stewart, claiming the family had withheld stocks he was entitled to as Kimberly's widower."

"Really? What was the result?" I asked.

"The Stewarts won, of course." Vince sliced through his stack of pancakes with his fork. "Kimberly didn't have a will, so while Ward was entitled to money from her personal accounts, Mac and Duff Stewart said her stock shares must revert back to the family."

"When did they put that arrangement in place?" Cam asked.

"Ah, there's the really interesting part. It was disclosed in the court records that Mac Stewart had changed that aspect of the stock options only *after* Kimberly married Ward."

Cam laid down his fork. "Which means either he thought his daughter's marriage wouldn't last . . ."

"Or that he suspected she might die early," I concluded, after dabbing my lips with a napkin.

"Because she had mental health issues?" Donna asked, looking puzzled. "But surely Macnamara Stewart should've been more concerned with getting his daughter help than holding onto stocks."

"You'd think," I said dryly. "But people like Mac don't always put family before business."

Cam shot me a sidelong look. "You mean, wealthy people?"

"Sorry, I didn't mean to generalize," I said, grabbing my coffee mug to take a long swallow.

"No, you're right. That is often the case, as I should know. Albert Clewe would've done the same." Cam pushed his half-eaten plate of food away. "Anything else?" he asked Vince.

"Only that Kaden Ward cut all ties with the Stewart family after the lawsuit."

"Then it isn't likely he'd have been at Finn's birthday party the night Gabe died," I said thoughtfully.

"I'd say not." Donna set down her coffee mug with a thump. "But that doesn't mean he couldn't have entered the house, sight unseen, does it?"

"I suppose it's a possibility, but I can't imagine why he'd want to murder Gabe. Sure, they argued, but what would be the motive at this point? It's not like Gabe would've had any control over the Stewart family stocks," I said.

Cam stared up at the hanging light fixture, obviously lost in thought. "What if Gabe knew, or at least suspected, something about Kimberly's death that Ward didn't want revealed?"

"You mean like Kaden Ward was an abusive husband, or he was cheating on Kimberly, which drove her to suicide?" Donna asked, her dark eyes widening.

"But why wouldn't Gabriel Neri have brought that up when Kimberly died?" Vince's forehead creased with concentration. "Why would he wait to expose such a thing?"

We all sat back as the waiter appeared to collect our plates and utensils. After he left, promising to bring the check soon, Cam intertwined his fingers and pressed them against his chest. "Gabe Neri was a drug addict for years. Where did he get the money for that? As far as I've been able to discover, he's always lived off a small stipend from the Neri family."

Vince frowned. "You think he might have blackmailed Kaden Ward?"

"Then changed his mind after he'd been clean for a while," Donna said, her expression radiating curiosity.

"It's just one possibility." When the waiter appeared with the check, Cam grabbed it before Vince could stretch out his hand. "I'll pay for this. You've all been helping with the latest investigations, after all."

"I'll get it next time," Vince said firmly.

Cam glanced up from calculating the tip. "There is one more thing I'd like your help with."

"Vanessa Gale," I said.

"That's right." Cam gave me an approving look before turning his gaze on Vince and Donna. "Has Jane filled you in on Ms. Gale and her offer to help find my father?"

"She mentioned something about it, but only in passing," Vince said. "She's a journalist, right? I assume you want me to look into her, using my contacts."

"If you would. I've had a couple of private investigators check her out, and she seems legit, but there's still something about her that makes me feel uneasy."

"Me too," I said. "I meant to ask for your help before this, Vince, but there's been so much going on that it kept slipping my mind."

Donna offered me a warm smile. "Oh heavens, Jane, don't chide yourself for that. Some days I think my mind has been greased with butter, so much is sliding out my ears."

"Anyway, if you could ask around about Vanessa Gale in journalistic circles, I'd appreciate it," Cam said.

"Glad to help." Vince nudged Donna with his elbow. "Ready to go, dear?"

"Sure." Donna flashed a bright smile. "Thanks so much for joining us today. Especially you, Cam. We've missed you."

A faint blush highlighted the freckles sprinkled across Cam's cheekbones. "Thank you. Sorry I've been out of touch. I really can't give you a good excuse."

"Oh, don't worry about it, dear," Donna said, waving the napkin she'd pulled from her lap. "We understand."

Cam's eyes shifted to me. "I suppose you've discussed everything with them."

"Not everything, and besides, they'd already figured it out. You aren't the only observant person in the world, you know," I replied, meeting his stern gaze with a lift of my chin.

Donna giggled. "Cam, if you could see your face . . ."

Clapping his hand on her shoulder, Vince gave her a little push. "Let's go before you say something I might regret."

Chapter Sixteen

After Vince and Donna left the table, Cam shifted to face me more directly. "Vince's information about Kaden Ward—does it track with your impressions of him?"

"You mean, do I think he's capable of killing his wife, either directly or by abuse or neglect, then paying off Gabe to keep that truth a secret?" I pursed my lips. "I'm not sure. He definitely doesn't seem weak or timid, so I suppose it's possible. But the thing is, Ward was very specific about Kimberly's mental state deteriorating rapidly after one family event. Which makes me wonder if she discovered something the Stewarts, or Neris, didn't want her to share. Perhaps that was what she was referencing in the note—she was threatened by one or more family members and tried to notify the authorities, but no one would believe her."

"What if Ward said that to throw suspicion on Kimberly's family rather than himself?"

I studied Cam's thoughtful expression. "There is that. He's certainly intelligent enough to plan out all his moves. But he seemed truly baffled by Kimberly's sudden decline. If that was an act, he missed his calling."

Cam glanced down at his watch. "Is it that late? I'd better get going. I have a call with the head of one of my charities in about an hour. I need to get back to Aircroft in time to prepare."

I slid out of the booth and stood up. "You go on ahead, then. I want to stop by the ladies' room before driving home."

After a swift goodbye, Cam hurried out of the café. I used the restroom and made my exit as well, but when I walked around one corner of the building to reach my car, I was met by a stranger in a black suit.

I bobbed my head in a brisk hello, assuming the man had just come from church and was headed into the café. Instead, he stepped in front of me, halting my progress.

"Ms. Hunter," he said in a voice remarkable only for its complete lack of any accent. "I'd like to have a word, if I may." Spreading his legs apart and placing his hands on his hips, he effectively blocked the sidewalk.

"It seems you're making sure I can't object." I looked around, hoping to spot a few other people in the parking lot. Unfortunately, I saw no one. "What is it you want, Mr. . . . ?"

"My name is unimportant." The stranger's appearance was as bland as his voice. His height and build were both average and his facial features unmemorable. He was also wearing reflective sunglasses that hid his eyes. "What is important is that you listen to my advice."

I looked him up and down. "OK then, share it, or move out of my way."

He quirked one eyebrow. "It seems my information was correct; you are rather unflappable."

"I'm just too old to be intimidated by someone who won't even introduce himself. Now"—I crossed my arms over my chest—"spit out your message. I want to get home before this afternoon."

The man's lips tightened into a straight line. "This is for your own good, Ms. Hunter, as well as the health and safety of your family and friends. Not that I wish you any harm. I'm just a messenger. But the truth is, it would be best if you and your boss stopped digging into things that don't concern you."

"Such as what?" I asked, feeling the first frisson of fear.

"Other people's business." The stranger lowered his sunglasses just enough to allow me to catch a glimpse of the threatening glare in his dark eyes. "Unfortunate deaths that don't need to be paraded out in public again. It just causes more pain for people who've been hurt enough as it is."

I narrowed my eyes. "Who sent you? The Stewart family? Or Lucas Neri? Or maybe Kaden Ward?"

"What does it matter? The point is that you and Mr. Cameron Clewe need to back off. Family tragedies should not be used for your amusement." The man turned on his heel and strode off, leaving me standing on the sidewalk, bemused and more than a little anxious.

* * *

As soon as I got back to my apartment I put in a call to Cam, but only received his voicemail in response. I left a brief "call me" message and headed into the kitchen to grab a glass of wine. Slumping down on my well-worn sofa, I set the wineglass on a side table and kicked off my shoes.

It was clear that someone had sent the man in black to warn me against investigating either Kimberly's long-ago supposed suicide or Gabe's more recent death. *Or both*, I thought as I sipped my wine. Once I finished off one glass, I contemplated another, but decided I'd rather distract myself with a good book.

I was absorbed in a reread of John Crowly's *Little, Big* when Cam finally called me back.

"So this person came across like some sort of enforcer?" Cam asked after I detailed my encounter.

"Not quite that frightening, but he did look like a stereotypical second-in-command to either a shady lawyer or a gangster."

"Not much difference between the two." Cam's humorous tone definitely sounded forced. "He mentioned me specifically as well, so he or whoever hired him knows about our sleuthing side-gig."

"Apparently. Which makes me wonder if he's connected to Kaden Ward. He definitely knows what we're up to."

"More likely one of the Stewarts," Cam said. "You met Ainsley. I can imagine her staging something like this. She's always been a bit too dramatic."

"It did feel as if someone had watched too many detective shows." I leaned back into my sofa cushions. "To be honest, I'm not really scared. The whole thing was a little . . . overdone."

"A warning without teeth?" Cam cleared his throat. "Still, we have to remain alert. It's obvious there are one or more individuals who don't want anyone looking into Kimberly's death, or Gabe's supposed overdose. They may become more dangerous if we don't back off."

"Are we going to back off?" I asked.

"Absolutely not," Cam replied with fervor. "This simply means we're on the right track. I'm convinced there's something mysterious concerning both deaths that needs to be exposed."

"I figured you'd say that." I fiddled with the fringe on the shawl I'd thrown over the back of my sofa. "Should I share this with Malcolm? Or do you want to keep it between us?"

A moment of silence told me Cam was thinking this through. "Let's not bring him into this particular scenario yet. I don't want him running off to confront his family or Ward or anyone else. Not until we have more solid information." There was another short pause. "Don't tell Vince and Donna either. Not yet."

"You're worried they might be put in danger," I said.

"I am. They don't need to be placed in anyone's crosshairs. Maybe they would still volunteer to help, but I dislike the idea that they could be targeted." Cam took a deep breath. "I don't like you being involved in something dangerous, either, but I know I can't actually stop you."

"No, you can't, so let that go. Besides, I think I've proven my mettle several times already."

"You've certainly done that. But don't get cocky," Cam said. "If you're over-confident, you could get hurt."

"Don't worry, I know my limitations. And I'm also quite willing to point out yours."

A brief burst of laughter filled my ear. "Like I'd ever doubt that."

Chapter Seventeen

I'd settled into a productive day of cataloging on Monday when Lauren appeared at the library door to inform me that Vanessa Gale had returned to Aircroft.

"Cam is busy, and I don't think he really wants to speak with her yet anyway," she said. "Would you mind talking to her? I hate to just turn her away. If she does have any info on Cam's father . . ."

I closed the book I was working on and rolled my task chair back from my desk. "OK, I'll see what she has to say. If it's anything important, we can alert Cam at that point."

"Thanks." Lauren's lovely smile lit up her dark brown eyes. "I left her in the entry hall. I'll go fetch her now."

After Lauren left, I crossed the room to sit in one of the armchairs placed on either side of a cherry-wood side table. Wanting to be on an equal eye-level with Vanessa, I preferred both us to be sitting down for this conversation.

Vanessa strolled into the library wearing what seemed to be her uniform of jeans and a muted plaid flannel shirt. I motioned toward the other armchair. "Please, have a seat, Ms. Gale."

"I hope you'll call me Vanessa," she replied as she sat down gracefully.

"Then it's Jane," I said. "But I'd suggest you refer to my boss as Mr. Clewe. He's a little stricter with the formalities than I am."

Vanessa crossed her long legs, allowing one booted foot to dangle. "Why doesn't that surprise me? Oh, by the way, I told Ms. Walker that I didn't need anything to drink. I hope you weren't expecting her to bring us coffee or tea."

"No, I usually get my own, and that's not really Lauren's job anyway. She's a valued assistant to our boss and is essential to running his business and charity concerns. She only offers to get drinks because she's a gracious person."

"I see." Vanessa blinked her pale eyes. "So, Jane, how much do you know about Rafe Glenn?"

"I know he's Cam's biological father and the son of Lily Glenn, who was romantically involved with Calvin Airley, the original heir of the wealthy family who built Aircroft. I'm also aware that Rafe is a photojournalist who has traveled the world for years, documenting places and events for publications like *National Geographic*." I toyed with the cork coaster placed on the cherry table next to my chair arm. "Rafe loved Cam's mother, Patricia, but felt he couldn't provide her with the medical help she needed for her chronic illness, so urged her to marry Albert Clewe. After Patricia passed away when Cam was just a toddler, Al lied, telling Rafe that Cam had died as well."

"A very cruel thing to do," Vanessa said, making a grimace of distaste.

"It was, especially since Al and Cam never had a warm relationship, and Cam never understood his coldness and disinterest."

I frowned. "Cam spent many years believing his only family didn't really care about him, because Cam didn't know that Al wasn't his father until he discovered some letters when he was older. They were love letters to Patricia Clewe, signed only with a capital R. Of course Cam tried every way he could to track down a man he only knew as R, but it wasn't until Lily Glenn finally came forward and confessed she was Rafe's mother and Cam's grandmother that Cam really knew the name and background of his biological father."

Vanessa cast me a sly smile. "My, my, you do know the whole story. Rafe was very angry over the deception, you know. He didn't find out that Cam was still alive until after Albert Clewe died, when Cam was already in his late twenties."

I decided to take advantage of this opening. "He talked to you about such things?"

"Yes, when we were on a shoot together in India. We were in an isolated location and there wasn't much to do except share stories." Vanessa brushed back a loose strand of her fair hair. "Rafe felt his mother and uncle should've told him the truth much sooner, but he grudgingly admitted they had a good excuse."

"They were afraid he would try to fight for Cam, and given Albert Clewe's money and influence, Rafe would be devastated, emotionally as well as financially."

Vanessa arched her wispy brows. "Exactly. I suppose you heard that from Lily and Gordy Glenn? I've contacted them but haven't met with them yet. I'm waiting to see if Mr. Clewe will support my expedition to find Rafe, or if I need to look elsewhere."

"Lily and Gordy don't have that kind of money," I said, not bothering to temper the sharp edge to my tone.

Vanessa shrugged. "Maybe not. But perhaps they could convince Mr. Clewe to fund my trip. Family leverage, you know."

"I'm not sure that would work as well as you think. They're rather at odds with Cam right now."

"Is that so? What a shame." Vanessa uncrossed her legs and leaned forward in her chair. "Listen, Jane, I really believe I can help. I've already got a lead on Rafe's location, but it's not the sort of information I can turn over to the authorities."

"Why is that?"

Vanessa pressed a finger to her lips. "My source isn't exactly operating on the right side of the law. Not all the time, anyway."

Studying her face, I observed excitement as well as determination. "Are you saying Rafe Glenn was or is involved with illegal activities?"

"Oh no," Vanessa said, waving one hand in a dismissive gesture. "Rafe is all about exposing looting or smuggling or anything shady. That's what made him a target."

"I see." Cam, who must've been loitering in the hall long enough to overhear at least the last portion of our conversation, strode into the library. "I ran into Lauren, and she told me that you were here, taking up my librarian's precious time."

Vanessa rose to her feet. "I actually wanted to talk to you, Mr. Clewe, but your very accomplished assistant was running interference. So I decided to speak with Jane instead."

Cam's expression gave no indication that he'd noticed the use of my first name. "You can sit back down, Ms. Gale. I'll pull over the desk chair so we can all chat."

I wasn't as taken aback by the grimness of Cam's tone as Vanessa seemed to be. "If you heard any of what I said, you should know why I'm here. I've learned your father could be in grave danger," she said when Cam, positioning my task chair so he could face her directly, sat down.

"Because he was attempting to expose looting of archeological sites?" Cam's eyes shone bright as emeralds.

"Well, yes." Vanessa squirmed in her seat. "I'm afraid he's run afoul of an organized theft ring that is vicious in its retaliation against perceived enemies."

"You didn't inform the local authorities about your suspicions?" Cam asked

"As I said, some of my information comes from sources who don't want to be involved with the authorities." Vanessa cast me a pleading glance. "Surely you can understand my dilemma, Jane."

"Not really," I said, earning a glare from Vanessa.

Cam leaned back in his chair, pressing his palms against his thighs in an effort I recognized as controlling any twitches in his hands and legs. "To be honest, your statements make me wonder if you're involved with this theft ring in some way, Ms. Gale."

Vanessa leapt to her feet. "How dare you! Here I offer to help you locate your father and protect him from possible harm, and you accuse me of being involved in illegal activities?"

"Please, sit, sit," Cam said, waving her back down. "I'm not accusing you of anything. I simply find it odd that you have a connection with someone who's allied with criminals, and yet you're assuring me that you can leverage this individual to locate my father."

Plopping down into her armchair, Vanessa focused her gaze on Cam's stoic face. "In my field, in order to uncover information, you sometimes have to play in a dirty sandbox."

"Hmm. Well, let's say that's true. What will you do if I provide enough funds for you to travel to Peru? Not with an entourage; just you. Will you use this slightly shady contact to find my father and then somehow free him if he is indeed in captivity? Or will you simply warn those who are opposed to my father's attempts to expose exploitation and collect a lucrative reward?"

"You seem to have a very dark perspective on things," Vanessa said. "Why suspect me of any alliance with thieves? I'm sure you've run extensive background checks on me. Did anything in that research indicate that I'm involved with criminals?"

"No." Cam examined Vanessa for a moment. "Jane suggested I fund you, and only you, on an expedition to Peru. Would you be willing to consider that option?"

"Of course." Vanessa straightened until her back wasn't touching the chair.

"Very well. I'll consider that proposal. But you need to submit an itinerary and estimated list of expenses first." Cam folded his hands in his lap. "Do that, and we'll see."

"I can email you those details by tomorrow." Vanessa stood up and took a few steps toward Cam. "I'll also provide my bank information, so you can send the money directly to my account."

"If I decide to do so," Cam said, looking up at her with narrowed eyes.

"Naturally." From Vanessa's triumphant smile it was clear she thought he'd acquiesce to her plan.

"Are you sure you want to take this on?" I asked, rising to my feet to face her. "If what you say is true, it could prove to be a tough challenge. You might end up captive yourself or worse."

Vanessa shook her head, making strands of her platinum hair sparkle under the overhead light. “I’m not an amateur.” She turned to me and flashed a self-confident smile. “I’m positive I can achieve my goals without placing myself in danger.”

“I’m sure my father thought that as well,” Cam said.

Chapter Eighteen

After Vanessa left the library, Cam stood up and rolled my task chair back behind my desk.

"Sorry for that interruption," he said. "I hope once I receive Ms. Gale's proposal, she'll undertake her self-appointed mission without disturbing us any further."

"Are you really going to pay her way to Peru?"

"If her statement of estimated expenses and her itinerary appear reasonable, yes." Cam smiled. "It's what you suggested, after all."

"True. I just hope she's actually on the up and up," I said, sitting down behind my desk. "Maybe Vince will provide us with some useful information soon."

"Hopefully. I'll touch base with him later today and see if he's been able to find out anything about Ms. Gale from his journalism contacts." Cam rubbed his left shoulder, as if trying to loosen up that joint. "Did she say anything about talking to my grandmother or great-uncle? I'm worried she's tried to ask them for money as well."

"She said she'd contacted them, but they hadn't met in person yet. I tell you what"—I rolled one of my pens back and forth under my fingers—"Why don't I see if I can visit them after work today? I know Lily is still staying with Gordy at the farm."

"That would ease my mind," Cam said.

"Good. I'll give Gordy a call shortly and make sure they plan to be home."

Cam thanked me and left the library, allowing me to get back to work. After calling and arranging to meet Lily and Gordy on my way home, I dove back into my cataloging. With no additional distractions, I was able to complete a decent amount of work over the rest of the day.

Although Gordy's farm was about five miles outside of town, it lay between Aircroft and Bradfordville, so at least I didn't have to backtrack. The winter landscape, studded with the stumps of crops and tangles of dun-colored orchard grass, provided a dull background for a few small brick houses, red wooden barns, and weathered white fences.

I turned onto a long, packed-dirt driveway. Post and wire fences burdened by the weight of leafless honeysuckle vines lined either side of the road. Behind the fences, the fields were choked with thistles and wild grasses. There was no livestock in sight.

I parked in front of a weathered shed that housed a vintage tractor with chipped red paint and bald tires. Parked next to the tractor was a battered truck I knew to be Gordy's main means of transportation.

Clumps of dried-out weeds filled the yard in front of a two-story white farmhouse with a sagging front porch and several missing shutters. I walked up the worn wooden steps onto the porch and rang the rusty doorbell.

Gordy Glenn was a tall man whose skin had been weathered into a web of wrinkles by many years of outdoor labor. His lanky figure was slightly stooped, but his silver hair was still thick and abundant. "Hello, Jane, so nice to see you again. It's been a while."

"Too long," I said, peering past him. Standing on the staircase that filled a major portion of the entrance hall was an elderly woman with hair styled like an old-fashioned Gibson girl. Her white hair framed her face like a cloud, softening her angular features. "Hi, Lily. Great to see you as well."

Gordy moved back to allow me to enter the hall, which ran straight to the back of the house. Doors with white porcelain doorknobs opened onto rooms on either side.

I waited for Lily to descend the staircase before following her and Gordy into one of the front rooms, which I knew they called the parlor. It looked much different from my first visit, when only Gordy had been living in the house. Then it had been dusty and sparsely furnished; now the furniture was polished to a high gloss and newer pieces had been added to provide additional seating. Colorful prints of flowers hung on the freshly painted white walls, and the old pine table and vintage television set had been replaced by a flat-screen TV and a sleek media cabinet.

Gordy's well-worn leather recliner hadn't been updated, though. He automatically claimed it as his chair, while Lily settled down at one end of a modern sueded sofa. When I sat in a wooden rocking chair facing both of them, I noticed that the old crocheted afghan that had once draped the back of the rocker had been switched out for a soft lemon-yellow chenille throw.

Gordy settled back in his chair and fixed me with his bright blue gaze. "It looks a bit different, doesn't it? That's all Lily. She swept in here like a hurricane and fixed it up real nice."

"I had help," Lily said, adjusting the hem of her navy wool skirt so it covered her knees. "There was no way I could clean the place by myself. Fortunately, Gordy knew a few folks from his volunteer work at the town museum. We've hired a regular cleaning lady now, as well as someone to take care of all the odd jobs."

"There's always something breaking in an old house like this," Gordy said. "I tried to keep up with things before, but it just got away from me."

Lily waved this off with one of her bony hands. "No one expects someone in their nineties to keep everything spic-and-span, much less fix the roof and those sorts of problems. You did the best you could, Gordy."

"Just needed a woman's touch, and better yet, her willingness to throw a little cash around." Gordy gave me a wink.

Lily's pale lashes fluttered over her bright blue eyes. "Don't listen to him, Jane. I'm not a spendthrift. Worked too hard for my money. But I couldn't live here in the state the house was in when I arrived." She cast her brother a sidelong look. "Guess I've gotten too used to a little more comfort over the years. Gordy never had that advantage, what with taking care of the farm by himself and all."

Gordy rolled his shoulders. "It wasn't much, really. I also worked at the local feed and seed store, so I was eligible for Social Security. Once I got that, I just gave up on farming. Never was that fond of it, anyway."

"Neither of us were," Lily said, sharing a smile with him.

"It's hard work, even if you like it," I said. "My grandparents had a small farm and after visiting them while I was growing up, I realized there was nothing idyllic about that life. It's an admirable endeavor, and I respect the heck out of those who do it, but it's no picnic."

"That's for sure." Gordy glanced at his sister. "Now, I know you're here to talk about that woman who says she knows Rafe. Vanessa something?"

"Vanessa Gale, a journalist who's worked with Rafe on several projects." I scooted to the front edge of the rocker. "She told me she spoke with you, but said you hadn't met in person?"

Lily nodded. "That's right. She called here and talked to me for quite some time. She seems to think Rafe might be in Peru."

"That's the same story she told Cam and me." I gripped my knees with my hands. "The truth is, Ms. Gale has asked Cam to fund an expedition to Peru. She claims she has contacts who might know where Rafe is, and that she can help bring him home."

Lily's eyes widened. "Really? She didn't say anything about that to me. I had the impression she was going to ask around; maybe sound out some of her contacts in that region, but she never promised to find Rafe."

Noticing the quiver of her lips, I sat up straight and looked her in the eyes. "I don't want to lead you astray, Lily. Both Cam and I are suspicious of Ms. Gale's promises. But he's basically agreed to sponsor a mission for her to go to Peru and see what she can discover. Just her, not a large expedition; not until we know she can be trusted."

"Is Rafe in danger?' The wrinkles around Gordy's mouth deepened.

"Possibly, according to Ms. Gale. But again, that's uncorroborated. If she sends word to Cam that can validate her concerns, he's more than willing to mount an all-out rescue. However"—I held up my hand, palm out—"that might not be necessary. Rafe may simply be out-of-touch because he's deep in the rainforest, completing a photography project. We can't be sure at this point."

"Cam will help, though, if necessary?"

The hopeful tinge to Lily's voice twisted something in my chest. *Does she think Cam will abandon his father, just because his family basically abandoned him?* I bit my lower lip to stop myself from saying those words out loud. It was clear that Lily was deeply worried about her son. I didn't need to add to her misery. "Of course. He's ready to spend whatever is required, depending on the situation. Don't worry about that. And don't feel like you need to give Ms. Gale any money, no matter what she says. Cam will provide her with what she needs for the trip."

Lily and Gordy shared a look that told me Vanessa had already broached the idea of them contributing to her expedition.

"She mentioned something about funds. Off-hand, like," Gordy said, confirming my guess.

"Then I'm glad I'm here to tell you to ignore any of her requests." I settled back in the rocker. "She may be truly honest and altruistic, but it's best to let Cam use his resources. He can afford a loss, and he can also find a way to bring her to justice if she's lying to us."

"Very well, we'll follow your advice," Lily said, dabbing at her eyes with a lace-edged handkerchief. "Thank you for looking out for us. And thank Cam too. I appreciate his help more than I can say."

I cast her a wry smile. "Perhaps you should tell him that yourself."

"You think that might help thaw the ice between us?" Gordy asked.

"It couldn't hurt." I said, meeting his questioning gaze. "Oh, one more thing, totally unrelated. Since you've farmed in this area most of your life, do you know anything about anyone in Macnamara Stewart's family?"

"You mean the tobacco kings?" Gordy wrinkled his brow. "Not much. I didn't move in their highfalutin society."

"Yes, but we mixed with them at sales sometimes." Lily shifted to look at me. "My father would take us to farm sales and auctions every now and then, when he was looking for a piece of machinery or some tools. Remember, Gordy? Mac was around our age. His father, Douglas Stewart, always seemed to show up at those events."

"And often out-bid our dad," Gordy said, nodding. "Yep, I remember that now. Macnamara Stewart was a little hoodlum, always causing a ruckus and then blaming it on other kids."

"Like you?" I asked, noting Gordy's sour expression.

"He tried it on me once. Filched a pocket-sized set of screwdrivers from one of the display tables, then tossed it on the ground near my feet. When I picked it up to place it back on the table, Mac claimed I'd taken the set." Gordy shook his head. "I stood up to him and called him a liar, which he and his father sure didn't appreciate. Douglas Stewart even threatened to call the police. Saving grace was that someone else saw the whole thing and pulled the older Mr. Stewart aside to set him straight. He and his hooligan son slinked off after that."

"With no apologies. And Gordy still got a beating from our dad for causing a commotion in public." Lily's lips tightened into a thin line.

"So, in your experience, the Stewarts were more than willing to throw the blame for their crimes on innocent parties?" I tapped my chin with one finger. *If Mac Stewart was raised in that environment, perhaps he was also willing to cover up the truth regarding family matters, like Kimberly's supposed suicide. But Macnamara Stewart wasn't alive when Gabe died, so if there was any family involvement in that tragedy, it had to be one of his children, perpetuating the tradition.*

"I'd say they were more than willing to do any number of questionable things." Lily met my gaze with a sad smile. "I heard Douglas even approached Calvin's parents right after he died, hoping to buy Aircroft while Bridgette and Samuel Airley were still in mourning."

"That does shed new light on the family," I said as I rose to my feet. "Thanks. I'll share that information with Cam, if that's all right with you."

"Please do. Also"—Lily pressed a hand to her heart—"tell him we want to see him again soon."

I offered her and her brother a warm smile. "I will. Lauren and I have been working on him, you know."

"Then I have hope," Lily said, with an answering smile.

Chapter Nineteen

A few days passed without incident, allowing me to complete a batch of cataloging I'd been working on for far too long. I reassured Cam that Vanessa Gale had not directly asked Lily and Gordy for money, which pleased him, and that they hoped to see him in person soon, which did not.

Leaving work on Wednesday, I decided to stop by a small café where I often ordered take-out. This was one option approved by Bailey, since they specialized in organic and healthy cuisine. I called ahead and ordered their hearty vegetable soup.

When I entered the café, one person was waiting at the pick-up counter ahead of me. It was a tall young man with broad shoulders and blond hair.

"Taylor, is that you?" I asked.

He turned and, recognizing me, smiled broadly. "Hello, Jane. What brings you here?"

"Same as you, it seems," I said, pointing toward his white paper bag. "Did you choose this place because it has Bailey's stamp of approval?"

Taylor's cheeks flushed. "You've caught me. She's always telling me that if I have to eat take-out, it should at least be reasonably healthy food."

"Same," I said. Taylor Iverson was a chauffeur Cam had hired to drive me to special events in the past. He'd also driven for Bailey when she'd last visited me.

Taylor looked like he could be a bodyguard, but he wasn't the rough and ready type at all. In fact, he was a writer trying to break into publishing. *Hence, the driver gig,* I thought with a smile. I looked him over, noting his worn jeans and down jacket. "You must be off duty now."

"Yeah, nothing on tonight, so I thought I'd pick up some food and have a proper dinner for a change." Taylor turned around to pay for his meal, then stepped away from the counter to allow me to ask for mine.

"You know," I said, after tapping my card and collecting my receipt, "Bailey suggested that we should have a meal together sometime, since we both often end up eating alone. Would you like to join me for dinner at my apartment? I promise I won't grill you about your relationship with my daughter," I added with a grin.

"Sure, that's certainly better than sitting in my apartment and watching the news." Taylor grimaced. "I can't seem to wean myself off the nightly news, even though most of it just makes me angry or depressed."

"Again, same. Why don't we leave the TV off and talk about something enjoyable, like books?"

"Sounds like a plan." Taylor offered me a warm smile. "I have to make another stop to pick up a laser ink cartridge at the office supplies store, but since I know where you live, I'll see you there."

"That's perfect, actually. I can make sure there aren't dishes in the sink before you arrive," I said.

"Alright, see you soon." Taylor lifted his take-out bag in a little salute and strode out of the café.

When I got home, I quickly changed into lounge pants and a sweatshirt. I didn't have to worry about washing any dishes, as my mother had trained me to never leave anything in the sink. I'd only used that excuse to put Taylor at ease over arriving a little late.

Filling a pitcher with ice water, I set it on my small dining table along with utensils, plates, and glasses. I'd just finished reheating my soup in the microwave when there was a knock on the apartment door.

"You can put the bag on the table and throw your coat over the back of the sofa," I said, as Taylor entered my small above-the-garage apartment. It was really one large room, with the bedroom area hidden from the rest of the space by several tall bookshelves. As in Malcolm's much more glamorous loft, there weren't any dividing walls, and no interior doors except for the ones leading to the bathroom and my closet.

"This is very nice," Taylor said, his gaze sweeping over my worn but comfortable furniture. "Cozy."

"It's not grand, but I like it. I get enough grand at Aircroft." I made a face. "It's nice to come home and escape all that, really."

Taylor took off his coat, revealing a slightly ragged beige sweater. He draped his coat over the sofa. "I'm sure I'd feel the same. I prefer less ostentatious spaces."

"You must like Bailey's place then. The amount she has to pay for that dinky little studio . . ." I rolled my eyes as I poured my soup into a bowl. "Would you like some of this? It's vegetable, and there's plenty."

Taylor waved this offer aside and pulled a bulky wrapped item from his take-out bag. "No thanks. This sandwich is huge. It should be enough, especially with the baked pita chips they always throw in."

We sat across from each other, arranging our food and taking turns filling our glasses with water. "Would you like anything else to drink? I don't have any beer, but I do have some wine."

"No thanks. I plan to call Bailey tonight, and I don't want to lie about drinking wine in the middle of the week." Taylor flashed me a smile. "She says it should be reserved for weekends, and then only a glass or two."

"Oh, I know," I said fervently. "I get the same lectures."

"She only does that because she cares." Taylor took a bite of his sandwich and chewed before adding, "Or at least, that's what she tells me."

"It's true. Maddening, but true."

We ate in silence for a moment before Taylor looked up from his plate and cast me a questioning look. "Bailey mentioned your latest amateur investigation. Something to do with the Stewart family, right?"

I nodded. "There was an interesting development involving Gabriel Neri, who recently passed away, and a book that once belonged to his late aunt, Kimberly Stewart Ward. Cam and I are looking into both deaths. Supposedly, Kimberly committed suicide, but according to Malcolm Stewart, Gabe wasn't convinced that was true. Now he's dead."

"The news reports called it an overdose." Taylor eyed me with interest. "Do you have suspicions about that as well?"

"His cousin, Malcolm Stewart, certainly does. He vehemently insists that Gabe had been clean for years." I stirred my spoon around in my soup. "Cam and I are trying to keep our minds open to all possibilities, but we're looking into both cases."

"Gabriel Neri," Taylor said thoughtfully. "I never met him, but I drove his brother Lucas to and from the airport several times. Interesting guy."

I laid down my spoon and leaned forward. "How so?"

"Very professional, but there was something off about him. He's one of those businessmen who exudes a false cheerfulness." Taylor frowned. "At least, I found it false. There was an edge to his words that seemed more brittle than bright."

"That must be your writer's brain, carefully analyzing everyone you meet," I said.

Taylor smiled ruefully. "Yeah, we're as bad as psychologists, or so I'm told. Anyway, Lucas Neri always tipped very well, so I suppose I shouldn't disparage him too much. That business acquaintance of his, though . . ."

"Who's that?" I asked before finishing off the last spoonful of my soup.

"The politician guy, or at least he hopes to be. Running for mayor of Winston-Salem this year."

"Roger Easton?" I slid back in my chair and considered this information for a minute. "He was the Stewart family lawyer for many years, before he decided to open his own office. I believe he may still act as an advisor to Duff Stewart on legal matters."

"And Lucas Neri, apparently." Taylor, who'd eaten his sandwich, wiped his mouth with a paper napkin. "I drove both of them a few times, and they were discussing business matters the entire trip. Typically, I try to ignore conversations between my riders, but Lucas Neri's voice carries too well, and Roger Easton wasn't much quieter."

"Not surprising, considering Easton is a lawyer. Now he's going into politics, which means he isn't opposed to giving speeches."

"He's not much for tips, though," Taylor said, with a wry smile. "When he wasn't riding with Lucas Neri he'd barely include fifteen percent. Even that much seemed to pain him."

"A Scrooge, huh?" I pushed my chair away from the table. "Which means he's probably overly fond of money."

"Could be. Or maybe he just feels superior to the help and doesn't believe in paying them any more than necessary." Standing, Taylor collected his plate and utensils. "I should leave soon, but let me help you wash these dishes before I go."

"No need," I said, rising to my feet to face him. "Just set stuff on the counter next to the sink. I have a small dishwasher, but it can handle this much easily enough."

"OK, if you're sure." Taylor stacked my dinnerware on top of his and carried everything to the kitchen, a trip that only took a few of his long strides. "I don't mind helping, though. I always wash the dishes when I'm at Bailey's place."

"Of course you do," I said, with a laugh. "I'm afraid she might have you wrapped around her finger, Taylor. Don't let her walk all over you."

"Don't worry, I've set healthy limits." He caught my eye and grinned. "It isn't easy, though. She's just so darn charming."

"Oh, I know. I had to steel myself against that when she was younger or she'd have turned into a total brat." I picked up our water glasses and strolled over to join Taylor at the sink. "As it was, she was only partially spoiled."

Taylor threw his arm around my shoulders. "Naw, Bailey may be feisty, but she's a sweetheart. Really caring and kind. You did good, Mom."

My eyes welled with tears. Setting down the water glasses, I rubbed the dampness from my lashes with one finger. "She'll always be my favorite person," I said, my voice cracking slightly.

Taylor's hold tightened into a side hug. "Mine too. But maybe don't tell her that yet."

"Don't worry," I said, wiping another tear from my cheek, "I'll allow you to confess to her when you feel the time is right."

"Thanks. I was planning to tell her when I got a book deal, but we'll see," Taylor glanced down at me with a smile. "I might not want to wait that long."

"You'd better not," I said, sniffling. "I think you're perfect for her, but you know there's a line of guys longing to take your place."

Taylor patted my shoulder. "Yeah, but never fear—I fully intend to do whatever it takes to stay at the front of the line."

Chapter Twenty

When I walked Taylor out to my landing to say goodbye, I noticed Vince was exiting his house carrying a large banker's box. He paused on the porch and looked up.

"Hi there," he said, setting down the box long enough to give us a wave. "Long time, no see, Taylor."

I followed Taylor at a slower pace as he clattered down the steps. "You two know each other?" I asked, when we reached the ground.

"Sure. We met when Taylor was driving Bailey around last year," Vince said. "Only briefly, of course, but long enough to find out that Taylor is a writer too."

Taylor crossed to the porch in a few swift strides and shook Vince's hand. "Nice to see you again, Vince. I was just sharing a meal with Jane. Her daughter thinks we should do that from time to time."

"Ah, that's right." Vince's eyes sparkled behind the lenses of his glasses. "I've heard you and Bailey are friends."

"A little more than that," Taylor said, without a shred of embarrassment.

Vince's eyebrows rose to meet a lock of steel gray hair that had tumbled over his broad forehead. "Really? Donna will be pleased."

"Oh dear." I shot Taylor a warning look. "She'll have them engaged and married by the end of the week."

Laughing, Vince nodded. "Sorry, should've thought of that."

"It's fine. Bailey will be amused too. She always says you can't be an actor if you care about what other people think of you." Taylor turned to me. "Speaking of Bailey, I need to head home, Jane. I'm supposed to call her for a video chat tonight."

"You'd better go then." I patted his arm. "Thanks for the company. We'll have to share a meal together again. Maybe I'll even cook next time."

Taylor's blue eyes brightened. "That would be great. Bailey tells me you're a great cook."

"I'm not bad," I said. "But I haven't done much of it lately, so I may need to practice first."

"You can always try out dishes on Donna and me." Vince flashed a smile. "We wouldn't object."

"I'll keep that in mind," I said.

After a flurry of goodbyes, Taylor drove off. "He's a nice young man," Vince said.

"I know, and it's such a shock. In the past Bailey has always picked the wrong guys." I exaggerated a sniffle. "I guess my baby is truly grown up now."

"She's a treasure," Vince said. "But you know that."

"I do. Now, changing the subject—have you learned anything more about Vanessa Gale from your journalist network?" I moved closer to the porch.

"Actually, that's one reason I came outside. I was headed up to your apartment to share my information on Gale, and to bring you these files." Vince bent down and picked up the box.

My eyes widened. "All that is info on Vanessa Gale?"

"Oh, no, no. Sorry to confuse you." Vince peered around the box to watch his feet as he carried the files down the porch steps. "This contains the information you wanted on the car accident that involved Duff Stewart and his cousins. I knew I probably had something stored in the basement, so I dug around a little and voila!"

"You found that much?" I stared at the box. "I didn't think there was a lot of coverage of the incident."

"This box isn't full. I actually file things by year, so there was a lot more shoved in here to start, but I took out anything unrelated to the accident." Vince shifted the box in his arms. "But it's still a little heavy. I'll carry it up to your apartment and leave it for you and Cam to investigate. While I'm there, I'll tell you what I heard about Vanessa Gale."

"OK, thanks," I said, leading the way to the garage's outside staircase.

After Vince entered the apartment and set the box on my kitchen table, I gestured toward the sofa. "Please, have a seat. I'm anxious to hear what you've learned about Gale."

"Not much, I'm afraid." Vince's rueful tone told me he must have diligently tried to discover more. "At least, nothing that would raise any red flags."

"She's legit?" I settled on the sofa as Vince sat down at the other end.

"That seems to be the consensus. Only one of my contacts—who wishes to remain anonymous, by the way—had any concerns about her past behavior." Vince leaned back and stared up at the ceiling, where some white paint had flaked off the beadboard. "I really need to get some painters in to work on this place. But I guess I'll need to wait until you go on another trip."

"Don't worry about that. It doesn't bother me," I said, scooting a little closer to him. "Tell me about this anonymous source. What were their concerns about Vanessa Gale?"

Vince cast me a sidelong glance. "It had to do with some of the company she kept. This contact worked mainly in Central and South America, so he was familiar with Rafe Glenn's mission to document the rainforests, as well as Vanessa Gale's articles about the region." Vince met my eager gaze with a solemn expression. "It was Vanessa's association with some rather disreputable people that raised red flags."

"She was connected to thieves or drug runners or what?"

"Not necessarily connected. You have to understand—journalists often have to work with people on the wrong side of the law, if only to get all angles on a story. It wouldn't be surprising for Vanessa Gale to associate with individuals who don't live within the law. But my contact said she was seen in their company outside of interviews, which is a little questionable." Vince shrugged. "Perhaps she was simply building a bond so they'd spill some secrets, but it's something Cam might want to look into before he gives her any money."

"I'll make sure he knows that. Thanks so much. And thanks for those files too," I said, motioning toward the kitchen table. But don't you want to go through them with us?"

Vince shook his head. "I'd love to, but one of Donna's childhood friends called out of the blue to say she was staying in Boone for a week. She wants Donna to meet her at a cabin she's renting in the mountains. Worst time of year for it, which is why I offered to accompany Donna, so I can drive if the weather turns bad."

"You'll both be gone for several days?"

"Yes, and I thought you and Cam would want to go through the materials in that box before I get back." Vince rose to his feet. "You can always text me with any exciting finds."

"And I will." I stood up as well. "When are you leaving town?"

"Tomorrow morning. Which is why I need to rush off. I still haven't packed, and Donna wants to get on the road early." Vince strode over to my front door. "It's best not to make Donna wait, you know," he added, with a grin.

"I bet. Well, tell Donna hello from me and have a great trip," I said, before wishing him a good evening.

After locking the door behind him, I wandered into the kitchen. I really didn't need anything more to eat or drink, but a glass of wine was calling me.

I answered the call, of course.

Settling back down on the sofa, I picked up my phone. There were no missed calls, which didn't surprise me. Cam never called this late, and Bailey was undoubtedly already video chatting with Taylor. However, there was one message. I peered at my phone screen, recognizing the number. It was from Malcolm Stewart.

Thought you'd like to know about a charity event this Sunday afternoon. It's to benefit cancer research and is being held at my dad and mom's house. Most of my family will be there, as well as a few others. I have the guest list from Finn's party too. Will you come? I can pick you up around noon. You can be my date.

He finished the text off with a smiley emoji.

I immediately replied—*It's a date. Only, not really.*

Malcolm sent back a crying emoji, which made me laugh. He really was a charming young man. If Bailey hadn't met Taylor, I would have found a way to introduce her to Malcolm, even if she was taller than he was by a couple of inches.

Not that such things mattered. While I knew most people placed a lot of value on looks, I'd long since discovered they were the least likely indicator of relationship success.

Let me not to the marriage of true minds admit impediments, I said aloud, quoting Shakespeare's Sonnet 116. The poem was a description of true, lasting, romantic love. The kind I hoped Bailey would find.

The kind I'd never had, but frankly, and fortunately, no longer missed.

Chapter Twenty-One

When I told Cam about Vince's files on Thursday, he was ready to drop everything and drive to my apartment to look through them with me. But after Lauren reminded him about a report he needed to approve and two important phone calls scheduled for the afternoon, he suggested we meet after work.

"Why don't I come as well?" Lauren asked. "Another pair of eyes will make quicker work of searching through the documents."

"Sounds good," Cam said, his gaze focused on his computer screen.

"It's a plan, then. I'll ask Mateo to make some sandwiches I can bring with me so we won't have to worry Jane with dinner." Lauren paused in the open doorway to Cam's office. "Wait—I've never actually been to your place, Jane. Text me your address, OK?"

"Sure thing," I said as she headed off down the hall. I glanced at Cam, who was frowning at something on his screen. "Speaking of extra help, would you mind if I invited Malcolm Stewart to come as well? He's just as eager as we are to find out more about that accident."

Cam looked up at me, his expression wary. "You're sure we can trust him? He's part of the Stewart family, after all, even if he claims to be estranged from most of them."

I squared my shoulders. "I trust him."

"Then yes, invite him," Cam said, after a moment spent examining me. "But you'd better go tell Mateo we'll need food for four people instead of three."

"Will do." I turned and hurried out of the office. There really wasn't any need to rush, but it looked like Cam had work to do, and so did I. We'd save any more discussion of our two cases for later.

I left work a little early, not sure if my apartment was in decent shape for guests. A quick text to Malcolm had garnered an enthusiastic *yes*, so at the very least I wanted to ensure I had enough clean plates and glasses for four people. I was so used to eating alone that I only ran my dishwasher after every piece of my dinnerware was dirty.

Fortunately, even though it had slipped my mind, I'd run the dishwasher the night before. I hadn't unloaded it yet, though, so I quickly pulled out enough items for four people. I was laying the place settings on the table when my doorbell rang.

"It's open, come on in," I called out.

Cam walked into the apartment shaking his head. "That isn't the safest choice, especially after getting a warning from some strange man." He was still wearing the black jeans and ivory cable-knit sweater he'd had on during the work day. Slipping off his coat, he hung it on one of the hooks near my front door.

"Didn't Lauren ride with you?" I asked while he crossed the room to join me at the table.

"No, she wanted to drive directly to her apartment after we finish here." Cam absently picked up a fork and laid it down again. "She's bringing the food."

"I assumed as much. Fortunately, Vince and Donna are out of town so there's plenty of space for everyone to park." I switched my gaze to the door as Malcolm strolled in. "Hello, come on over and let me introduce you."

Cam turned on his heel to face Malcolm. He was taller by a good six inches, but Malcolm's vibrant presence allowed him to hold his own.

"Cam, this is Malcolm Stewart," I said. "Malcolm—my boss, Cameron Clewe."

As the two men shook hands, Malcolm stared at Cam with a question in his blue eyes. "I think we may have met before."

"When we were children, perhaps," Cam said. "Your grandfather occasionally visited my stepfather at Aircroft, and I remember him bringing along some young kids from time to time. I was a bit stand-offish back then, though, so I doubt we had much to do with one another."

I blinked rapidly, amazed that Cam was willing to share anything about his introverted nature with a virtual stranger.

Malcolm snapped his fingers. "That's it—I recall playing hide-and-seek in the gardens when I was only five or so. There were glorious gardens, weren't there? One section was strictly maintained, but the back portion was allowed to grow wild. That was the best place to hide."

"The gardens are still there." A line creased Cam's brow, indicating his attempt to remember details about this event. "Your older brother Finlay suggested hide-and-seek. He was twelve and I was nine, I believe. Your sister wasn't interested in playing, but he convinced her to do the searching."

"Yeah, Ainsley was already a teenager. She's ten years older than me, so she must've been around fifteen." Malcolm swept back the lock of wavy brown hair that had fallen over his forehead. "She never did find you, did she?"

"No, but I knew the wild section of the garden like the back of my hand," Cam said with a shrug. "I had the advantage."

"That's an amazing coincidence," Malcolm said, looking Cam over. "Your hair had more red in it back then, so Ainsley was sure she'd find you. Red stands out against green foliage, you know. But she didn't." Malcolm's rueful smile was charmingly crooked. "Funny, I think that's one of my first clear memories. How strange that we should end up working together now."

Cam, his attention caught by Lauren standing in the doorway, didn't reply. "You're here at last," he said.

Lauren held up two insulated food bags. "Bringing food, so you should be grateful." She strolled over to the table to set down the bags. "You must be Malcolm Stewart," she said, extending her slender fingers. "Very nice to meet you."

Malcolm clasped her hand, his gaze fixed on her face. "And you must be Lauren Walker. Trust me," he added, flashing a brilliant smile, "the pleasure is all mine."

Cam cleared his throat. "Should we sit down? The quicker we eat, the sooner we can get to the files."

"There's no rush, is there?" Malcolm let go of Lauren's hand but continued to stare at her, his eyes alight. "Unless Jane wants us to get done and get out, of course."

"I have no other plans tonight," I said dryly. Sneaking a glance at Cam, I couldn't help but notice his stony expression. It was clear he hadn't missed Malcolm's immediate attraction to Lauren.

For her part, her warm smile told me she wasn't averse to Malcolm's attentions. As she sat down at the table and began to remove wrapped sandwiches and a plastic container of fruit from the bags, Malcolm reached for the chair next to hers.

Cam's hand shot out, grabbing the chair before Malcolm's fingers could land. He sat down, forcing Malcolm to take a seat across from Lauren. Swallowing back a pithy comment, I settled in the chair beside Malcolm.

The truth was, Cam's action backfired. Malcolm and Lauren began chatting across the table like a couple on a first date, leaving Cam eating in glum silence. I attempted to engage him in a conversation that would tie in with what the other two were discussing, to no avail.

After we finished eating, Malcolm helped me clear the table. "They aren't dating or anything?" he asked me, sotto voce, while I stacked plates and utensils in the sink.

"Well, no, but . . ."

Cam's voice cut me off. "Why don't you leave that? Let's dig into the files. The dishes can wait."

Malcolm washed his hands while I dried mine on a kitchen towel. "We have been summoned," I told him, handing him the towel.

"It seems so." Malcolm raised his eyebrows and gave me a brief grin. Hanging up the towel, he strolled over to the living room area, where Cam and Lauren were seated on the sofa, the open box between them.

I followed more slowly, my thoughts whirling with this new development. It was obvious that Malcolm and Lauren had hit it off, which was bound to create tension with Cam. As I approached the sofa, Lauren stood up.

"You sit on the sofa, Jane. I'll plop down on the rug beside Malcolm," she said. "After all, we are the two youngest ones here."

Cam's lips thinned into a tight line. Yanking a handful of files from the box, he handed them to Lauren, who was now sitting in the lotus position on the floor. "Share these with Malcolm," he said, his words clipped short.

I reached in the box for my own portion of the files. "There'll probably be a lot of repetition in these articles and reports, but who knows—maybe we'll discover something unique."

"Something useful," Cam said, picking up the first file in the stack next to him and flipping it open. "Unique may be entertaining, but unless it provides real information, a bit useless."

I gave him the side-eye which, as usual, he ignored.

Chapter Twenty-Two

Several minutes passed, the silence broken only by the crinkle of paper and Malcolm humming under his breath. Suddenly, he straightened, holding up a newspaper article encased in a clear plastic sleeve. "I had no idea what a terrible scene that must've been," he said. "No wonder Gabe was traumatized. I mean, I know he was badly hurt, but apparently the other driver . . ."

"Joseph Carson," Cam interjected without looking up.

Malcolm stared at him for a second. "Right. Anyway, when the police and emergency personnel arrived, Mr. Carson was screaming hysterically and searching around the area on his hands and knees. It seems his wife, who wasn't wearing a seat belt, was ejected from the car and thrown against a roadside boulder, causing terrible injuries, while his two-year-old daughter was crushed when my cousin's car spun after being hit head-on. The back of Lucas's vehicle apparently slammed into the side of Carson's car where the toddler was strapped in a child seat."

"I'm sure it was devastating," I said, thinking of the damage that would have been inflicted on everyone involved, psychologically as well as physically.

Cam's restless fingers fiddled with a loose piece of tape on the banker's box, tearing it free. "Every report says Joe Carson was at fault," he said, shaking the tape from his thumb. "But a blood alcohol test proved he was sober. In fact, everyone involved was, except your father."

"Who was a passenger," Malcolm said. "I believe the police assumed Carson lost control after hitting a spot of black ice."

Lauren looked up at Cam, her feathery black brows drawn together over her nose. "There *was* ice on the road, according to everything I've read so far."

"Which is one reason Neri's car spun out so wildly," Cam said. "I wonder if both vehicles were going too fast. That information doesn't appear to have been included in the reports."

Malcolm's expression grew thoughtful. "Gabe never knew, one way or the other. Of course, he was badly hurt, so the fact that his mind blocked out some of the details was a normal reaction."

"What about your dad and Lucas Neri?" Lauren asked. "Have they ever mentioned anything about Carson speeding?"

Malcolm frowned. "They never talk about the accident. Whenever Gabe would bring it up at family gatherings, Dad or Lucas would shut him down immediately."

"Maybe they remembered too much." Lauren twirled one of her tight black curls around her finger. "You said Gabe had some level of amnesia, but perhaps they never did. It could've been too painful for them to talk about."

"Hmmm." Cam leaned back against the sofa cushions and stared up at the ceiling. "That's one option."

I lifted another photocopied report from the file open in my lap. Glancing over it, a name jumped out at me. "Malcolm, did you know Roger Easton represented you dad and cousin in this matter?"

"No, I never heard that. It seems odd. Roger mainly dealt with business-related cases. Still does, as a matter of fact. He focuses on things like trademark violations or mergers and acquisitions. To my knowledge he was never involved in legal issues related to accidents or criminal activity."

I flourished the paper. "Well, maybe not, but his name is listed as the legal representative for Duff Stewart and Lucas and Gabriel Neri in this accident report."

"Let me see that," Cam said, snatching the paper from my hand.

"Roger has always been close to the family," Malcolm said. "Since my relatives weren't at fault, maybe they didn't think they needed a real defense attorney. Roger might have simply gotten involved to protect their rights and provide advice."

"Perhaps." There was a distant look in Cam's eyes.

He's processing this new fact, trying to click it into place in the puzzle, I thought. Shifting my position on the sofa, I returned to my examination of the paperwork.

We finished going through the files in the next hour, discovering nothing unexpected, or truly helpful. Lauren did come across a fairly detailed description of Joseph Carson's arraignment and trial. He'd been convicted of vehicular manslaughter and reckless driving, but only served a year in jail.

"I'm sure the judge felt the loss of his wife and child was punishment enough," I said, when Malcolm expressed some surprise at this light sentence. "Also, he wasn't under the influence of drugs or alcohol, and they couldn't really determine his car's exact speed before the accident occurred."

"And hitting black ice isn't necessarily something you can avoid," Lauren said, with a sidelong glance at Malcolm. "It seems like he was simply terribly unfortunate."

Cam placed the file he was holding on the side table next to the sofa. "It appears we've gone through everything. Why don't you two head on out? I'll stay and help Jane re-box the files and clean the dishes."

"I'm happy to stay if you want to get home, Cam." Lauren's questioning gaze swept over his stoic face.

"I can help as well," Malcolm said.

Cam waved this aside. "No, I insist. Jane and I hold the responsibility for this case. You should go."

This last statement was spoken with such firmness that both Malcolm and Lauren immediately stood up. "I'll see you tomorrow, Cam. And Jane, of course." Lauren's troubled expression informed me that she suspected Cam was hiding something from us.

"Goodnight, then," Malcolm said, sharing a glance with Lauren. "I'm delighted to have met you, Lauren, as well as you, Cam. I'm sure we'll see each other again soon."

Passing by me on the way to the door, Malcolm tapped my shoulder. "I know I'll see you very soon, Jane. With that guest list, which I forgot to bring this evening. Sorry."

"No problem. See you Sunday at noon," I followed Lauren and Malcolm to the door so I could lock it behind them.

By the time I walked back into the living room area, Cam had already shoved most of the files into the box. He cast me a raised-eyebrow glance. "Sunday?"

"He invited me to a charity event being held at Duff and Sharon Stewart's home. I thought it would offer me a good chance to sound out a few more members of the family."

"Good thinking." Cam placed the lid back on the box. "Now for the dishes."

"You forgot a file," I said, pointing to the manila folder laying on the side table.

"No, I didn't. I'm keeping that one. You can return it to Vince separately."

"What's so important about it?"

Cam rose to his feet holding the box, which he set on the floor in front of the side table. "It contains an article detailing Joseph Carson's testimony. He never wavered in his statements, no matter how much evidence was stacked against him. And, even though he was convicted, he's always claimed to be innocent."

"You mean . . ."

"Yes, Joe Carson has stubbornly maintained that the court got it wrong." Cam met my gaze with a wry smile. "In his testimony, he swore Lucas Neri's vehicle was the car that actually crossed the center line."

Chapter Twenty-Three

"But how could the investigators get that wrong? Wouldn't there be tire marks and that sort of thing?" I asked, mentally readjusting my assumptions about the accident.

Cam shrugged. "It depends on whether the investigation was thorough enough. Lucas Neri had no drugs or alcohol in his system, so neither driver was under the influence. The authorities couldn't use that as evidence against either driver."

"Does Joe Carson have anything to back up his claims?"

"Not that I've seen. But there's someone who could undoubtedly offer more insight," Cam said, crossing his arms over his chest.

"Carson himself?"

Cam shook his head. "I doubt he would tell us anything other than what I've read in his testimony. No, I mean Roger Easton. He provided legal advice for Duff Stewart and his cousins, so he's likely to recall any unusual details that may have cropped up. Or, if he doesn't remember, he surely kept a record of the case."

"Would he talk to us?" I asked as I headed for the kitchenette. "You meant that offer about the dishes, right?"

"Of course." Rolling up his sleeves, Cam joined me at the sink. "As for Easton—he'll talk to me. In fact, I bet Lauren can set up a meeting for tomorrow."

"Did you donate to his mayoral campaign or something?" I turned on the faucet and squirted dish soap over the dinnerware. "I'll wash; you dry. I'd hate to see that beautiful sweater ruined."

"I never give money to politicians. There are much more worthy causes," Cam said, grabbing a clean kitchen towel. "The truth is, Roger Easton's firm does work for many large businesses and corporations, but he's never signed a contract with me. Primarily because Al didn't want to work with him, and I've continued that tradition. If Easton thinks I might be ready to change my mind, he'll happily embrace an opportunity to consult with me."

"I get it. He wants his firm to make money off of your businesses and foundations."

"Exactly." Cam looked over at me, "I might as well leverage his avarice, don't you think?"

"Absolutely," I said. "Of course, he could be disbarred if he reveals anything that violates attorney-client privilege, so he might not be willing to talk about anything related to the Stewart or Neri families."

"Perhaps. I suppose it depends on how much he wants my business, and how little he truly cares about legalities. I suspect he may have ignored such things before. We shall see," Cam said.

We fell silent as I concentrated on washing the plates, glasses, and utensils. In perfect rhythm I set them in the drying rack and Cam picked them up and dried them off. *That says something,* I thought, *about our odd synchronicity. We're so different, yet we complement each other. It's why we can successfully pursue sleuthing together.*

But on one subject I felt at a loss. "Malcolm seemed very interested in Lauren," I said, as Cam finished drying the last glass. "Of course, it's hardly a surprise. She's smart and beautiful and can talk about any number of subjects."

Cam carefully placed the glass inside the upper cabinet next to the sink. "I noticed," he said, closing the cabinet door a little too firmly.

"I don't think you have to worry, though," I dried my hands on another towel.

Cam shot me a fierce look. "Worry about what?"

"Oh"—I snapped the towel in the air before hanging it on a wall rack—"that Lauren might quit working for you if she gets seriously involved with a guy. I think she'd want to keep her job even if she got married. You probably won't lose her, no matter what."

Cam lowered his head, staring at his shoes as if they held the answer to some mystery. "Is that what you truly believe?"

"It's what I hope. But that could be just wishful thinking. Now, if someone could give her another reason to want to stay at Aircroft . . ."

Cam snapped up his head and turned to face me. "I appreciate a lot of things about you, Jane, and I know you mean well, but please don't interfere in my private life. Not concerning my grandmother and great-uncle, and not in reference to . . . anyone else."

"You mean Lauren," I said calmly. "Honestly, Cam, don't you think someone needs to interfere or, better yet, give you a good, swift kick in the posterior?"

His stare would have pierced a less hardened heart, but I'd been through too much to allow a thirty-something man to intimidate me. Especially when I knew I was trying to improve his life.

"I think I should go now," Cam said, breaking our staring contest with the flick of his hand. "Be prepared to visit Easton and Associates tomorrow. Do a little online research on them tonight."

"Is that an order, boss?" I asked his back, which he'd turned to me to stride toward the front door.

"It's a request." He threw his long coat over his shoulders and was halfway out the door before he added, without turning around, "Which I expect to be fulfilled."

* * *

I arrived at work on Friday to the news that Cam and I had an appointment with Roger Easton at one o'clock that afternoon.

"You worked wonders, as always," I told Lauren.

She shook her head. "I didn't have to try very hard. All I did was mention Cam's name, and they immediately shifted other appointments to accommodate him."

"Money talks," I said.

"That's the truth." Loitering just inside the open doorway of the library, Lauren took a quick peek up and down the hall before turning back to me. "What's your opinion of Malcolm Stewart, Jane? I know you've spent more time around him than I have."

"I think he's handsome and charming and extremely nice. He appears to have rejected his sister's haughtiness and his father's belligerent attitude. He comes from a wealthy family but doesn't have that spoiled rich kid attitude," I said, ticking off these observations on my fingers.

Lauren beamed. "That's what I think too."

"Did he ask you out yet?"

"No, but we did exchange phone numbers." Lauren bit her lower lip. "If he asks, I'm inclined to say yes. Is that wrong of me?"

"Of course not. You're both single and around the same age, and it seems like you clicked last night. What could be wrong?"

I tapped the top of my desk with my short fingernails. "There's nothing to stop you from dating Malcolm."

"I know." Lauren cast me a pleading look. "I can't wait around forever, Jane."

"And you shouldn't," I said. "Don't torture yourself. Have some fun and see what happens. The only happiness you're responsible for is your own."

She offered me a warm smile. "Thanks, that's what I needed to hear."

After Lauren left, I concentrated on cataloging until noon then took a short lunch break and headed outside, where Cam was waiting in his luxury sedan.

"Our appointment is at one," he said.

I snapped my seat belt into its clasp. "Which is why I'm here at twelve-twenty. Besides, the way they cleared the decks for you, I'm sure Easton and Associates will wait if we get held up in traffic."

"I like to be prompt."

A quick glimpse to my left revealed the tension in his jaw and his death grip on the steering wheel. "I know you're peeved with me right now, but why don't we call a truce? My intentions are always to help you. I think you understand that."

"Easton and Associates is in downtown Winston, so I plan to park in one of the public garages," Cam said. It was clear he wasn't going to address my last comments, but a sidelong glance told me the tension in his face and hands had eased.

"No problem. I wore my walking shoes," I said.

"Don't you always?"

"Ninety-nine percent of the time, anyway. I prefer comfort and safety over fashion, you know."

"You don't say," he replied, but this retort was softened by a faint smile.

The office building that housed Easton and Associates was only a few blocks from the parking garage, so Cam and I arrived in the law office's lobby a few minutes before our appointment.

"Swanky," I said while Cam checked in with the receptionist. It was obvious that Roger Easton wanted to present an atmosphere of subdued luxury. Leather sofas were flanked by antique walnut side tables and a vintage gold-framed mirror hung over an elegant sideboard. The dense beige carpeting and heavy damask drapes muffled sound while projecting an air of seclusion. It was a calming, cocoon-like space, which was probably deliberate, given the conflicts undoubtedly occurring beyond the reception desk.

A stylish young woman appeared at the door to the inner chambers. "Mr. Clewe and Ms. Hunter? Mr. Easton is ready for you. Please follow me."

She led the way down a corridor filled with the portraits of Easton and the other lawyers at the firm, past and present. At the end of the hall, double doors opened inward with one push from the assistant's hands. She stepped back to allow us to enter the office.

"Sir, they're here," she said, before leaving and pulling the doors closed behind her.

The luxurious carpet was soft under the soles of my loafers. Crossing to Easton's desk, I was stuck by the expansive corner windows that looked out over a city park. They screamed wealth and prestige, as did the vintage décor.

Cam leaned in and whispered, "Remember what we discussed. Stick to the strategy."

I nodded, then plastered on a smile as Roger Easton turned away from his corner office view to greet us.

Chapter Twenty-Four

Roger Easton's trim figure was complimented by the impeccable cut of his charcoal gray suit. A man of average height, he had a sharp-featured face framed by perfectly coiffed russet-brown hair. His dark brown eyes surveyed us, unblinking.

He reminds me of a fox, I thought, glancing over at Cam to catch his reaction to the man.

Cam's face didn't betray any emotion. "Hello, Mr. Easton. Thank you so much for making time to meet with us today."

"No worries. It took a bit of shuffling, but that's what my staff is for. Please, have a seat." He motioned toward three armchairs clustered around a small cocktail table. A crystal pitcher filled with water sat on a pewter serving platter, accompanied by four glass tumblers.

Cam and I sat in the two chairs facing a taller-backed wing chair. I assumed that chair, with its throne-like aura, belonged to Easton.

"Help yourself to water," he said, sitting down without reaching for a glass himself. "I can also ask my assistant to get you coffee or tea, or even a soft drink, if you prefer."

"I'm good, thank you," I said.

Cam didn't bother to reply. I knew he was fighting an internal battle, but unlike when we'd first met, he wasn't betraying his unease. He'd curled the fingers of his right hand into his palm to prevent them tapping the upholstered armrest and maintained a neutral expression that gave nothing away.

Bravo, Cam, I thought. *You've obviously been working hard, learning methods to mask any signs of your anxiety.*

"What can I help you with today?" Easton asked, settling back in his chair. "I wanted to speak with you first to see what type of legal assistance you might need, before I recommend one of my gifted colleagues. They all specialize, you see."

"I think you're getting a little ahead of yourself." The slight tremor in Cam's voice made me nervous. I didn't want to see him lose control of his emotions in front of Easton. Fortunately, the lawyer appeared oblivious. "I'm here to get a handle on your guiding principles and how you conduct business."

"I see." Roger Easton leaned forward, resting his elbows on his chair arms and clasping his hands under his chin. "How can I display such a thing, Mr. Clewe? The guiding principles are available in our business statement, of course, but as to how we conduct business . . . we work to ensure our clients' best interest. As I'm sure you understand, we must protect the confidentiality of our clients. I can't really share any step-by-step descriptions of how we've managed our cases without violating that."

Cam studied Easton, his sea-green eyes narrowing. "That's the thing, though. I'm dedicated to handling all of my business ventures in an aboveboard manner. I won't take shortcuts or try to juggle the numbers or anything of that nature. I assume you agree with that philosophy?"

"Of course." Easton's tone remained friendly, but the lines bracketing his mouth and fanning out from his eyes deepened.

"Easton and Associates prides itself on its transparency and honesty. We uphold and vigorously champion the truth."

Cam's heel bounced soundlessly against the thick carpet. "It's funny, though. I was speaking with someone from the Stewart family—you know them well, I believe?"

Roger Easton straightened, dropping his hands to grip the chair arms. "Yes, I've worked with them for many years."

"That's what I was told. My contact said you even represented Duff Stewart and his cousins Lucas and Gabriel Neri when they had an unfortunate car accident several years ago."

Easton's knuckles blanched as he tightened his grip. "Represented? I think that's a misstatement. I offered some advice and support, that's all. They really didn't need more than that, since they were the victims, not the guilty party."

"I did think it was odd that you'd be involved, since you aren't a defense attorney. But then again, as you say, they weren't the ones at fault." Cam glanced over at me. "Does that answer your question, Jane? I know you were puzzled by Mr. Easton's involvement in the case when you conducted some research for Vince Fisher."

Easton's head whipped to the left so quickly I was afraid he was going to snap his neck. "You're working with an investigative reporter?"

"Not exactly. Vince is my landlord, and we're friends. I sometimes help him with his research, but that's all. He's retired now, so he isn't writing for the paper, but he's working on a couple of ideas for books based on his reporting in the past." I smiled disingenuously. While it was true that Vince wanted to write a book, his focus was on telling the story of the Airley family and their estate. He certainly wasn't planning to write a book based on the Stewarts, but Roger Easton didn't need to know that.

"If he includes me or my law practice in any of his writings, he'll have to clear it with me first," Easton said, jabbing his finger at me. "You'd better tell him that, Ms. Hunter. I won't put up with being libeled."

"I'll make sure he understands, Mr. Easton." Fearing that my fake smile was morphing into a grimace, I switched to a neutral expression.

"He should practice caution when referencing the Stewart and Neri families as well. I may not handle libel cases, but I know many other excellent lawyers who'd be happy to do so."

"I'm sure Mr. Fisher will be circumspect in his writing," Cam said, his gaze fixed on Roger Easton's disgruntled face. "Especially considering the recent tragedy that has befallen the Neri family."

Easton audibly sniffed. "You mean Gabriel Neri's death? That was an accident waiting to happen. He had an addiction to opioids, and you know how that goes—users keep wanting more and more until their habit eventually kills them."

"His cousin Malcolm claims he'd been clean for years," I said.

"How would Malcolm know that? He's been estranged from the family for quite some time." Releasing his grip on the chair, Easton folded his arms over his chest.

"He and Gabe remained close, regardless," I said. "Apparently they visited each other and communicated frequently."

These words appeared to strike Roger Easton like a slap across the face. He exhaled a rattling breath and jumped to his feet. "I suspect you may be here under false pretenses," he said, looking from Cam to me and back again. "It's clear you're more interested in ancient history than any legal advice, Mr. Clewe."

"I'm sorry you have that impression," Cam said, standing to face him across the cocktail table. "Like I said, I'm just testing the waters. Unfortunately, I don't think we're a good fit, businesswise. It seems we're inclined to misunderstand one another."

I stood as well. "Please believe me, I didn't mean to cause you any distress, Mr. Easton."

He cast me a furious glance. "What do you mean by distress? I assure you—nothing you've said today has caused me the least concern."

"That's good to hear," I said. "You seemed a little upset there for a minute, but I must've been reading you wrong."

He looked me over with a sneer. "Forgive my bluntness, but it's clear your perception is flawed, Ms. Hunter."

"Really? You feel entitled to insult my personal staff? I'm afraid that seals it—I cannot work with your firm, Mr. Easton. Not now and not in the future." Cam turned, allowing his long coat to sweep across the cocktail table, knocking over the water pitcher. While the thick carpet cushioned the fall, the handle of the pitcher still snapped off. "Oh, sorry," Cam said, looking down at the mess. "On my way out, I'll let your assistant know that you need assistance. Come along, Jane. Just watch for broken glass."

I followed him out of the office, grinning as Roger Easton's string of invectives filled the air.

Chapter Twenty-Five

On Sunday, the day of the fundraiser, I chose a simple gray wool dress and hip-length black velveteen jacket, which I dressed-up with the black-and-silver marcasite jewelry Bailey had given me on my last birthday.

Malcolm arrived promptly at noon, driving an all-electric compact car.

"This is just what I pictured," I said, as I climbed in the passenger side of the vehicle.

"The car, you mean?" Malcolm grinned. "Do I really come across as the crunchy granola type?"

"Yes, but I wouldn't think you'd mind."

"I don't," Malcolm said, as he pulled out onto Bradfordville's main street. He cast me a sidelong glance. "People will think we color coordinated," he added, giving the lapel of his gray suit jacket a tug.

"Ah yes, gray jacket and black pants to match my black and gray outfit. Some guests may get the idea that you're dating a much older woman. Shall we set them straight from the get-go?"

Malcolm waved this aside. "Let them think whatever they want. It'll give them something to talk about other than all the stuff they bought over the past week or their last luxury vacation."

"That's fine. Honestly, I'd be flattered if anyone thought a young man like you would date a woman like me." I gazed out the window. We'd gotten on the highway, which was busy despite it not being a work day. "By the way, did you bring that birthday party guest list?"

Malcolm patted the left chest section of his coat. "I have it right here. I'll hand it over when we reach the house."

"Great. I'm interested to see who was there other than your family." *Like Roger Easton*, I thought.

Malcolm lifted one hand off the steering wheel and flexed his fingers. "Finger cramp. I use my hands a lot in my work and sometimes I overdo it."

I turned my head to study his handsome profile. "I bet you're the type who can't quit working once you're in the zone."

"You're very perceptive." Malcolm flashed me a smile. "That's probably why your boss brought you in as a partner in his sleuthing hobby."

"It's more serious than a hobby," I said, my tone a little sharper than I'd intended. "People's lives and reputations are often at stake. We don't view it as a game."

"Sorry, I meant no disrespect."

Malcolm fell silent for several minutes after that statement, and I decided to follow suit. I knew outsiders viewed our efforts as part of the peculiar affectations of a wealthy, but eccentric, young man, but it was more than that. Both Cam and I were driven by a quest for justice and a desire to reveal the truth. I shook my head, thinking how that made us sound like old-fashioned superheroes. *You have to admit you enjoy solving the puzzle, too,* I reminded myself. *Cam's the same. Our amateur detective work isn't entirely altruistic.*

"There is an element of enjoying the chase," I said, earning a quizzical glance from Malcolm. "I mean, in our sleuthing pursuits. I can see why you might call it a hobby."

"No, I should know better. I've had enough people denigrate my career as an artist by calling it that. You'll probably see that in action, soon enough," Malcolm said as he turned onto his parents' driveway.

"I assume your mom and dad think you should be involved in the family business and simply paint on the side?"

"My father does. My mom says she just wants me to be happy." Sorrow flitted across Malcolm's face. "I'm not sure why she thinks that's something easy to accomplish. She's never been able to do it."

After Malcolm parked the car, he reached inside his coat and pulled out a folded piece of paper. "Here you go. Keep it safe to look at later."

"I will," I said, tucking the paper into my purse.

We walked side-by-side to reach the imposing front doors.

"Did you meet my mom when you were here before?" Malcolm asked as I pressed the doorbell.

"No, only your father and Gabe. And a housekeeper," I said, as that same woman opened one of the doors.

The cloying scent of lilies wafted out of the front hall behind her. "Please, come in," she said, staring at Malcolm as if she'd seen a ghost. "We didn't know you were coming. Your mother will be pleased."

"My father, not so much." Malcolm offered her a smile. "Don't worry, Ms. Warner, I'm not here to cause trouble."

"Well . . ." The housekeeper's cheeks were tinged pink from embarrassment. "It's good to see you looking so well." She turned to me. "And Ms. Hunter. I didn't realize you were acquainted with anyone in the family."

"Malcolm and I met recently," I said as I followed her into the front hall, holding one finger under my nose. The entire space was filled with banks of flowers. Pots of lilies and roses were set on tiered plant stands, with ceramic urns filled with greenery interspersed throughout.

"But we've become good friends in that short time, haven't we, Jane?" Malcolm offered Ms. Warner another brilliant smile.

"We have," I said, slipping off my long wool coat.

"Here, let me take those." Ms. Warner slung our coats over her arm. "I'll put these in the closet over there. Please feel free to grab them whenever you wish to leave." She trotted across the front hall, but paused for a moment to call over her shoulder, "Everyone's in the great room. Mr. Malcolm."

Malcolm touched my arm. "This way," he said, heading off toward one of the arches under the sweeping staircase.

I trailed him down a wide hallway with dark wood floors, celery-green walls, and an elaborate coffered ceiling. White plaster plant stands held more lilies.

"Heaven help anyone who's allergic to flowers," I said.

Malcolm shared an amused glance. "That's the Stewarts for you—more is more." He paused at the end of the hall, where a wide arch opened onto a room almost as large as the ballroom at Aircroft.

It certainly lived up to its name as a Great Room. The white ceiling that rose high above the dark wood floors featured rafters that resembled the flying buttresses in historic cathedrals, and there were several of the icicle-style crystal chandeliers hanging over different seating areas. The pale wood or white-painted furniture offered little contrast with the taupe, beige, or white cushions and upholstery. Everything except the floor was light and bright. Asian-inspired ceramic vases filled with flowers provided the only splashes of color.

"Not a room friendly to red wine," I murmured to Malcolm, who gave my shoulder a light squeeze.

"I just spotted Ainsley and Finn. Let me introduce you," he said.

"I've already met Ainsley so . . ."

My words were cut off by the approach of Duff Stewart.

He stopped short directly in front of us, fixing Malcolm with an intimidating glare. "What the hell are you doing here?"

Chapter Twenty-Six

A roomful of guests turned as one at Duff's bellowed words.

"I'm here to support a worthwhile cause," Malcolm said, remaining perfectly calm in the face of his father's aggression. His self-possession revealed he'd had plenty of experience dealing with similar attacks.

"Hello, Mr. Stewart," I said. "I'm not sure you remember me . . ."

"I know who you are, Ms. Hunter. I may be getting older, but I'm not senile yet." Duff adjusted the open collar of his lime green shirt, which he wore with a plaid jacket over tailored khaki pants. It was an outfit that would have been more appropriate for the country club after a golf match rather than a semi-formal charity event, but I supposed he could wear whatever he wanted in his own house.

A petite woman hurried forward, the sleeves of her peach chiffon cocktail dress fluttering like butterfly wings. Her short, walnut-brown hair and blue eyes told me that this must be Malcolm's mother, Sharon Stewart.

"Duff," she said, in a breathy voice, "what are you doing?" She gave Malcolm a quick hug before stepping back to stand beside her husband. "Of course we're delighted to have you here, Mal. It's been far too long."

"Yeah, I'm sorry about that, Mom. I've been very busy lately, teaching and preparing for an exhibition."

Duff snorted. "Busy? Slapping paint on canvas? Now, if you were helping to run things at Stewart Enterprises, you'd know what busy is."

"Come on, Dad, you have Ainsley and Finn. You don't need me," Malcolm said. "Anyway, please allow Ms. Hunter to mingle a bit. We've been working on a little project together, and I invited her here today to introduce her to the rest of the family."

Duff glowered as Sharon reached out and clasped my hand. "But first, let me make sure you have some refreshments. Leave the men to chat." She cast a warning glance at her husband, who huffed and turned aside. "This way," she told me, leading me a few feet away before she dropped my hand.

I glanced back, observing that Duff had stalked off to join a group of men discussing golf. Malcolm, shrugging, jogged over to catch up with us. "Dad isn't in a talkative mood," he told Sharon. "At least not with me. But it's OK. I'll make sure Jane gets something to drink and eat. You can go back to making the rounds and drumming up money for the cause, Mom."

"Alright, dear. Just try not to annoy Ainsley this time, please?" Although Malcolm was not tall, his mother had to lift her chin to look up at him.

"Scout's honor," Malcolm said, making the sign of the cross.

"Silly boy, you were never in the Scouts." Sharon gave him a fond smile and a pat on the arm before she headed back into the crowd.

"Your mother seems sweet," I said, following Malcolm as he maneuvered through clusters of chattering guests.

"She is, unfortunately for her." Malcolm led me to a linen-draped banquet table that held platters of appetizers as well as a variety of elegant desserts. He handed me a small crystal plate. "Here you go, help yourself to some food. The bar's over in the corner. I'm going to step outside for some fresh air before I dive into the required greetings." He popped a tea sandwich into his mouth and hurried off toward the French doors.

I sat down at a café table near the bar to munch on a couple of crustless sandwiches and a few pieces of raw vegetables. As I was sipping from my glass of lemon-infused water I heard a young girl's voice.

"Can I sit here with you?" she asked. "All the other tables are full."

I met her luminous dark-eyed gaze with a smile. "Of course."

She was petite enough to be mistaken for a younger child, but I could tell by her figure and manner that she was in her early teens. Her black hair was pulled back in a high ponytail and her face was devoid of make-up.

"I'm Ara," she said, settling into the chair across the table from me.

"I thought you might be. I'm Jane Hunter. I bet your dad is Finn Stewart?"

"Yeah. My mom's name is really Soo Jin but everyone calls her Sue. I don't think that's cool, but my mom says I shouldn't make a fuss about it." Ara wrinkled her pert nose. "My grandparents, I mean the ones on Mom's side, don't like it either, but they live in Korea and don't have much of a say about what goes on here."

I studied her for a moment. She had delicate features I assumed she'd inherited from her mother and the poise and posture of a successful athlete. "A friend of mine told me that you're an equestrian. She said you're quite good and win a lot of the competitions another friend's granddaughter also participates in."

Ara toyed with the three petit fours on her plate. "I'm not bad. We haven't found the perfect horse yet, though. The rider and horse must both be at a top level if you want to enter something like the Olympics."

"Is that your dream?" I asked.

Ara bobbed her head, bouncing her ponytail. "Yeah. It's pretty hard to reach that level, but I want to try."

"Well, it's difficult to become a working actress too, but my daughter did it. Like you, she wanted to try, so she worked as hard as she could and didn't give up even when she got a lot of rejections. So I definitely think you have a chance."

"Really? What's her name? Have I seen her on TV or anything?" Ara's expression brightened, revealing her true beauty.

"Her name is Bailey Hunter. She mostly works on the stage, but she's had a few TV and film roles." I fished my wallet out of my purse and opened it to a photo of Bailey. "Here she is," I said, holding out the wallet so Ara could see the picture.

"She's really pretty." Ara's voice sounded wistful.

I pulled back my arm and slipped my wallet back into my purse. "You're quite pretty, too. But more importantly, I can tell you have the same sort of drive to succeed. Please don't give up on your dream."

"I won't." Ara's smile faded as she looked at something over my shoulder. "Ugh, I hope he doesn't come over here."

I swiveled in my chair to see who she was looking at. "Mr. Easton? Don't you like him?"

"Not at all. He always talks to me like I'm five years old, and he doesn't treat Mom right." Ara took a bite out of one of the petit fours.

"What do you mean? Is he rude to her?"

"No," she replied, after she finished chewing. "It's like he's always hitting on her. Which is gross because he's so old."

My research had confirmed that Roger Easton was sixty-five, only three years older than me, but I let that go. "You mean he flirts with her?"

"Kind of." Ara finished off the little cake cube and wiped her hands on a napkin. "Mom says he thinks she's *exotic*, which she really hates. It's like she's some animal in a zoo, you know?"

"It's very rude, is what it is," I said. "By the way, is the man standing near Mr. Easton your cousin Lucas Neri?"

Ara pursed her lips. "Yeah. He's OK, but he's always so loud."

Since I could hear his voice over the rest of the crowd, I had to agree. "I guess they're friends, huh?"

"I dunno," Ara said with a shrug. "They talk about business stuff a lot. I don't really pay attention."

"I wouldn't either." I stared at Lucas Neri, who bore a close resemblance to his brother, Gabe. The major difference was that Lucas appeared much healthier, despite being the elder of the two by a good ten years.

I'd just started to turn back around when a commotion erupted near the French doors to the patio.

"What's going on?" I said, standing to get a better look.

Ara climbed up on her chair and peered over the heads of the crowd. "It's Cousin Malcolm and some guy I don't know. I think Mal dragged the guy in off the patio."

"Malcolm is holding onto him?" I asked, rising up on my toes to get a better look.

"He's got the guy's arms yanked behind his back." Ara whistled. "Whoa, looks like the stranger must've been trespassing or something and Cousin Malcolm caught him."

Raised voices filled the room as Malcolm herded his captive over to where Duff had joined up with Roger Easton and Lucas. A short, slender woman with straight dark hair scurried across the room, zig-zagging around the tableau of angry men to reach Ara and me.

"Ara, get down from there," said the woman, who I assumed was Soo Jin Stewart. "The last thing we need is for you to break an arm or leg."

"What's happening, Mom?" Ara asked as she climbed down off the chair. "Who's that guy?"

"Someone who doesn't belong here." Soo Jin cast me a quizzical look. "I don't believe I know you, Ms. . . .

"Hunter. Jane Hunter," I replied. "I'm Malcolm's guest today."

Soo Jin swept her silky black hair behind her narrow shoulders. "I'm Sue Stewart. Nice to meet you. Sorry for the commotion."

"It's fine. I just hope everything is all right," I said, focusing on the group of men who were clustered in the center of the room. All the other guests had stepped away, leaving Duff, Lucas, and Roger facing off with Malcolm and his captive.

The stranger lunged forward, breaking free of Malcolm's grip, and spat on the floor. "Don't you treat me like a criminal. It's time you compensated me for all my pain and suffering," he shouted.

Soo Jin squinted as she stared at the scene, then stepped back, her face pale as milk.

"Oh no, it can't be. Not Joseph Carson," she said.

Chapter Twenty-Seven

Soo Jin grabbed her daughter's hand. "Come with me, Ara. We can slip out the back door. No need to witness this." Turning to me she added, "You might want to join us, Ms. Hunter."

"I think I should stay," I replied. "I'm Malcolm's guest, after all. I don't want him to wonder where I am."

"Mom, why can't we stay?" The whiny note in Ara's voice brought back vivid memories of Bailey's teenage years. "Dad's with Granddad and Cousin Lucas now. Don't you want to make sure he's OK?"

I switched my focus to the group of men engaged in a faceoff with Joe Carson. The man who had joined them resembled Duff Stewart, although he was leaner and had more finely etched features. His dark blonde hair, styled in a typical businessman's cut, gleamed like burnished gold.

"Dad will be fine. It's five against one," Soo Jin said, dragging Ara toward a door positioned behind the bar.

But is it? I mused, staring at the men. Malcolm hadn't switched sides to stand with his relatives and Roger Easton. He was still on Joe Carson's side.

"Leave or I call the police," Duff demanded, his face as red as a rooster's crest.

Carson's angry expression slid into a sneer. "Sure, why not? You've got them in your pocket. I'm sure they'd be happy to arrest me again."

"You're treading on thin ice." Roger Easton's voice, though perfectly calm, was emphatic. "This isn't the first time you've disrupted an event sponsored by the Stewart family. They've been lenient with you before, but now you've gone too far. You could easily be charged with trespassing as well as stalking."

"Liar!" Joe Carson leapt forward, fists raised, only to be blocked by Duff and Finn. They stepped in front of Easton, forming a bulwark against Carson's charge.

Joe Carson was not a big man. Short and wiry, he was easily dwarfed by the Stewarts and Lucas Neri. Even though they were only of average height, their broad-shouldered, well-muscled builds made Carson look like a skinny teen.

"My father said get out," Finn said. "You'd better listen if you don't want to end up back in jail."

Carson sputtered a string of obscenities, igniting gasps from the crowd. Malcolm rushed forward and took hold of his arm, pulling him back.

"Let's go, Mr. Carson. This is a waste of time," Malcolm said.

I narrowed my eyes. It almost seemed as if Malcolm was protecting Joe Carson rather than his family. Perhaps he was simply trying to de-escalate the situation, but the fact that he was the one who'd escorted Carson inside, albeit a little roughly, and was now attempting to remove him before any punches were thrown felt a little suspicious to me.

Carson shook off Malcolm's hand and straightened his back. "I'll go. Continue on with your stupid party. It doesn't change the fact that I know the truth."

Duff Stewart laughed. "The truth? The truth is you killed your wife and daughter and can't live with that fact so you've convinced yourself you weren't at fault, despite the court's verdict. You can't accept the truth, so you blame others."

"Enough," Lucas Neri said, shooting Duff a sharp look. He took a few steps forward, moving closer to Carson, who had dropped his head and begun to sob following Duff's comments. "Mr. Carson, we understand the depth of your loss. It was a terrible accident. But this behavior can't continue. It pains me to see you throwing away your life over an old tragedy."

Lucas Neri's words resonated throughout the room, generating murmurs of approval from the guests. I shifted my focus to Malcolm, whose face was as still as a stone mask.

"Please, let me take you outside," Malcolm said to Carson, his voice surprisingly gentle.

Joe Carson, tears still dripping off his chin, nodded. Muttering something over and over that sounded like *liars*, he allowed Malcolm to guide him over to the French doors and escort him out of the house.

Duff, catching my eye, marched over to stand in front of me. "Sorry for the disturbance, Ms. Hunter. I assure you our parties are not always so . . . lively."

Lucas and Finn had followed him. They looked me up and down and asked to be introduced.

"This is Cameron Clewe's personal librarian, Jane Hunter," Duff said, baring his teeth in the semblance of a smile. "Ms. Hunter, my son, Finn, and our cousin, Lucas Neri."

"Pleasure to meet you," Lucas said, pumping my hand in a strong shake. "Please forgive our little contretemps. I'm afraid Mr. Carson has been suffering from delusions for quite some time."

"I see," I said, acknowledging Finn's nod in greeting. "But don't worry about me. I worked in a university library for many years. I've seen worse."

Duff's booming laugh was echoed by a chuckle from Finn. Lucas, on the other hand, only managed a faint smile. "I believe you met my brother Gabe before his unfortunate passing, Ms. Hunter. He spoke highly of you."

I blinked, confused by this statement. Gabe had been pleasant when we'd interacted in the Stewart's library, but we hardly spent enough time together to allow him to make any sort of assessment. *Unless he'd already done a good deal of research on Cam and me,* I thought, further convinced about our theory that Gabe had deliberately chosen to include Kimberly's book and note in the stack headed to Aircroft. "Yes, we met, and may I say I'm very sorry for your loss, Mr. Neri."

"Thank you." Lucas shifted his weight from foot to foot and stared at a point over my shoulder.

"It was definitely a shock," Finn said, laying a hand on his older cousin's shoulder.

Duff's lips twisted into a grimace. "Unfortunately, that's what often happens when someone just can't seem to kick the habit. Very sad, but not really that much of a shock," he added, side-eyeing his son. "I'd been expecting it for years."

"Really, Dad?" Malcolm appeared at my side. "Gabe was clean and had been for over a decade. But it's not surprising you wouldn't know since you hardly ever interacted with him."

Duff huffed. "Nonsense. It's you who've abandoned the family, Malcolm."

"More like I was driven out," Malcolm said, his tone edged with anger. "But let's not quarrel in front of Jane. I'm sure she isn't interested in our family dynamics."

Of course, I was, but didn't plan to share the reasons for my interest.

"At any rate, I should introduce Jane to a few other people." Malcolm lightly clutched my bent elbow. "I know you said you've already met Ainsley, but we should say hello, and I'm sure my mom would like to talk with you a little more." He slid his hand down to my forearm and pulled me closer to his side. "If you'll excuse us . . ."

We walked away without any goodbyes. Malcolm introduced me to a few other guests before I came up with the right question to ask about the day's events. "I didn't expect to see Joe Carson here," I said, with a sidelong glance at Malcolm's profile. "It seems like such a coincidence, considering the research we were doing just the other day."

Malcolm met my inquisitive gaze with a wry smile. "Coincidences do happen."

"True, but they can also be *made* to happen," I said.

Ignoring this remark, Malcolm ushered me over to a group of guests that included Ainsley and Sharon Stewart. "Hello," he said, releasing my arm. "Please welcome my guest, Jane Hunter. She's a librarian who works for Cameron Clewe. We met over some . . . special research."

Ainsley's carefully sculpted brows arched over her hazel eyes. Pinning me with a piercing stare, she placed her hands on her narrow hips. "Good afternoon, Ms. Hunter. I didn't realize you had such a chummy relationship with my baby brother and, frankly, I can't imagine what sort of research he'd be doing. Mal never was that interested in academic subjects."

She's still determined to squash any investigation into Gabe's death, I thought. *I wonder who she's trying to protect?* "It's nothing big," I said, flashing my best professional smile. "Just a topic that interests both of us."

Ainsley's intense gaze shifted to Malcolm. "And what might that be?"

"Come now, dear," Sharon said. "This isn't the time or place to interrogate your brother. Let's just be happy he decided to join us today." She gave me a smile and a nod before turning away to speak with a group of younger women.

"That's true, this is the first time you've been home in forever. With a guest, no less." Ainsley's supercilious gaze swept over me. "Robbing the cradle, aren't you, Ms. Hunter?"

Malcolm opened his mouth as if to form an appropriate retort, but I patted his arm and replied instead. "I thought you were interested in younger men as well, Ms. Stewart, judging by your behavior at Aircroft. Or did I read that wrong?"

Fury contorted Ainsley's face. "Not the same thing," she snapped.

"I know. And trust me, I also know better than to romantically pursue a man young enough to be my son. Malcolm and I are friends, nothing more, and I don't believe there are any age restrictions on friendship."

"Why are you here, anyway?" Ainsley said, speaking directly to Malcolm. "I thought you found such events far too bourgeois for your artistic sensibilities."

Malcolm shrugged. "I have my reasons. None of which should concern you."

I glanced at him. *Does he mean that?* I wondered. *Or is he simply trying to goad her into revealing something? She publicly supports the official report on Gabe's death, so any investigation that contradicts that story will certainly impact her.*

Ainsley dropped her arms to her sides and tossed her honey-blonde hair. "Whatever. I'm not really that interested." She turned to me. "Pleasure to see you again, Ms. Hunter. Tell Cam I said hello."

I simply smiled in response. "I hope you raise a lot of money today, Ms. Stewart, despite the strange interruption."

"That will probably help the cause. Excitement often makes people open their wallets wider," she said. "Now, if you'll excuse me, I have to go speak to a few potential donors."

As she sauntered off, Malcolm leaned in closer and whispered, "You seem to be harboring some suspicions about today's incident, Jane. I hope you don't think I'm keeping things from you."

"Sorry, Malcolm, but I suspect everyone, even you. Cam taught me that it's the best tactic when sleuthing."

Malcolm examined me for a moment. "He's right, of course. You shouldn't trust anyone. Not completely."

"Don't worry," I said. "I don't."

Chapter Twenty-Eight

Malcolm smiled. "Good, glad we settled that. Now, are you about ready to leave? I know I am."

"Yes, definitely," I said.

At that moment Soo Jin and Ara reappeared, entering through the same door they had used to make their stealthy exit. Malcolm, seeing them, touched the back of my hand. "Sorry, but I need to talk to my sister-in-law and niece for a moment. I haven't seen them in quite some time."

"Of course," I said. "Why don't I give you some space? I'll head to the main entry hall and grab our coats. Take your time; I'll wait for your there."

"You're sure you know where you're going?" Malcolm asked

"Never fear—if I can make my way around Aircroft, I can certainly navigate this house."

I told Soo Jin and Ara that it had been lovely to meet them, but they were too excited to see Malcolm to pay me any attention. Shrugging, I walked away, heading for the corridor leading to the entry hall.

Crossing the hall, I spared one glance for the death-trap chandelier. When I lowered my gaze I noticed a familiar figure standing in front of the coat closet's open door.

"David, I didn't know you were here or I would've greeted you before this," I said.

David Benton, handsome as ever in a three-piece navy suit, turned around with a broad smile. "Jane, I'm so sorry I missed you. There was such a crowd, though. It was hard to meet everyone."

"It really was. I never even caught a glimpse of you, even though you were probably one of the tallest people in the room. I suppose you came to support the charity?"

"And to mingle with the excessively well-heeled. Comes with my job, I'm afraid." David shrugged on his coat and swept back an unruly lock of his gray hair. The co-owner, with his mother Gloria, of Benton House in High Point, he and I had become friends during the events of the last major case Cam and I had undertaken. Benton House was well-known in the area. They handled high-end art and antiques and catered to professional interior designers and their wealthy clients. David also dabbled in acquiring and selling valuable manuscripts and vintage books, which was the first thing that had sparked our friendship.

"Of course, today was a little different. That strange confrontation . . ." I watched David's face for his reaction. He had a lot of contacts in the world of the rich and famous, and I hoped my prompt might encourage him to share some useful information.

"Very odd indeed. I remember a little about that accident, mainly because I was seventeen and my mom used it as a warning about the dangers of driving. I'd just gotten my license, and she was terrified I'd drive recklessly and end up dead on the side of the road."

"Sadly, two people did end up dead from the crash involving Joe Carson and our host and his cousins."

"Yes." David's smile faded. "I suppose I'd react the same way as Carson if I'd killed my family. You don't want to believe it, so you have to find others to blame."

"He claims it wasn't his fault," I said. "But, as you say, that could simply be a defense mechanism. If he had proof, I'd expect him to have produced it by now, so it's just his word against the Stewarts and Neris."

David's expression grew thoughtful. "Who did have a lot more money and power than a day laborer like Carson."

"Is that what he did? I never really heard," I said.

"Yes, but only before the accident. Afterwards . . . Well, he had some serious injuries, which probably limited him physically, and there was the jail sentence. I expect he's had to struggle mightily over all these years."

"It's sad any way you look at it." I cast a glance toward the hallway that led to the Great Room, but Malcolm was still nowhere in sight.

"Are you waiting for someone?" David asked. "I planned to ask you if you needed a ride, but I expect you have that covered."

"I came as a guest of Malcolm Stewart." I raised one hand. "Not as a date. You know me—I don't even date men my own age. I'm certainly not going to get involved in a romantic relationship with a thirty-year-old."

"The thought never crossed my mind." David's smile returned. "On another topic, do you happen to know someone called Vanessa Gale? She visited Benton House, looking to sell some artifacts from Central and South America. I was a little dubious, so I put her off, but she did namedrop your boss."

I widened my eyes. "We've met. She came to Aircroft begging Cam to fund an expedition to Peru. She claimed to know Rafe's whereabouts, and suggested that she could connect Cam with his biological father. For a cost, of course."

"What did you think of her?"

"Both Cam and I felt something was a little off, even though all our research hasn't turned up anything concrete." I tapped my foot against the polished floor. "Was that the end of it, or did she plan to come back and try again?"

"Actually, she said she was going to collect some personal references and documents tracing the provenance of the items and return. Based on her eagerness to sell, I expect her to show up in the next day or two."

"Would you let me know if she does? Just text me when she arrives, and I'll try to get to Benton House before she leaves. I'd like to see those references myself."

"Certainly. I'll even make sure she stays put until you show up." David thrust his hands into his coat pockets. "You're trying to protect Clewe from a scam, right?"

"Yes. Although he isn't easily fooled, his father has been missing for a while. Something like that can distort your perception."

"Absolutely." David slid one hand from his pocket and reached out to pat my shoulder. "Don't worry, Jane. I'm not really close to Cameron Clewe, but I know you are. That means I'm more than willing to help you help him."

"Thanks." I lifted my chin to look up at him and smiled. "It's too bad I'm not interested in dating. You're definitely a good catch."

"Ah well . . ." A faint hint of color flushed David's cheekbones. "Honestly, at first I'd hoped you might change your mind about going out with me, but since you've turned down several of my invitations over the past months, I've finally accepted the fact you only want to be friends."

"I'm glad to hear that," I said. "I do like you as a friend, and certainly don't want you to miss out on someone great because you're thinking I'll change. You should use your good looks and charm to enchant some other woman."

David opened his mouth to reply but immediately tightened his lips at the sound of footsteps. I turned to see Malcolm entering the hall.

"Sorry it took so long, Jane." Malcolm looked David over. "But it seems you've met a friend, so I don't feel so bad."

"You shouldn't. It gave us the opportunity to catch up," I said. "Have you two met?"

"Not officially, but I know who you are," Malcolm said, extending his hand. "I'm Malcolm Stewart, nice to meet you, Mr. Benton."

David stepped forward to give Malcolm a quick but firm handshake. "The painter? I saw one of your recent exhibits. Excellent work. We should talk."

"I'm open to that." Malcolm's eyes shone like sapphires.

I suspected he was thrilled that David had identified him as an artist rather than one of Duff Stewart's sons. "I have your numbers, so I'll text you both. That way you can talk shop to your hearts' content." I grinned at both men. "All I ask is a teeny, tiny commission."

Malcolm laughed. "Done, for my part."

"How about dinner instead?" David asked.

I rolled my eyes. "Excuse me, I need to grab my coat." I brushed past David to reach the closet. "I can get yours as well, Malcolm. You two go ahead and chat amongst yourselves."

"So I have a question—you've known Jane longer than I have. Is she always so bossy?" Malcolm asked.

David cast an amused look in my direction. "Always. I find it's best to obey."

Chapter Twenty-Nine

By the time Malcolm dropped me off at my apartment, all I wanted to do was to change my clothes, grab a glass of wine, flop onto my sofa, and watch the 1995 film version of *Sense and Sensibility*. It was my go-to comfort watch and worked its magic this time as well.

When the movie was over, I wandered into the kitchen to see what might be available in my refrigerator or cabinets. I found some canned soup and crackers and decided that would be dinner.

My phone buzzed right after I finished the last spoonful of soup.

"Hello," I said, not recognizing the number. "May I ask who's calling, please?"

"You don't need to know that," said a husky woman's voice. "What you do need to know is simple, but essential—you should drop your investigation into Gabriel Neri's death. The authorities have closed the case, and any attempt to reopen it will only cause confusion."

"Excuse me, I don't think you have any right to tell me this," I said, fighting to keep my voice from shaking. "I don't know who you are and sincerely doubt you have any official authority to warn me off."

"I possess a different, but equally compelling, authority." The voice dropped to a lower register, making me question if the caller was actually a man masquerading as a woman.

"To do what, exactly? Are you saying I'm putting myself in danger if I pursue the leads I've already discovered?"

"Not just you, but some of your acquaintances. Including, of course, Mr. Cameron Clewe. But if you persist, anyone in your orbit could become a target."

"Then this is a real threat." I didn't pose this as a question.

"It is, and if you're smart, you'll leave the Gabriel Neri case where it should remain—closed and forgotten."

The caller hung up before I could reply. I shoved my cell phone in the pocket of my sweatpants, poured another glass of wine, and headed over to my sofa.

I didn't bother to turn on the TV, preferring to sit in silence and consider the warning I'd just received. It was clear that someone didn't want me, or Cam, digging into Gabe's death. Perhaps it would be best to turn this information over to the police, but as the caller had said, the authorities considered the case closed. Would they listen to me and try to track the call, or simply dismiss the occurrence as the product of my over-active imagination?

"I should call Cam," I said, talking to the air. "He needs to know about this."

Of course, we'd planned to discuss what had transpired at the fundraising gala on Monday, but this was more urgent. I tapped his contact in my cell and sat back as his phone rang on the other end.

"I thought we were talking tomorrow," he said, picking up after the fifth ring and eschewing any polite greeting. "I'm in the middle of looking over some reports for an important meeting on Tuesday. Can this wait?"

"No, it can't." I took a deep breath and described the mysterious and threatening phone call. "I felt you should know right away, in case they attempt to contact you as well."

"Was there a number to trace?" Cam asked, after a minute of silence.

"Yes, I'll text it to you. But I suspect it's a burner. Also, I don't believe the caller was the person behind the threat. I think they were just the messenger."

"Still, I can have my personal investigators look into it." Cam cleared his throat. "Do you feel safe, Jane?"

"Tonight? Yes. This was a warning. If we were to drop the case, I believe we'd never hear from this caller or anyone similar again. They're giving us a chance to back off."

"Which I don't intend to do, so we do need to take the threat seriously." Cam's deep sigh resonated across the ether. "I can hire private security, if necessary. But first, text me that number. If my PI's can track down the caller, we may be able to discover who's the power behind the curtain before resorting to bodyguards or other intrusive measures."

"OK, I'll do that as soon as I hang up. Don't worry, my doors and windows are locked, and I'm not about to welcome in a stranger. I'll be fine, so get back to your reports."

After our mutual goodbyes, I checked my phone log and wrote down the number from the mystery caller. Texting it to Cam, I added a message: *We should meet first thing in the morning. The events at the Stewart home need your insight as well.*

Sinking down in my sofa cushions, I laid my phone on the side table, trading it for my glass of wine. "This sure has been an interesting day," I told the books on my overflowing shelves. "If

I weren't so brain-dead, I'd read one of you, but right now I'm going to drink this wine."

I sipped my drink, not minding the silence or the fact I was alone. It was something I'd learned over time—I wasn't a person who was lonely when alone. Not that I didn't enjoy company and lively conversation and friends, I simply didn't require them to feel happy and whole.

Setting down my empty glass, I allowed my head to drop back against the cushions and closed my eyes. Before I knew it, I must have fallen asleep, because I sat up with a start when my cell phone vibrated itself off the side table and fell onto the sofa arm. I grabbed it and rubbed my eyes while peering at the screen.

"Bailey," I said, swiping to answer the call.

"Hey Mom, did I wake you? It's only ten, but I know how you old folks like to go to bed early."

"Yes, you woke me, but I wasn't in bed. I fell asleep on the sofa after experiencing a rather dramatic day." I rubbed my right foot, which had apparently fallen asleep along with me. "Wait—why are you calling now? Shouldn't you be at the theater?"

"That's the thing. I have a couple of weeks off, starting today, because"—Bailey tapped her fingers against her phone like a drum roll—"our show is moving to Broadway!"

Wide awake at this news, I leapt to my feet. "And you're moving with it?"

"Yes, yes, yes!" Bailey's excitement bubbled through her words. "My first actual Broadway role! Can you believe it?"

"Of course I can. You're spectacular in that part." I flicked a tear from my lashes. "I'm so proud of you, darling, but darn it, you're going to make me cry."

"Good. I need someone to cry happy tears with." Bailey sniffled. "Seriously, Mom, it feels surreal. And of course, you have to come back to New York to see the show again."

"Someone would have to chain me down to keep me away," I said, wiping my cheeks with the back of my hand. "What now? Do you get a break while the show transitions?"

"Yes. Two full weeks. It'll take longer to get the show up and running, but I'll need to go back for additional blocking and rehearsals and all that, so I can only take a short break. But still, there's plenty of time to come down for a visit. I mean, if that's OK with you."

"Why wouldn't it be? Unless you plan to simply use my tiny apartment as a home base and flit about, spending most of your time with Taylor. Hmm, I bet that's what's going to happen, isn't it, and you're hoping that's going to be alright with me?" I clucked my tongue. "Well, of course it is, you silly goose. I don't mind if I only see you in your spare moments; I just want to see you."

"Thanks, and I promise to spend time with you as well as Taylor. I mean, he has his driving gigs and has to work on his writing too."

"Sure, sure. Anyway, I'll be working during the day. It's not really a good time for me to ask Cam for days off."

"That's OK. You know I'm quite capable of taking care of myself." Bailey sneezed. "Sorry, allergies, not illness. I won't bring anything infectious along with me."

"Except your laugh," I said, earning a chuckle. "When will you arrive? I'll need to stock up on food you'll actually eat."

"Next weekend. Don't worry about picking me up from the airport, I know a guy . . ."

I smiled. "That chauffeur's license sure is handy."

"Yes, and the driver is too," Bailey said slyly.

I burst out laughing. "TMI, TMI! Have some pity on your poor old mother."

"As if I ever needed to feel sorry for you. I think your life is often more exciting than mine," Bailey said.

I took a deep breath to silence my giggles. "Actually, I could do with a little less excitement some days."

"Then quit helping Cam with his cold cases."

"I can't do that."

Bailey sighed. "You mean you don't want to."

"I plead the fifth," I said.

Chapter Thirty

Immediately after arriving at Aircroft on Monday, I dropped off my tote bag, purse, and coat in the library and headed to Cam's office.

He was already there, seated behind his desk, examining a printed report.

I sat in the other office chair and cleared my throat. "We have a lot to discuss this morning."

"I know." Cam looked up and slid the report to one side of the desk. "First, that anonymous call last evening. You were right; it was a burner phone and untraceable."

"I was afraid of that. Well, it can't be helped." I leaned forward. "But there's other important news to share, including the guest list from Finn Stewart's birthday party." I pulled the folded note from my pocket and slid it across the desk

"No surprises here," Cam said after looking over the paper. "Everyone on our current suspect list was there."

"At least it confirms that supposition," I said. "Now, let's discuss the fundraising event at the Stewarts' home yesterday."

Listening to my recital of the events, including Joe Carson's confrontation with Duff and company, Cam closed his eyes. I knew he wasn't ignoring me—he was evaluating the information and trying to piece together the puzzle.

"You seem unsure about Malcolm's actions," he said when I finished speaking.

"It's just that he was the one to drag Carson into the house and then he didn't display true allegiance to his dad, brother, or cousin. I had this errant thought . . ."

"That Malcolm and Joe Carson were in on the drama together?" Cam leaned back, rocking his chair. "I believe that's possible, especially since Malcolm seems determined to expose the truth about Gabriel Neri's supposed overdose. He may have hoped Carson's accusations would elicit some useful leads."

"You're saying Malcolm believes his father and Lucas, and possibly even his brother, had something to do with Gabe's death?"

"Or they're covering for the actual killer," Cam said. "Think about who else was there."

"Roger Easton?" I asked, with a lift of my eyebrows. "But why would Easton want Gabe dead?"

Cam pressed his elbows against the chair arms and rested his chin on his clasped hands. "I don't know, but I suspect it would have to do with his political aspirations. Perhaps Gabe knew about a scandalous incident in Easton's past and threatened to expose him."

"It's possible, I suppose." I pondered this idea for a moment. "That theory could apply to the other men as well. I doubt Duff Stewart's past is squeaky clean, and Lucas and Finn are both involved in the Stewarts' business interests."

"True. That particular motive to kill Gabe Neri could fit any of them." Cam's eyes were sparkling with excitement. "Finally, something my private investigators can look into. If any of those men have a scandal in their past, particularly in terms of embezzlement or otherwise cooking the books, there's probably a way to reveal their crimes. Nothing can be hidden forever, especially not when money is involved."

"But why drag Joe Carson into the mix? If Malcolm had anything to do with that, I mean."

Cam straightened, lowering his arms to rest on the glass desktop. "Carson developed an intense hatred for Duff and his cousins. Perhaps he discovered something in his quest to pin the accident on them. Malcolm might've hoped to leverage that knowledge to put the others off-balance."

"Or it was what it looked like on the surface—a man with a vendetta crashing a party to confront his enemies." I shrugged. "I think we need to interview Malcolm again before we can be sure he was involved."

"I agree. Besides, one of my contacts who works in publishing shared information that could point to another suspect."

I sat back in my chair and stared at Cam's animated face. It was clear he was dying to share this news. "Who's that?"

"Kaden Ward. To be clear, this is all based on rumors, but apparently Ward and another aspiring author, Lee Jenson, were close friends in college. They often critiqued each other's manuscripts by reading drafts, something neither man allowed anyone else to do." Cam drummed his fingers against the tabletop. "Unfortunately, Jenson died in a hiking accident before he was able to acquire an agent or publisher."

"Was Ward a suspect in his death?"

Cam shook his head. "No. Kaden Ward was five states away when the accident occurred. Not to mention all reports describe him as devastated. But, six months later, when Ward scored his first book deal, a rumor made the rounds. No one knew who started it, or why, but my contact claims the rumor definitely existed."

I snapped my fingers. "Someone claimed Kaden Ward stole Jenson's manuscript and passed it off as his own?"

"Exactly. The thing was, no one knew where this story started, and then it spread like a game of telephone. Someone heard someone else say they'd overheard someone else claim they'd gotten a peek at Jenson's manuscript, and it was essentially the same as Ward's first novel."

"Was there actually evidence to back up the rumor?" I asked, recalling my conversation with Kaden Ward. He didn't strike me as the type of person to pull such a con, but I knew first impressions weren't always accurate.

"There was not. Which is why the story floated away like dandelion floss in the wind."

"After all these years, and many other published books, why would someone want to hurt Ward's career? Unless . . ." I gazed up at the ceiling for a moment to clear my thoughts. "Gabe somehow stumbled onto that old rumor and decided to share it again, this time on social media, which could be much more damning than the simple word-of-mouth smear campaign that happened back in the eighties."

"That sort of threat could definitely be a motive to silence someone," Cam said.

I met his gaze with a nod of agreement. "Gabe was very close to Kimberly Stewart Ward. What if he'd always felt Kaden Ward's mistreatment of her contributed to her suicide? I don't know that any such thing happened, but it could have. Which would have meant Gabe might've been nurturing a grudge for years. Then if Gabe recently discovered Ward's rumored plagiarism scandal, he might've seen that as having been another stressor bearing down on an already fragile woman."

"Then you agree Kaden Ward belongs on the suspect list?"

"Yes." I counted off on my fingers, "Ward, Easton, Lucas Neri, and Duff and Finn Stewart are all viable suspects. Although Lucas killing his brother seems like a stretch, at least to me."

"Not like it hasn't happened before," Cam said.

A rap on the door halted our discussion. "Sorry," Lauren called out. "I have some news I think you should know right away."

"Come in. We're talking about our investigation but it's nothing you can't hear," Cam said.

I swiveled my chair to face the door. "Yes, please share. You aren't going to disturb anyone."

Lauren entered the office and crossed to us, her high heels tapping a staccato beat against the wooden floor. "Honestly, it could be seen as disturbing," she said, shooting darting glances at us both "But I felt it was important you know, since it ties in with what I learned about your recent sleuthing activities." She took a deep breath before adding, "Joseph Carson is dead."

Chapter Thirty-One

Cam and I both leapt out of our chairs.

"Was it a suicide?" I asked, remembering Carson's devastating sobs after his confrontation at the fundraiser.

Lauren used both hands to shove her curls away from her forehead. "No, it was an accident. Apparently, he liked to bike. He'd ride every day the weather was fit. An acquaintance who was interviewed said Mr. Carson much preferred biking over driving."

"Not surprising, after that car crash," Cam said.

"Anyway" Lauren blinked rapidly, as if staving off tears, "he was riding his bicycle on a quiet road, so I'm sure he felt safe. But someone drove off the edge of the road and hit him. They didn't even stop, and it wasn't a busy road, so he might've lain there for a while." She hiccupped.

Cam strode over to stand at her side. "I'm sorry you had to hear all the details just to report to us. It isn't an easy scene to contemplate."

In my head I was willing him to put his arm around her shoulders, but he didn't. Still, recognizing and honoring her emotions was a good first step.

"A hit and run?" I sent Cam a questioning look. "Could it have been deliberate?"

"There's always that possibility," he said.

Lauren pulled a tissue from the pocket of her dress and dabbed at her eyes. "Forgive me for being so emotional. It's just that I remember reading about Mr. Carson's tragic life in those files we looked through. It seems so unfair for one person to endure so much."

"Agreed," I said, crossing to give her the side hug Cam would not. *Or could not,* I reminded myself. Although I knew my boss had experienced other, albeit short-lived, relationships in the past, I didn't think any of them truly mattered to him. His feelings for Lauren appeared to be on another level; one which ignited his anxiety, creating a barrier between them.

Cam, who'd strolled back to his desk and picked up his cell phone, swiped through several screens. "The police have set up a perimeter to check any vehicles leaving the area where Carson was struck. They're also going door-to-door to discover if any residents saw the accident, but the area is sparsely populated, so they aren't pinning their hopes on that."

"I wonder if Carson often biked the same route? If so, he could've been targeted by someone who'd followed him previously," I said, "Given his grievances with the Stewart and Neri families, I don't think we can rule them out."

Lauren's dark eyes widened. "You really believe someone might have deliberately hit him?"

"We have to consider that option," Cam said. "Though I doubt it would've been one of our well-known suspects, like Duff Stewart or Lucas Neri, who would've done the deed themselves."

"Right," I said. "They would've hired someone. Easy enough to do if you have money, and less likely to leave traces."

"Because a hired killer could've found an old junker car, something without GPS or any other tracking devices, and also used fake plates," Lauren said thoughtfully.

"And dumped the car at a junkyard or somewhere else it's unlikely to be found." Cam set his phone back on the desk. "It'll be difficult to solve this case if that's what happened. Everyone will end up writing it off as a tragic accident."

"So unfair, especially if your theory is true," Lauren said, lifting her hands. "I know I seem awfully invested in the sad life of a man I didn't know, but it's just . . . Well, from what I've seen, Joeseph Carson had so many strikes against him even before the car crash. He came from poverty and fought hard to make a living and support his family. I know a lot of people like that. They work and struggle just to get by and then get hit with tragedy after tragedy." She shook her head. "No offense, Cam, but I don't think you can possibly understand what that sort of life is like."

I stared at her, my mouth half-open. It was the most Lauren had ever shared about her personal life and experiences, at least in my presence.

Cam shoved his hands in his pockets and rocked back on his heels. His face had paled, making his freckles stand out like tiny drops of blood. "You're right, Lauren, I can't comprehend living under those circumstances. Please forgive my ignorance."

"It isn't your fault," Lauren said, shoving the damp tissue back in her pocket. "But sometimes I just like to remind you that not everyone's enjoyed your enviable upbringing. Not to be accusatory, simply to help you understand the lives of others."

"And I appreciate that. I realize one of my flaws in terms of investigating cases is that I don't always view things the way someone less privileged might." He cast me a faint smile. "That's why it's so important to have Jane as a partner. She knows a lot more about the real world than I do."

"At least you admit that," Lauren said, with a sniffle. "Excuse me, I need to get back to the paperwork on my desk and leave you to your detecting." She managed a tremulous smile before crossing to the office door.

Cam and I remained silent as she paused with her hand on the doorknob. Turning slightly, she called out, "I meant to ask—is it OK if I get off work a little early today, Cam?"

"Ah, do you have a date?" I asked slyly.

"As a matter of fact, I do," Lauren replied. She flashed us a bright smile before leaving the room.

I wandered back to my chair and sat down, staring at Cam, who'd slumped into his own chair. Judging by his glum expression, it was clear that Lauren's announcement about a date—no doubt with Malcolm—had hit him hard.

It was time to change the subject. "There's one more thing I need to tell you," I said. "When I was leaving the fundraiser I ran into David Benton. We were both grabbing our coats at the same time. Anyway, David asked me about Vanessa Gale. She showed up at Benton House wanting to sell some Central and South American antiquities, and it seems she mentioned your name. David didn't entirely trust her, so he asked about our impressions of her."

"That is odd." Cam rubbed at his tensed jaw. "Did David buy anything?"

"No. He wanted more information on the provenance of the items. Vanessa seemed pretty desperate to sell something and said she'd gather more documentation and return."

"We should intercept her, if possible," Cam said.

"I already thought of that. I asked David to let me know when she showed up again and he said he'd text me." I folded my hands in my lap. "He even promised to keep her at Benton House until I could arrive. Or you and I, if you'd like to go."

"I think I'll leave that to you if you don't mind."

I started to say I actually *did* mind—I would have preferred back-up when confronting Vanessa—but clamped my mouth shut when I noticed the defeated expression on Cam's face. "That's fine," I said instead. "David will be there, so I won't be facing her alone."

"OK. Keep me posted." Cam reached for the report he'd shoved aside earlier.

I waited to see if he had anything else to say, but after a few minutes of silence I stood and made my way to the door. Since Cam's face was buried in the report, I didn't bother with a goodbye.

Rubbing my temples, which were starting to throb, I realized the problem—my caffeine addiction was reminding me I hadn't had any coffee yet. I hustled to the kitchen, where I ran into Lauren again.

"He didn't take it well," I told her after inhaling the heady scent of the coffee I'd poured into a ceramic mug.

She didn't ask what I was referring to, and I didn't explain. I was sure she already knew.

Chapter Thirty-Two

I'd just completed a batch of cataloging on Tuesday when my cell phone buzzed, alerting me to a text. I took a quick peek. It was from David.

Vanessa Gale just walked in. Do my best to keep her here until you arrive.

I immediately grabbed my coat and purse and hurried down the hall and out to the circle driveway, where I'd parked my car. High Point wasn't that far, but it would still take about twenty minutes to get to Benton House. I hoped that David could ensure that Vanessa didn't leave before I got there, but I knew it might not be the easiest task, especially since he wasn't likely to buy anything she was selling.

Benton House was located in a large, cream-colored brick building that looked more like a warehouse than a store. There wasn't a sign; the only indication of the purpose of the building was *Benton House* etched into the entrance door windows in an elegant script.

I'd finally learned after several visits that I didn't need to park on the street. A narrow alley that ran between the art and antiquities emporium and another furniture store led to a large gravel lot behind both buildings. It made sense—High Point hosted an international furniture market twice a year, drawing buyers and sellers from all over the world. The various businesses involved with this event obviously needed additional parking.

Except during Furniture Mart, Benton House didn't get many walk-in customers since most of their sales were by appointment. They typically kept the front doors locked and required visitors to ring the bell but, on a hunch, I tried the doorknob. As I'd hoped, David had left the front doors unlocked for me. *So it won't alert Vanessa,* I thought, opening the door as quietly as I could.

I didn't see anyone when I walked in, which wasn't unexpected, given the building layout. The store was arranged with a wide aisle that bisected the front half from the back. Along each side of the aisle, tableaus of furniture, art, and decorative items were arranged to showcase specific styles or eras. I hurried past sections displaying the rustic charm of American Primitive items, the extravagance of Victorian pieces, and the stark sleekness of Mid-Century Modern furniture and abstract art.

A bevy of chandeliers, lamps, and other light fixtures hung from the black metal rafters of the high ceiling. I knew everything in the store was for sale and items were often replaced with acquisitions. The Tiffany chandelier I'd once admired was gone, but an equally beautiful tiered chandelier dripping with crystals hung in its place.

The sound of voices drew me to the far end of the room. Standing between a reproduction of a nineteenth-century Parisian apartment and a dining room that would not have looked out-of-place at Monticello, David and Vanessa faced one another.

Vanessa was breathing heavily. "I brought the documentation, as you requested, and you still have no interest in my offer?"

"All I've seen are photos. I'd need to visit your warehouse or wherever you've stashed the items to get a good look at them." David's smile was more sardonic than friendly. "There's Photoshop and, heaven help us, AI now. Photographs aren't enough to prove authenticity, no matter how many documents you produce."

"If you don't agree to my offer now, you'll miss out. I'll sell the pieces to someone like Cameron Clewe instead."

"He won't buy them either," I said, approaching them.

Vanessa spun around, her eyes flashing. "What are you doing here?"

David calmly flicked an invisible flake of lint off his jacket. "I called her. When we recently ran into each other at an event, she confirmed my guess about Clewe's opinion of you. He doesn't entirely trust you, and neither do I."

"Is this an ambush?" Vanessa squared her shoulders. "I don't know what your boss has against me, Ms. Hunter. All I did was offer him an opportunity to find his missing father."

To his credit, David masked any astonishment he felt over this announcement. Although it was now common knowledge that Albert Clewe had been Cam's stepfather, most people didn't know the name of his biological father. They certainly weren't aware he was missing.

"How did you plan to do that?" David asked.

"Ms. Gale apparently knows Cam's birth father, whose name is Rafe Glenn, because they worked together in the past. As you're aware, she's a journalist, and Cam's father is a photographer who freelances for the National Geographic Society, among others." I crossed my arms over my chest. "Ms. Gale volunteered to mount a mission to locate Cam's dad."

"If Cam foots the bill?" David asked, sharpening his tone.

"Exactly." I met Vanessa's furious gaze with a lift of my chin. "You seem awfully desperate for money, Ms. Gale. First approaching Cam, then Mr. Benton. What's your real angle?"

"I visited Mr. Clewe in good faith." Vanessa practically spat out the words. "I wasn't asking for charity."

David frowned. "Maybe not, but I have to agree with Jane. Your attempt to sell me Peruvian artifacts reeks of desperation. Typically, such sales take time and due diligence, yet you expect me to hand over a great deal of money for items I haven't even seen in person."

Conflicting emotions flitted across Vanessa's face. "I'm simply trying to fund a rescue mission. Rafe may be in serious danger. The people who could be holding him prisoner . . ." Tears welled in her eyes.

"Are you that close to him?" David asked, after a questioning glance at me.

Vanessa sniffled. "We're friends, that's all. But when a friend is in trouble, you have to help, don't you?"

I dropped my arms to my sides, fists clenched. "It depends on what kind of trouble it is. To me, it sounds like we'd be better off talking to the Peruvian authorities. If he's in the hands of some drug cartel or gang of thieves, they'd be more equipped to rescue him."

Vanessa burst into tears.

Shocked, I shared a look with David. "What's really going on, Ms. Gale? Are you honestly afraid for Mr. Glenn, or"—a sudden idea occurred to me—"is this actually about your own safety?"

David slipped a white cotton handkerchief from his pocket and moved closer to Vanessa. "Here, take this. It's clean. And perhaps you'd better sit before you fall down."

"Thanks," she blubbered, pressing the cloth to her face as he led her over to one of the sturdier looking chairs in the dining room display.

Vanessa buried her face in her hands. Her shoulders heaved for a few minutes before she sat up abruptly, the handkerchief wadded up in one hand. "I have to get the money, one way or another. Yes, I'm in danger, but so is Rafe, and it's all my fault."

"Tell us what you did," I said, crossing to stand in front of her chair. "No more lies and evasion. Spill it."

Her pale skin blotchy and her light eyes rimmed with red, Vanessa looked up at me. "We were documenting the rainforest when a storm blew up, and we had to take shelter in a small cave. Inside the cave we stumbled over a cache of rare artifacts. At first we thought it was a legitimate find, but we soon realized that the items had been looted from another location and simply stored in the cave until they could be smuggled out of the country. Rafe planned to alert the authorities, of course." Vanessa inhaled a deep breath. "He's worked with several organizations over the years, helping to repatriate stolen art and artifacts. Of course, that meant he was on radar of the region's organized theft rings."

"They found you and kidnapped him?" David asked. "But why did they let you go?"

"To acquire the money to ransom Rafe." Vanessa wiped her nose with the handkerchief. "This particular ring of thieves saw the chance to double their windfall. They gave me photos of a few of the artifacts and ordered me to go back to the US to sell the lot." She sniffled. "Well, to scam someone into buying the pieces and then skipping town. Of course, I don't actually have them."

"Did they know about Rafe's connection to Cam?" I rubbed my throbbing temples.

Vanessa bobbed her head. "But I learned later, when I was holed up in Lima, waiting for further instructions. One of the gang's minions came to see me and told me they'd gotten that much out of Rafe."

David muttered a swear word under his breath.

"You mean they tortured him?" I asked, my voice rising to a higher register.

"Maybe. I don't know." Vanessa clasped her hands in her lap as if trying to hold herself together. "They could've simply asked him if he knew anyone who had the money to pay a large ransom," Vanessa said. "Rafe was definitely aware of Cam's status, even if he hadn't learned his son was still alive until Lily Glenn told him when Cameron was already a preteen."

"That sounds about right. Did Rafe share all this during one of your expeditions?" I asked. "Just how close were you two, anyway?"

Sensing my disapproval, Vanessa cast a resentful glance at me. "We were never lovers—Rafe always carried a torch for his lost love—but we did share a lot of stories and personal recollections. The truth was, Rafe didn't want to interfere in Cameron's life. He said the love of his life, Patricia, had married Albert Clewe to provide for her son's future. She knew Rafe would be traveling the world, unable to give Cameron a safe and secure home. She also wanted Cameron to inherit Aircroft, especially since Rafe was the son of the original heir, Calvin Airley."

"Still, as his father . . ." David shook his head. "I really don't get it."

I remembered the letters I'd discovered at Aircroft—messages sent from Rafe to Patricia after her marriage. "There was a lot more to it," I said, feeling a need to defend Cam's birth father. "Patricia had been ill, and Rafe was afraid she might relapse at any time. Rafe encouraged her to accept Al's proposal primarily because Albert Clewe could foot the bill for the expensive medical treatments she required. He was very concerned about her survival. It wasn't just about the baby or the inheritance."

Vanessa nodded. "And then Albert Clewe told Rafe his son died not long after Patricia passed away. Rafe was devastated by that news. It's one reason he became a globe-trotting photojournalist."

"He wanted to escape the pain." David appeared lost in thought. "He should've contacted Cam after Al's death, though. At least in my opinion."

"Like I said, he didn't want to interfere. Rafe's mother kept him informed about Cameron, including the fact that he'd inherited all of Al's businesses and properties. Rafe thought he shouldn't do anything to interfere with that."

Vanessa pulled the front edges of her flannel shirt together over her turtleneck. "I'm cold," she murmured. "May I have my coat?"

"I'll get it," David said, sharing a warning glance with me.

I assumed he thought she'd run off if given half a chance, and he was probably right. "So what was the plan? You'd get some money from fraudulently 'selling' the artifacts, then more money from Cam to fund a fictitious mission to rescue Rafe Glenn? But in reality, all the funds would be funneled to the people holding him hostage?"

"That's right." Vanessa rubbed her watery eyes.

David, returning with her navy wool peacoat, handed it to her. "Here. Now perhaps you'd better leave. I'm obviously not buying anything from you, and I don't trust you enough to hand over money for a possibly fake rescue."

Looking up at him, I noticed his mouth set in a straight line and his brows drawn together over his nose. He wasn't going to bend, no matter what Vanessa said. It was obvious he didn't believe her.

I wasn't so sure. Vanessa was a liar who was not averse to running a scam, but if her stated motive was true, we could be playing with Rafe's life by ignoring her. "Alright, put on your coat and come with me. Did you drive?"

"Uber," Vanessa said.

"Then I'll drive you where you need to go."

"Where's that?" Vanessa asked, as she slipped on her coat.

I looked her directly in the eyes, my expression grim. "Aircroft, of course"

Chapter Thirty-Three

David escorted us to the front doors. "Be careful," he whispered as I paused on the front stoop.

"Always try to be," I replied, offering him a smile.

He pointed his forefinger at me. "Text me when you're safely at Aircroft."

I nodded, then called out to Vanessa, who'd already reached the sidewalk, "Wait for me. I'm parked around back."

Vanessa slumped down in the passenger seat of my car and remained silent for most of the drive. I glanced at her from time to time, attempting to gauge her emotional state. But it was as if she'd donned an expressionless mask.

"I expect you to explain this situation to Cam, just like you did to David and me," I finally said. "He needs to hear all the details."

"What good will that do?" Vanessa replied in a hollow voice. "He'll probably call the police. Which wouldn't necessarily be a bad thing, for me. At least, if they arrest me, I'll be out of reach of my adversaries. But it won't help Rafe."

I parked in the circle in front of Aircroft. "You could've asked for the ransom directly, you know. Why create a false narrative about heading up a rescue mission?"

"I still thought I could get away clean, and I didn't want Cameron Clewe to involve the authorities," she said. "I believed if the thieves noticed signs of such interference, they'd kill Rafe without a second thought."

I sent David a brief text, then climbed out of the car. "Come on, let's get this over with."

Vanessa trailed me into the entry hall and down the corridor that led to Cam's office. Along the way we ran into Lauren, who was carrying a sheaf of papers. "Hello," she said, examining Vanessa with curiosity. "Are you looking for Cam? He's taking a walk around the garden. If you want to talk to him, head outside."

I rezipped my coat. "Thanks." Turning to Vanessa, I added, "We'll go out one of the back doors. Follow me."

Striding off toward the door just beyond the entrance to the office, I led Vanessa outside. The winter sun was bright in a clear sky, and I shaded my eyes to catch sight of Cam standing near the covered koi pond.

"Hey there," I called out, waving one hand over my head.

Cam glanced over, straightening to his full height when he noticed Vanessa. He took a few steps toward us.

"No, wait there," I said. "We'll come to you."

I took off at a fast pace while Vanessa lagged behind. At one point, she stopped in her tracks and I had to turn and grab her by the wrist to pull her forward.

"To what do I owe this honor?" Cam asked, shooting me a questioning glance before focusing on Vanessa.

"She has some things she needs to tell you." I gestured toward the marble stairs leading up to the pavilion. "You might want to sit down."

Cam raised his eyebrows and took a seat on one of the steps. "What about you?"

"I'll stay on my feet. I've already heard it," I said.

Vanessa shuffled over and sat next to Cam, although she maintained some distance between them. She stared at me. "Are you going to tell him?"

"Nope. That's on you," I said, taking a step back. "Go ahead. Nothing's going to change if you hesitate."

Vanessa cleared her throat and launched into the same story she'd told David and me.

Cam's expression froze halfway through her recital. He stared straight ahead, flexing and unflexing the fingers of his right hand. "The money was never for an expedition," he said, when Vanessa finished speaking.

"No. It was for a ransom," Vanessa replied, biting her lower lip.

"Then why not present it as such?" Cam turned his head to gaze at Vanessa, his eyes narrowed.

"I didn't want the authorities involved or even private investigators. I know you employ a few PI's from time to time," Vanessa said, squirming on her hard seat. "I worried that might anger the people holding your father."

"Really? Wouldn't they be happier to receive the money directly from me without it having to pass through your hands? After all, they had to suspect you might skim a little off the top." Cam stilled his restless fingers and pressed his palm against his upper thigh. "I know I would."

Vanessa gnawed on one of her fingernails. "It was the plan they proposed. I'm sure they had their reasons."

"Hmmm." Cam stared steadily at Vanessa, making her blink rapidly. "I do employ PI's, as you said. They dug up a little dirt on you, Ms. Gale. Something about a small but priceless gold sun disc that was discovered at an archeological dig but then mysteriously disappeared. Along with you, I might add. This was right before an organized gang of thieves hit the site. I imagine the thieves scoped it out ahead of time and were very displeased to find the disc already gone."

I swore under my breath. "Is that true?" I asked, glowering at Vanessa.

Ducking her head, she muttered, "Yes, but . . ."

"This ring of thieves you claim kidnapped my father, they're actually after you, aren't they?" Cam's voice was as cold as the wind biting my exposed fingers.

I thrust my hands into the pockets of my coat. I was dressed for driving, not loitering outside. "What were you planning to do? Grift money from Cam and David and then use it to pay off your pursuers? Then you'd do what? Disappear into the wilderness you know so well, in some far corner of the world?"

Vanessa lifted her head and met my disdainful gaze with a smirk. "You think you're quite intelligent, don't you? But you didn't figure it out. He did." She jabbed her finger at Cam.

"Yes, stupid me. I actually brought you here thinking to convince my boss that he should pay the ransom to free Rafe Glenn and save your life." I shook my head. "But you don't even know where Rafe is, or who's holding him, do you?"

"I doubt she even knows he's actually been kidnapped," Cam said, standing. "It was all a ruse, from start to finish."

Vanessa leapt to her feet. "My life is at stake!"

"Why not just give the thieves the disc?" I asked. "That would've been far simpler."

"I'd sold it already," Vanessa said.

I rolled my eyes. "Then give them the money."

"I don't have that either. I owed another debt. I used the money from the disc to pay that off," Vanessa said between gritted teeth.

Cam tapped a waltz beat against the paving stones. "Your life seems to be one big tangle, Ms. Gale. Robbing Peter to pay Paul. Not a very smart way to live."

"I'm not going to live!" Vanessa wailed. "Don't you understand? If I can't put together enough money, I'll be marked for death."

"I'm not sure how that's my problem," Cam said calmly.

I nodded in agreement with Cam's words. "The best bet is what you mentioned before—turn yourself into the police and let them protect you."

Vanessa stepped closer to Cam. "I do know your father, and I can assure you the last place he was seen by anyone was in a rainforest in Peru. Isn't that information worth something?"

Cam looked her up and down. "Not really. My PI's could probably figure out that much, given enough time. But your comments about an organized crime syndicate and their vendetta against my father because he was working to expose the theft and smuggling of looted artifacts is interesting. Perhaps I could spare a little cash for that intel, if you'd supply the names of the leaders of the organization."

"How would I know that?" Vanessa stilled her rapid breathing before speaking again. "I only dealt with a go-between; someone on a low level. I never met the higher-ups."

"There you are then—your new mission. One I'll happily bankroll. I'll even pay off your debt to get those crooks off your tail, and support your life in Peru." He held up his hand, palm out. "Not a lavish life, but comfortable enough. All you have to do is to uncover a few names."

Vaness clutched a fist to her heart. "I might as well shoot myself in the head. Even if I can get close enough to find out anything, do you know what those people do to snitches?"

"No, but I know what's going to happen to you if you decide to turn down my offer." Cam faced her, his expression grim. "You'll be arrested and end up in jail. No more traipsing the globe for stories; just four walls and a roommate who'll probably be more than happy to kill you if you cross her."

I watched this scene with a certain amount of awe. It always amazed me how cool and collected, not to mention slightly dangerous, Cam could become when the chips were really down. It was as if he automatically switched into robot mode, encasing his anxiety in steel.

"So what's it going to be?" I asked. "Cam's offer is more than generous, especially considering how far down the literal and metaphorical garden path your lies have dragged us."

Standing straight as a ramrod, Vanessa squared her shoulders. "Very well. I'll take the risk. But only after you prove you've paid my debt."

"I assume it's going to some offshore account? Just give me the details, and I'll take care of it. Then I'll buy you an airline ticket and give you a little money for expenses. You don't get more until you're in Peru and start sending me reports on your progress." He held out his slender fingers. "Deal?"

"Deal," Vanessa said, shaking his hand.

"Alright, head back inside and find Lauren Walker. You can provide her with the information about bank accounts and so on." Cam slid his fingers free of her grip.

"I don't want to explain this to anyone else." Vanessa's words held a hint of belligerence.

"You won't have to. Lauren isn't going to ask you anything." Cam said. "That's one reason why she still works for me."

Glaring at him, Vanessa tossed her head. "You'd better keep your end of the bargain."

"I will if you will," Cam said.

I waited until Vanessa strode back into the house before I said anything to Cam. "You do realize that she might disappear once you've cleared her debt, don't you?"

"Of course," he said, with a wry smile. "I'm well aware it's a gamble. But in this case, I'm willing to play the odds."

Still cold, I flipped up the collar of my coat. "Hopefully, they'll fall in your favor. But even if she does do a runner, you'll still have saved her life."

"And there's that," Cam said.

Chapter Thirty-Four

The following day, when Lauren stopped by the library, we chatted about the Vanessa situation.

"I gritted my teeth and sent off those funds yesterday afternoon," Lauren said. "I suppose Cam sees it as some sort of charitable act or a way to garner good karma, but I suspect I might as well have thrown that money in the koi pond. I don't think Ms. Gale is going to provide any actionable information."

"I know, but if there's even the faintest chance Vanessa can supply names associated with any gang who may have targeted Rafe, Cam has to take it." I twirled my pen between two fingers. "He needs to talk to Lily and Gordy. They should be given the news about Rafe, even if it's mostly supposition."

"I agree, but I don't know if I can convince him." Lauren playfully batted her eyelashes. "Would you like to try?"

"Why not ask me to climb to the top of the pavilion roof?" I smiled. "I'll give it a go, but don't expect miracles."

"I believe in you." Lauren pulled a folded piece of paper from the pocket of her lemon-yellow dress. "One more thing—when you talk to him, can you deliver this?"

I took the paper from her fingers and unfolded it. "An invitation? Didn't this come via email?"

"It did, and I could've forwarded it to Cam, but then I thought twice. I was afraid it might not get the best response if it just popped up in his inbox."

"A wise move," I said, staring at the words printed on the paper. It was from Duff and Sharon Stewart, inviting Cam and guests to a dinner party at their home on Saturday evening. "He's allowed to bring up to three guests? That's a little odd, isn't it?"

"I thought so too, so I immediately called Malcolm." Lauren ignored my smile over this confirmation of their connection. "He said his parents were trying to make peace. Well, mostly his mother, but it seems his dad is humoring her. They decided to throw a party that would celebrate some of his paintings and thought inviting a few extra people might help the atmosphere, since most of the other guests will be family and business associates. Malcolm asked that they include Cam, and by extension, you."

"You don't feel comfortable mentioning this to Cam?"

Lauren's lips twisted. "Not really. I'll be going as Malcolm's guest, so . . ."

"Say no more," I said. "Sure, I'll let him know. Even though he doesn't enjoy socializing, especially at someone else's house, he'll probably be willing to attend this particular dinner party. It'll be a great opportunity to observe many of the suspects associated with the Kimberly Ward and Gabe Neri deaths."

"That's what I thought too." Lauren focused her attention back on me. "I'm sure Cam will want you to accompany him. The other two guests? I don't know."

"I do," I said, thinking about the weekend. "Bailey is coming into town on Friday evening, so she'll be available. With Taylor Iverson as her date, that'll make the right number."

"Great, I'll leave that to you then." Lauren strolled to the door. "You can tell Cam I already have a personal invitation," she added, before leaving the library

I stared down at the paper. It still seemed odd that the Stewarts would extend an invitation out of the blue, but I wasn't going to look a gift horse in the mouth. With the knowledge we'd gained over the last few weeks, Cam and I should be able to conduct a more nuanced investigation of our various suspects.

Because of that opportunity, I knew I could easily get Cam to accompany me to the dinner party. Convincing him to visit Lily and Gordy was another story. Walking to his office, I rehearsed a few options in my mind. *If nothing else,* I thought, *I can appeal to his sense of honesty and justice. Whatever his feelings toward his long-absent family, surely he'll agree they need to know the latest news about Rafe.*

My first rap on the half-open office door elicited a "Come in, Jane," from Cam.

"How'd you know it was me?" I asked, crossing to the guest chair facing his desk.

"Lauren wears heels. You and Jenna don't, but Jenna wouldn't interrupt me at this time of day, and Mateo's footfalls are heavier. Thus"—Cam spread wide his hands—"it had to be you."

"A clever deduction," I said, sitting down.

"It wasn't really that difficult." Cam slid forward in his chair. "What brings you here this morning?"

"Two things. First, you've received an invitation to attend a dinner party at the Stewarts' on Saturday evening." I slid the paper across the desk. "I know it's not your favorite thing . . ."

"But it will provide a great opportunity to pursue our cases." Cam examined the invite with a frown. "Three guests? Of course, you'll be one, but I can't think of anyone else at the moment, except for Lauren. That still leaves one more."

"Two, actually," I said. "Lauren has her own personal invitation. But never fear, I have the answer—Bailey's coming on Friday for a visit so she can be number three, and her boyfriend, Taylor Iverson, can be four. Not to mention, Taylor can drive us. You don't even have to pay him this time."

"They're still seeing each other, then?"

"Whenever they can."

As Cam gazed down at the paper again, his eyes were veiled by his lowered lashes. "And Lauren received a personal invitation? From Malcolm Stewart, I suppose."

"Yes. He's actually the guest of honor. Apparently, his parents want to turn over a new leaf by celebrating his artistic achievements instead of disparaging them."

"That's good." Cam raised his head. There was an absent look in his eyes that told me his thoughts were occupied with something else. *Probably mulling over the idea of Lauren dating Malcolm.*

"You agree to go?" I asked.

"With you, Bailey, and Taylor, yes. You can tell Lauren to respond accordingly." Cam shoved the paper back across the desk. "You said there were two things. What's the other?"

"Can't you guess?"

Cam studied my face for a moment. "You believe I should visit my grandmother and great-uncle to inform them about my father's current situation. Or what we've been told about it, anyway."

"Bingo," I said.

Cam stood and began pacing the office. "Logically, I admit you're right, but we know so little at the moment. I've been debating about waiting until we have more concrete information to share."

"I don't think you can wait that long. Your grandmother's been worried for a long time, waiting for even the tiniest scrap of news. I believe she'd at least want to hear that it's highly likely her son is in Peru."

"I suppose." Cam stopped walking and turned to face me. "You'll accompany me when I visit them, I hope."

"If you want me to, of course I will. I'll even drive you to the farm," I said.

"Very well, I'll do it." Cam massaged one temple with his fingers. "It's already giving me a headache but I know it's necessary. So—when?"

"Tomorrow?" I suggested. "I'll call Lily to find out if that works for her, but I'm sure she'll be willing to adjust any other plans in order to see you."

"What about your daughter? You said she's arriving tomorrow." The hopeful lilt in Cam's voice was a dead giveaway that he wanted to put this visit off as long as possible.

"That's not a problem. Bailey doesn't get here until evening, and Taylor's picking her up at the airport. I'll be home in plenty of time to prepare for her arrival." I met Cam's glum gaze with a smile. "Cheer up, it won't be that bad. Anyway, I'll go now," I added, rising to my feet. "I need to tell Lauren about the RSVP for the dinner party as well as call Lily."

Cam strolled back to his chair and sat down. "Text me the time for the meeting after you speak with my grandmother."

"Will do," I said.

"And ask Lauren to order some flowers we can take with us tomorrow." Cam met my quizzical gaze with a sardonic smile. "I may be a social misfit, but I've learned that much."

"Good to know," I said before crossing to the office door.

Now if only you'd learn a few more things, like how to tell a certain young woman you like her, I thought as I exited the room.

Chapter Thirty-Five

On our drive to Gordy's farm on Friday, Cam shared some news concerning Joe Carson's death.

"They found the car," he said, reading from his phone screen. "As expected, it had been dumped in a junkyard."

"Maybe the police will still be able to pull some evidence off of it. Fingerprints and that sort of thing." I turned onto Gordy's driveway.

"Sadly, it had also been set on fire," Cam said. "It looks totally burnt out, judging by the photo on the news site."

"So, a thorough, professional, job." I grimaced as my car hit a pothole on the beaten-down dirt road. "Aren't you glad we're using my car? You wouldn't want one of your luxury rides bouncing down this lane."

"I do appreciate that," Cam said, still focused on the news on his phone. "It seems Carson didn't really have any family to speak of, or at least none still alive. One of the police officers set up a go-fund-me page to pay for his funeral and burial expenses."

"Again, such a sad life." I parked in front of the shed. "OK, we're here. Are you ready for this?"

"No." Cam held up a bouquet of sunflowers in his trembling hands. "Promise me, if I start having a panic attack, get me outside. I really don't want my grandmother and great-uncle to witness that."

"I don't think it will come to that." I climbed out of the car and waited near the front of the vehicle for Cam to join me. "Let's go. I'm sure Lily and Gordy are waiting anxiously."

"Not as anxiously as me," Cam muttered under his breath.

Standing on the slightly sagging front porch, I rapped on the door. It swung open after the second knock.

"Thanks so much for coming." Lily's slender figure was outlined by the golden-hued light from the hallway fixtures, lending her a spiritual aura. The effect was particularly striking where the light played off her white hair, creating a spun-sugar halo around her face. "I'm delighted to see you again, Jane." Lily stepped back, leaving the door open. "And you," she said, her gaze locked on Cam.

"Hello." He thrust to bouquet at her. "I came because I have news about your son."

"Your father," Lily added with a gentle smile. "Yes, Jane mentioned as much. Please, come in, both of you."

We entered the parlor and chose seats at either end of the sofa while Lily disappeared with the flowers. She returned with the bouquet arranged in a vase that she set on a console table placed against one wall and then sat across from us in the rocking chair. Gordy followed her a few moments later, carrying a tray laden with glasses of amber liquid and a platter of cookies.

"Who wants tea?" he asked.

"Sweet tea?" Cam scrunched up his nose.

"No, I always make it plain," Lily said. "There's sugar you can add if you wish."

"I don't," Cam accepted a glass of tea from Gordy but waved aside the offer of cookies.

I wasn't able to display that restraint. Setting my tea on the coaster placed on a side table next to the sofa, I took one of the napkins from Gordy's tray before grabbing two of what looked like homemade sugar cookies. "Thanks," I said, while Gordy turned away to serve Lily. As expected, she followed Cam's lead and refused anything to eat.

Gordy placed the tray next to the flowers on the console table. "You're missing out," he said, settling into his leather recliner. Clutching a glass of tea in one hand, Gordy held up a cookie in the other. "Lily made these, and she's one heck of a cook."

"I'll get one later," Cam said, placing his half-full glass of tea on the side table near his end of the sofa. He slid to the edge of the cushions and leaned forward, gripping his knees. "First, I want to be honest—you shouldn't get your hopes up. The truth is, I haven't found Rafe yet. All I know is that there's a good probability that he's somewhere in the Peruvian rainforest."

"That's quite a large area, and difficult to search." The light in Lily's blue eyes faded. "But I suppose it's better than having no idea at all."

"True, at least it's not the entire world," Gordy said.

Cam glanced at Gordy before fixing his gaze on Lily. "I know it isn't the news you wanted to hear."

"Any news is good at this point," Lily said. "I'm sure you've been spending a lot of time and money to locate your father, and I have to bless you for that."

"Trust me, he has," I said.

Color rose in Cam's face. "I've done what any decent person would do and will continue to do so. I promise to support the search until Rafe is found and brought home safe and sound."

"It's all I can ask," Lily said, with a beatific smile.

I snuck a sidelong glance at Cam, trying to gauge whether he intended to share the possibility of Rafe being in grave danger. I wasn't sure I should mention such a thing, but felt I had to reference Vanessa in some way. "There is a woman, a journalist, who knows your son fairly well. Apparently, they've often worked together on projects. She contacted us and has promised to share any information she might be able to collect from her acquaintances in Peru."

Without looking at me, Cam made a surreptitious slicing motion with the hand he'd laid on the sofa cushion next to him. "I hope she can help, but we can't base all our efforts on that," he said. "I'll also continue to engage other people to help with the search. I have several business contacts in South America. I hope to leverage their connections as well."

"That's wonderful, dear. I know you'll do your best. We'll stay out of your way and simply wait for more news. But in the meantime, Cam, I hope we can overcome our differences and become better acquainted." Lily's expression turned rueful. "You know, so many businesses and organizations are out there, promising to treat everyone like family, which always makes me cringe. Not all families are happy, and certainly many are not something to be emulated."

"That's the truth," Gordy said, sharing a look with her.

Lily sighed. "We always want to believe people will never harm their family members and, instead, will do anything to protect them, but bad things still happen. Sometimes it's deliberate, but often I think it's just an individual looking out for their own interests. It's easy to come up with excuses for why they don't spend time with their family, like they're too busy making the money they feel they need to provide for them. And they often justify certain actions and behaviors because they claim it's best for the family as a whole. You can have one member of the family harming another and feeling it's OK, as long as the family unit survives." She shook her head. "I believe that was my father's thinking, when he did the things he did."

Gordy glanced over at Lily, sympathy filling his eyes. "That would be a gracious way to look at it, I guess."

Lily cast him a gentle smile before shifting her gaze to Cam. "Anyway, dear, I've come to realize how much of a shock it was for you, meeting Gordy and me after so many years. I hadn't thought about what you must've felt when we crashed into your life, not really. Not until after Christmas dinner."

Gordy took a sip of tea and eyed Cam over the top of his glass. "Yep, you made things pretty darn clear then, son."

Cam sat back, crossing his arms to grip his elbows with both hands, as if giving himself a hug. "I apologize for my behavior that day. Sometimes my emotions get the better of me."

"Don't beat yourself up. That happens to everybody, one time or another," Gordy said.

"We do understand better now, dear. We've heard from some people"—Lily cast me a swift glance—"how hard your life was when you were young. We honestly didn't know you had such a difficult relationship with your stepfather. We should've known; we should've made sure to know, but we didn't. That blame falls on us."

Cam dropped his arms, switching his tension to a constant jiggling of his right leg. "I don't want to blame you, but it's difficult . . ." He sucked in a deep breath. "The honest, absolute truth is that I was terribly lonely. I didn't really have anyone who cared the least little bit for me, other than my nannies and a few kind cooks and housekeepers. My mom passed away when

I was very young, and my stepfather was always distant and cold. That is, when he was around, which wasn't often. To be fair, he wasn't cruel, and he gave me everything I needed, except . . ."

"Love?" Lily's eyes misted over. "I'm so sorry, Cam. I thought you were being well cared for. Once we knew that Albert Clewe had lied to Rafe and that you were still alive, Gordy kept tabs on you as best he could."

Gordy scratched at the stubble on his jaw. "Anyway, I tried. From the outside it seemed like you were healthy and were getting a good education along with every other opportunity. I wasn't connected to anyone who could provide me with any more details. I mean, I was a farmer. I didn't have anything to do with the people in Albert Clewe's social circle."

"I know it sounds like we're simply making excuses," Lily said, wiping her eyes with a tissue she'd yanked from her pocket. "And I also know there isn't any excuse. We shouldn't have abandoned you. And I should never have backed Rafe when he decided to go about his life without ever trying to fight for you. All three of us failed you, Cam. We can't make it up to you. All we can do is admit how wrong we've been and ask for your forgiveness."

The silence following this confession hung heavy in the air. Gordy busied himself with finishing off his tea, while Lily sat as still as a statue, staring at Cam.

For his part, Cam seemed to have shrunk into himself, his chin lowered and his shoulders hunched. I scooted over to him, close enough to lay my fingers on his forearm.

He didn't shake off my hand. "Well," he said, lifting his head and meeting Lily's gaze. "It will take time. I have some issues, you see. You haven't been around me long enough to notice, but as Jane can tell you, I'm something of a mess."

"I wouldn't say that," I retorted, tightening my hold on his arm. "Cam has a few social challenges, and, I'm sure, some undiagnosed OCD and anxiety. It isn't easy for him to deal with other people unless it's in a transactional, businesslike way. Regulating his emotions is difficult for him too. But that doesn't make him a mess; just someone who needs empathy and understanding." I offered Lily and Gordy a warm smile. "Like everyone else in the world."

Lily gaze flitted from Cam to me. "Thank you, Jane. I'm glad you're his friend."

"Yep, he's lucky to have you," Gordy said.

I shook my head. "It's not like I'm some saint. He's a good boss and trust me, he pays me well."

"All of which you earn, and then some," Cam said, surprising me by laying his hand over the fingers I'd used to clutch his arm. "And I do feel fortunate to have met you, Jane." He lifted his hand and held it out to Gordy and Lily. "I hope to feel the same about you one day, Gordy, and . . . Grandmother."

Hearing that title, Lily swallowed back a sob. "That will be a good day," she said.

Chapter Thirty-Six

On the return drive to Aircroft, Cam leaned back in the passenger seat and closed his eyes.

After several minutes, I decided to break the silence. "What are you pondering so deeply? Your grandmother's apology? Which was truly heartfelt, I must admit."

Cam cast me a glance from under his lowered lashes. "It was, but that's not what's on my mind."

"What else then?"

"I've been thinking about my grandmother's observations about families." Cam sat up and stared out the side window. "I think she made an important point that could affect the way we look at our current cold cases."

"That not all families get along?" I asked, as I turned onto Aircroft's long, paved, driveway. After leaning out the window and punching in the gate code, I threw a quick look at Cam. "I think that's a pretty well-accepted truth. It certainly applies to portions of the Stewart and Neri families, but I'm not sure how . . ."

"That's not the part that caught my attention," Cam said as I drove through the open gates and headed down the driveway.

"What interested me were her comments about individuals taking actions that hurt another family member, but the perpetrator rationalizes it because it benefits the larger family. She also mentioned the idea that we often tell ourselves we're doing something to help someone else when really, we're just helping ourselves."

I considered these points as I parked in the circle. "You mean, perhaps someone in the Stewart or Neri families murdered Kimberly or Gabe and justified it to themselves by saying it was necessary to protect the rest of the family?"

"Which means the perpetrator may not display much guilt, because they don't think they did anything terribly wrong." Cam jumped out of the car but waited for me at the steps leading to the main doors.

"If you think about that way, the family business could rank higher in some of our suspects' minds than another individual's life," I said, when I reached him.

"It could also add more suspects to the list." Cam opened one of the front doors and motioned for me to enter the front hall ahead of him. "Like Finn or Ainsley Stewart. Of course, they weren't even born when Kimberly died, but it's possible the two deaths aren't actually connected. I think either Ainsley or Finn might've been willing to kill Gabe if he posed a direct threat to the family fortune."

"True." I lingered in the hall, not wanting to lose this train of thought. "When we attend the dinner party we'll have to keep our eyes on all of them, young or old. Although I think we can eliminate Sharon and Soo Jin, and Ara, of course."

"I'm not removing anyone from the list, except for the girl," Cam said. "Just because the two wives don't seem that involved in business matters doesn't mean they didn't have other reasons to eliminate a threat."

"We'll be busy, then." I shook out my hands, which were cramping for some reason. Perhaps because I'd been gripping the steering wheel too tightly. "I assume you're including Malcolm Stewart as a suspect as well?"

"Of course. The fact that he's been at odds with his family for years doesn't exclude him. He says he and Gabe were close, but if his cousin threatened his inheritance or trust fund . . ."

Yanking off one glove, I waved it in his face. "Just don't mix up your feelings about him with the facts."

"I don't know what you mean. I harbor no feelings about him whatsoever." Cam turned to face the entry hall's curving double staircase.

"Hah! Now you're practicing that same comforting delusion Lily was talking about," I said to his back.

Striding off toward the hallway that led to his office, Cam didn't bother to reply.

* * *

When I got home on Wednesday evening, I was greeted by Vince and Donna, who were sitting in the Adirondack chairs on Vince's porch despite the chilly weather.

"Hi, were you waiting for me?" I asked when I'd reached them.

"Yes, and enjoying some hot chocolate," Vince said, holding up an indigo-glazed mug. "Come and join us."

"I'll get you your own mug," Donna said, scrambling out of the low chair. "Sit here next to Vince, he's the one who wants to share some info with you." She winked at me as she headed for the door. "He's practically bursting at the seams to tell you. We can chat later."

"How was your trip?" I asked, as I settled in the chair Donna had abandoned. "I don't think we've talked since you got back."

"Fun, for Donna and her friend, at least. I felt a bit like a third wheel." Vince grinned, indicating his acceptance of this state of affairs. "They had so much to talk about, it gave me lots of excuses to go on long hikes. Great for the old constitution." He patted his only slightly rounded belly.

"That's good. Now—what's this news you're excited to share? I'm all ears."

Vince leaned back and stretched his arms over his head. "It has to do with the accident involving Duff Stewart and his cousins."

"Really?" I shifted in the chair to look at him. "Have you heard what recently happened to the other driver?"

Vince nodded. "Poor soul. He was the poster child for bad luck, wasn't he? Living through a car crash only to be hit by a car while cycling." Vince set his mug down on the patio table between our chairs. "Tell me—do you and Cam suspect foul play?"

"We've considered the possibility." I told Vince about the confrontation at the fundraiser. "We wondered if someone had had enough and decided to shut him up."

"By hiring a killer to mow him down? Yeah, I wondered about that too, when I read the news about the car being found completely burnt out and dumped at a junkyard."

"The police don't appear to be pursuing the murder angle, though," I said.

Vince tapped his chin with one finger. "You never know. Sometimes they keep things close to the chest while they investigate, so they don't scare off the perp or push those involved into destroying additional evidence."

"I suppose . . ." I looked up with a smile as Donna bustled out of the house carrying a steaming teal mug emblazoned with the statement, *Journalists make headlines when they do it.*

"I can move," I said, taking the mug. "I stole your chair, after all."

"How could you steal it when I offered it to you?" Donna's broad smile illuminated her round face. "Stay. I'll pull over one of the folding chairs."

While she busied herself setting up her chair next to mine, Vince sent me an amused glance. "Don't try to outdo Donna's hospitality, Jane. That'll never work."

"I know, she's the queen of social graces," I said, earning a grin from Donna. "But, Vince, you were just about to tell me something about the car crash involving Duff Stewart and Lucas and Gabe Neri. What've you found out?"

"Right. Well, it's all based on gossip and rumors, which hurts my newsman's soul, but I thought it was interesting enough to share, given your interest in the case." He used his thumb to shove his drooping wire-rimmed glasses up to the bridge of his nose. "The gist of it was that there was one reporter covering the accident who thought there could have been a few shenanigans during the original investigation. He was at the crash site not long after the accident and told some of his colleagues that the final report didn't match what he initially saw."

"In what way?" I set my mug down and leaned forward.

"Something about the positioning of the vehicles, and the fact that Gabriel Neri was awake and talking, but the official report later stated he was unconscious when emergency personnel first got to him."

"Are you suggesting that someone tampered with the case?" I asked.

Vince shrugged. "Again, this is hearsay. But one of my old colleagues swears that the reporter on the scene was adamant about what he heard and saw, and shocked when he read the final report."

"You have to remember the power the Stewarts could wield, especially back in those days," Donna said. "They were some of the wealthiest people in the state and probably had a lot of influence over organizations like—oh, I don't know—the police perhaps?"

"Maybe Joe Carson was right," I said, talking more to myself than the others.

"I just thought you'd like to know. You can share the story with Cam, of course," Vince said. "If the case was rigged to find Lucas Neri innocent and Joe Carson guilty . . . Well, it wouldn't be the first time that money and power interfered in an official investigation. I know that because I've seen it happen myself."

Lifting my mug, I took a swallow of the hot chocolate and pondered this new possibility. "Roger Easton represented them. Duff, Lucas, and Gabe, I mean. He told Cam and me that he simply got involved to offer legal advice, but what if he did a little bit more?"

"The guy running for mayor of Winston-Salem?" Donna's deep brown eyes widened.

"That's the one," I said.

Vince's face radiated excitement. "If he was involved in a cover-up of that magnitude, where two people died, for goodness sake, he wouldn't want that information getting out."

"It could sink his political career," Donna said. "His chances of a mayoral seat would drop like an anchor in the sea."

"According to his cousin, Malcolm, and others, Gabe always claimed he couldn't remember anything about the accident. Maybe that was true, but what if, at some point later in life, he did remember?" I looked from Vince to Donna, noting their fascination with this hypothesis.

Vince held up a finger. "If there was corruption involved in the case, his recovered memory could've been seen as a real threat."

"Indeed. To quite a few people, all of whom were at the party the night he died," I said.

Chapter Thirty-Seven

After finishing my hot chocolate and discussing Donna and Vincent's recent trip, this time from Donna's point of view, I decided to head up to my apartment.

"I need to share Vince's very intriguing information with Cam," I said, demurring when Donna urged me to stay for dinner. "I have all evening, but I don't like to call him too late. I know he needs his solitude to recharge." I walked down the front porch steps but paused at the bottom to share another piece of news. "By the way, Bailey is coming for a visit. She'll be here Friday evening and plans to stay for about two weeks."

"Great," Donna said, clapping her hands. "I'll start planning a dinner party for you and Bailey and that handsome young man who drove her around last time. If they're still seeing one another, that is."

"They are, and that sounds like fun. But not this Saturday evening, please. We already have plans for that night." I waved goodbye, leaving them chatting on the porch while I climbed the stairs to my apartment.

I changed into my loungewear and plopped down on the sofa with my cell phone in hand.

"What do you think?" I asked Cam after sharing Vince's information.

"It certainly tracks with some of our other intel," Cam said. "If Gabe actually recalled the accident not long before he died, and realized there'd been a coverup, he could've felt the need to right the wrong. Perhaps he would've even considered supporting Joe Carson in an attempt to reopen the case. That scenario would not only destroy Easton's political career, it could also cause a scandal that might tank the Stewart and Neri family stocks."

"There was a lot at stake," I said. "More than enough to incite a murder."

"Absolutely. Of course, Kimberly's death doesn't seem to have any connection to the accident, so perhaps it was a suicide after all."

"What if she was driven to it, though? That wouldn't be murder, but it could still be a scandal. Gabe and Kimberly were close, so perhaps he knew enough to suspect someone in the family was pressuring her." Feeling a wave of exhaustion, I stretched out on the sofa. "We've already speculated that Kaden Ward might have been abusive, but what if the stress came from another source? Remember the rumor Vince shared about Ward being accused of plagiarism?"

"A rumor that seemed to come out of nowhere." The sound of Cam's fingers tapping the phone case filled the pause that indicated he was thinking through several possibilities. "We keep assuming Kimberly had a bad marriage, simply because she was suffering from anxiety and depression before she died. What if she actually deeply loved her husband, and at least part of her stress derived from someone threatening to destroy his career?"

"Which would mean what? That someone in her family was behind the rumor? Why would they do that?"

"Someone in her family or someone close to the family," Cam said. "Someone who was afraid she knew a dangerous secret. Somone who was using the threat to Ward to silence her."

"Knew something? About what?" I snapped my fingers. "The accident!"

"It's possible. I said the two cases might not be related, but what if they are? Kimberly was close to Gabe. She probably spent a lot of time with him in the hospital and throughout his recovery. Even though he later said he didn't remember anything, perhaps he talked in his sleep or shared his suspicion that something wasn't right."

"That could have driven her to find out more, for Gabe's sake, and her snooping into family secrets put a target on her back." I sighed. "This is all theoretical. How can we prove any of it?"

"By using our theories as a framework to develop questions to pose at Saturday evening's dinner party," Cam said. "I'll work on that, but jot down whatever you feel is important too, and we'll share our notes at work on Friday."

"Ah, so this is part of my job? Do I get a bonus for the extra time and effort?" I asked, infusing a lilt into my words.

Cam snorted. "As you told my grandmother, you already get paid quite well. Consider this as a contribution to a good cause."

"Alright, but if I have to talk to my union rep . . ."

Cam laughed and ended the call.

* * *

We spent an hour going over our suggestions for questions on Friday, consolidating them into a more concise, and precise, list.

After completing that task, I asked Cam if I could get off work early to prepare for Bailey's arrival, a request he was more than willing to grant.

By the time Bailey and Taylor arrived at my door, I'd laid out an enticing, organic, feast of vegetables, fresh bread and crackers, various cheeses, and fruit. It was the kind of dinner I also enjoyed, but rarely took time to put together.

"Mom!" My tall, willowy, daughter enveloped me in a hug the minute she entered the apartment.

Taylor strolled in behind her, carrying a bottle of something in a wine bag as well as Bailey's luggage. Despite her need to pay attention to her appearance, Bailey's stints performing in national touring companies of Broadway shows had taught her how to pack light, so at least Taylor hadn't had to lug too much stuff up the apartment stairs.

"Hey, Jane, good to see you again," he said, setting down a compact suitcase and small duffle bag before also giving me hug. "We're having that dinner together again before I thought we would."

"You two should be meeting up every Friday night." Bailey swept her long, wavy auburn hair behind her slender shoulders.

"Why? To keep us both out of trouble?" I asked, accepting the wine bag from Taylor.

"To make sure you aren't eating alone every night of the week," Bailey said, patting my shoulder. "You can hang your coat on one of the hooks by the door," she told Taylor as she handed him her padded jacket. "Mine too, if you would. Thanks."

I smiled. That was Bailey all over—assuming people would happily do anything for her, but always remembering to thank them. "Dinner is being served buffet-style," I said. "Once you're settled, grab a plate and fill it with whatever you want. I thought we could eat in the living room since the table is full."

By the time we'd all sat down with our plates and glasses of wine—Bailey and Taylor on the sofa and me in the rocking chair—I was almost too tired to eat. Almost.

"We'll have to make a special trip to New York to see our Broadway star's show," I said, waving a celery stick at Taylor. "What do you say? Will you drive me there in style?"

"Yes, ma'am." Imitating the stableboy in some period drama, Taylor tugged the lock of hair falling over his forehead.

"Maybe you should be the one on stage," Bailey said, elbowing him.

"Nope." Taylor pulled a grape off its stem and popped it in Bailey's mouth. "I'm going to write the words; you're going to do the acting."

"Have you written a play for her yet?" I asked, with a wicked smile. I knew Bailey wanted Taylor to create a character just for her, but I also knew he'd been too busy trying to acquire an agent to represent his first book.

"No, he hasn't." Bailey sighed dramatically. "It's all about the novel. The next great American novel, or the next great worldwide sensation novel," she said, whipping one hand through the air in a grand flourish.

Taylor appeared unperturbed by this jab. "Don't pay any attention to her, Jane. She's the one supporting me behind the scenes, always boosting my ego when I think the book is pure, unadulterated crap. This is just dinner and a show."

"I'm familiar with that," I said, shaking my head at Bailey. "I know you're teasing. You should be glad Taylor does too."

"We wouldn't have lasted this long if he didn't," Bailey said blithely. "I don't know why, but he puts up with all sorts of nonsense from me." She leaned closer to Taylor, laying her head on his shoulder. "I guess it's because he's such a sweetheart."

"Watch out or you'll get my red wine all over your extremely pretty but also very white sweater," Taylor said without shifting his position.

Bailey sat up, squaring her shoulders. "A sweetheart but not a pushover," she told me.

"I'm glad to hear that." I cast Taylor an approving glance. "Good work, sir."

He grinned and took another swig of wine.

Bailey placed her plate on the side table and folded her legs up under her, yoga style. "So, Mom, what's going on with your amateur sleuthing these days? You told me a little about the two cases you and Cam are investigating, but haven't given me any updates."

"We have more information, but no answers," I said. "Honestly, tomorrow night will be our best chance to glean more clues."

"Saturday evening? That's the dinner party at the Stewart mansion, right?" Taylor set his empty plate on the other side table and scooted a little closer to Bailey. "I'll be your chauffer, you know."

"And my date," Bailey said, tapping his nose with her finger.

Taylor arched his golden eyebrows. "You don't mind being seen with the help?"

"No, it's very romantic. *Lady Chatterley's Lover* and all that," Bailey said with a toss of her glorious mane of hair.

"Whoa, I'm not sure that's the reference I'd use, sweetheart," Taylor said, his cheeks blushed rose-pink. "Have you even read that book?"

Bailey made a face at him. "No, Mr. English Literature major, but I've seen the movie."

Taylor pressed a hand to his forehead. "Do you hear that, Jane? She's *seen the movie.*"

"I know, I've failed as a mother. Forgive me," I said, with a laugh.

Bailey elbowed him again. This time she was close enough to dig into his ribs.

"Hey, that hurts," Taylor said, pulling away from her.

"Just like your snooty comment." Bailey adopted the pouty expression she'd perfected for some of her early ingenue roles. "I know I'm not as *erudite* as you two, but I do have my own talents."

"Indeed you do, and plenty of them," I said, giving Taylor a wink. "We both think you're brilliant, don't we, Taylor?"

"Absolutely." Taylor stretched his arm around Bailey's shoulders and pulled her close.

She settled against him with a happy sigh. "I forgive you, then."

For the next hour we chatted about other things, including Taylor's writing and Bailey's recent theater experiences. That was always an amusing topic, since Bailey could recount the misadventures that had happened to her and others on stage in a way that never failed to elicit laughter.

"Oh, I have a funny story too," Taylor said, when Bailey finished sharing her hilarious anecdotes. "You can imagine, with all the people I drive around, that one or two passengers turn out to be pretty weird."

"Only one or two?" I said. "I'd call that a win."

"Yeah, but this latest one"—Taylor rolled his eyes—"was a real winner. He'd hired me to drive to his new girlfriend's house. Turns out he'd lost his license due to a DUI, but of course he didn't want to tell the girl that, especially since their relationship was brand spanking new. Anyway, we go along, like normal, with him in the back and me up front. But when we reached his date's apartment complex, and I parked in front of her building, he ordered me to switch places with him. Well, not exactly switch—he wanted me to get out of the car and hide while he climbed in behind the wheel."

"He wanted to pretend that he was the one driving?" Bailey asked, her dark lashes fluttering over her brown eyes.

"That was his plan. The thing was, then he had to lie to the girl and say he'd forgotten his wallet and didn't want to drive her anywhere in case he got stopped."

"Making it sound like he didn't want to involve her in a traffic violation?" Bailey shook her head. "Pretty clever, but wow, what a scumbag."

"What happened? Were you forced to wait around, hiding in the bushes or whatever, until you had to drive him home?" I asked, amazed by one more example of selfishness combined with stupidity.

"He probably would've liked that, but I'd had enough," Taylor said. "I got back in my car and texted him that I was leaving and would refund his return trip. Then he frantically texted back, asking how he'd get home. I just told him to walk or get a taxi and drove away."

"Good for you," I said. "Imagine trying to fool someone like that. Switching seats . . ." I sat up with a start. "Wait a minute, what if someone switched seats, not to con a date but to mislead the police?"

"Are you talking about that old car crash you're investigating?" Bailey asked.

"Could be," I said, my mind clicking a puzzle piece in place. "Very well could be."

Chapter Thirty-Eight

I called Cam on Saturday morning to discuss my new theory.

"It would make sense for Duff and Lucas to switch places before the police arrived since Duff was driving under the influence and Lucas had little to no alcohol in his system," Cam said. "Lucas, at least, would've been aware of how badly a drunk driving incident causing such devastation would affect the family businesses."

"Yes, but playing devil's advocate, they were both injured, although not as severely as Gabe. Could they have managed it?"

"It's amazing what people can do when adrenaline kicks in. You should be well aware of that." Cam's tone held a hint of irony, which I recognized as a reference to his own actions during our last major case. "Also, my research has uncovered the fact that neither Duff nor Lucas spent more than two days in the hospital following the crash. Obviously, they weren't so seriously injured that they couldn't have accomplished the switch, especially in the heat of the moment."

"OK, but what about fingerprints on the steering wheel? Surely the police checked that," I said.

"Of course, they would've done at least that much. But remember—it was a cold enough evening in December to allow for ice on the road. Both men were probably wearing gloves."

"Oh, of course they were." I pondered this possibility and its implications. "According to Vince, the reporter who was first on the scene said Gabe was awake and talking right after the crash, but it seems from the EMT statements that he was already unconscious when he was taken from the car. So it's possible Gabe saw the switch happen, yet only remembered it much later."

"The trauma might have given him amnesia," Cam said. "His mind could've blocked everything out related to the crash. Not to mention he was a drug addict for years, so perhaps the memories only returned after he'd been clean for quite some time."

"Malcolm claims that pain from his injuries is what hooked Gabe on drugs in the first place, but I wonder . . ." I took a second to compose my thoughts. "If he did see the switch, what Lucas and Duff did would've still been buried somewhere deep in his mind. Perhaps he always felt tortured by that knowledge, despite not consciously remembering the scene. Early on in his recovery, he may have conveyed that unease to Kimberly somehow, which is why she could've questioned the truth of the official statements from Lucas and Duff." I snapped my fingers. "Kaden Ward told me that Kimberly's mental state went downhill right after a family dinner where she had a private conversation with Gabe. Apparently Gabe was high on something that night. His pain medicine, I assume. Maybe he was rambling and expressed his suspicions about the accident. Even if he didn't remember it clearly yet, he might've said enough to clue Kimberly into the truth."

"Which might have driven her to confront Duff or Lucas, or even Roger Easton. If she did, she would've become as much of a threat to the family as Gabe was later," Cam said. "Which is why someone connected with the case concocted the plagiarism charge against Kaden Ward and used that to keep her quiet."

"Even if that's true, we still don't know who that was," I said. "It could've been Duff or Lucas or even Roger Easton."

"Or Macnamara Stewart." Cam's voice took on a thoughtful tone. "He was alive and still running the family businesses back then. I would be greatly surprised if he didn't know what had actually happened."

I hadn't considered that angle, but it made sense. "So how do we get anyone to give us more answers tonight?"

"Use our question list. It's still valid," Cam said. "You can focus on Ainsley, Soo Jin, Malcolm, and Sharon. Also, Easton, who probably won't want to talk to me after our last encounter. I'll try to use an innocuous discussion of business topics to segue into the questions I want to ask Duff and Finn Stewart and Lucas Neri."

"Unfortunately, Kaden Ward won't be there, so we can't get any confirmation of our theories from him."

"True, but I honestly don't think he was involved in either murder. If Kimberly's death *was* a murder, of course."

"It could've been a murder-by-proxy," I said. "Whoever threatened Kimberly, and we know someone did, given that note, knew how mentally fragile she was. They harassed and bullied and maybe even blackmailed her, using her husband's career, driving her to suicide."

"It's possible, although I'm not entirely convinced that she wasn't murdered by someone lacing her food or drink with excessive amounts of her prescribed medication."

"True enough. Since she died from an overdose of medicine she took regularly, it would've been easy to stage that as a suicide."

"I think we may have a clearer picture now, which should help direct our questions tonight. Right now, I need to do a little more digging into the information I've collected on the car accident to discover if we've missed anything. See you later," Cam said, before ending the call.

Later, after Bailey insisted on helping me choose an outfit and apply my makeup, we stood together in front of my full-length mirror. As always, Bailey looked beautiful in her burnt sienna dress. It was constructed from a soft wool that clung to her lovely figure without appearing too tight. She'd left her hair loose and only accented the dress with a gold pendant and drop earrings. I looked short and dumpy beside her, although she chided me when I made that observation.

"Don't be silly, Mom. That black dress fits you perfectly, and goes so well with your hair and silver jewelry. It's very elegant."

"As you say, less is more," I said. "Of course, less on you only highlights your beautiful looks."

Bailey, peering into the mirror, flashed a broad smile. "It does, doesn't it?"

"Maybe a little more humility," I muttered as I turned away.

Throwing her arm around my shoulders, Bailey gave me a side hug. "But my good looks had to come from somewhere. Your genetics had something to do with it."

I shook my head. "You don't look like your father or me. You're one of those chance genetic mutations. What do they call it in botany? Oh right, a *sport*."

"A good sport?" Bailey twirled in front of the mirror to get a view of the back of her dress. "That sounds about right."

"Very punny," I said dryly, just as I heard knocking on my front door. "That must be Taylor."

"He told me he was going to pick up Cam first, so I have an idea," Bailey said, as she crossed the room.

"What's that?" I asked while collecting my coat and purse.

Bailey grabbed her own tiny purse and oversized coat before opening the door. "You sit up front with Taylor and I'll sit in the back with Cam. That will give me a chance . . ."

"A chance for what?" Taylor asked, leaning in to kiss her before greeting me. He looked carelessly elegant in a brown suede jacket worn over a beige cable-knit sweater and dark brown pants.

Bailey flipped her shining fall of hair behind her shoulders. "Never you mind. I just have a few things to say to Cam, based on some info Mom's given me recently."

Locking the door behind us, I turned and eyed her with suspicion. "What info? Not anything to do with his personal life, I hope."

"We'll see," Bailey said, following Taylor down the stairs.

I sighed and trailed them to the car. Although I was dubious about Bailey's intentions, I couldn't stop her from jumping into the back seat with Cam. I reluctantly sat up front.

Cam appeared startled by this turn of events. "Hello, Bailey. Good to see you again," he said after giving her a onceover.

"Same." Bailey's cheerful tone made me even more nervous.

"I hear congratulations are in order," Cam said. "Your first Broadway starring role. That's wonderful."

I glanced in the rearview mirror. Cam's expression was wary. I knew he and Bailey had established a friendship-only relationship not long after they first met, so he wasn't acting anxious around a potential love interest. No, he had to sense her desire to talk about things he preferred to ignore. *Well,* I thought, *that is Bailey's specialty.*

"How are you, Taylor?" Cam asked. "I haven't seen you in a while either."

"You have Jane now, so you haven't needed me to take you anywhere you don't want to drive." Taylor turned his head to offer Cam a smile. "But it's good you decided to let me act as your chauffer this evening." He pointed at the small display screen on the dashboard. "The weather might be a little dicey."

"I thought it was just supposed to be light snow showers," I said, peering at the windshield.

Taylor shook his head. "That was earlier. Now they say the storm track has shifted and we might get some substantial accumulation. But don't worry—this car can handle snow, and its driver can too."

"Good to know," I said, buckling my seatbelt. "Normally, given the possibility of bad weather, I'd say we should send our regrets, but I don't want to miss this opportunity . . . I mean, this event."

"Mom wants to support Malcolm Stewart," Bailey said. "It seems they've become good friends."

"Have you?" Taylor cast me a sidelong glance. "I guess he must be an OK guy, then. Which is surprising, given his family."

Bailey laughed. "He's a sport. Right, Mom?"

"Right," I replied.

"A good sport?" Taylor asked, with a glance at her via the mirror. "Is it that funny?" he added, as he pulled the car out onto Bradfordville's main street.

After stilling her laughter, Bailey replied, "Sorry, inside joke."

We drove along making pleasant conversation for some time. I even thought Bailey had abandoned any plans to talk seriously with Cam. But I was wrong.

"So, Cam," she said, out of the blue. "Have you told Lauren how much you like her yet?"

Chapter Thirty-Nine

My sudden coughing fit was punctuated by sputtering from Cam.

"She isn't here with us, so I assume she has another date." Bailey sounded perfectly composed, as if she hadn't just dropped a bomb in the back seat. "I think you're making a grave mistake, Cam. It isn't every day that you meet someone you really care about who cares about you too. I know, because I'd had nothing but bad luck in relationships until I met Taylor." She blew a kiss toward the driver's seat.

Taylor kept his eyes on the road while the color rose in his face.

"I don't think that is any . . . any of your business," Cam finally choked out.

"Maybe not, but someone has to tell it to you straight, and everyone else is too intimidated to do that. Well, not Mom, but since you're her boss, it's a little awkward."

A quick glance over my shoulder showed Bailey casually examining her buffed nails. "I don't think it's the time or place for this conversation," I said.

"Why not? Does anyone think the situation will magically change?" Bailey asked. "Well, it won't. It requires action. Serious, thoughtful action from you, Mr. Cameron Clewe."

"I can take care of my own relationships, thank you very much." Cam's tone was taut as a violin string.

"Doesn't seem like it. Otherwise, Lauren would be your date, not Malcolm Stewart's."

"We don't have that kind of relationship," Cam said, anger clipping his words.

"I know, and that's a shame," Bailey replied. "It's clear to anyone who's been around you and Lauren that both of you are suffering from unrequited love. Which is very poetic, but also pretty useless."

"How much longer?" I asked Taylor.

He cast me a tightlipped glance. "About ten minutes."

"Not good, not good," I said under my breath.

"Bailey," Cam said after a long, uncomfortable pause, "I'm sure you have great intentions, but I haven't engaged you as my relationship counselor, nor do I intend to do so."

"Shame. I believe I could really help," Bailey said airily.

Silence descended again. I clutched my purse in my lap and kept my gaze fixed on the windshield. I didn't disagree with Bailey's opinions, but felt she'd chosen the worst possible time to spring them on Cam. We had to have clear heads to accomplish our goals tonight, and I wasn't sure that was possible for Cam now.

By the time Taylor parked the car under the portico in front of the Stewart home, I was ready to bolt from the vehicle. Leaning into Taylor, I murmured, "Wait outside with Bailey until I get Cam inside the house."

He nodded. "Understood."

Immediately after I climbed out of my seat and closed the door, I opened the passenger side back door. "Let's go," I told Cam. "We have a lot to accomplish tonight."

He crawled out of the car and straightened, his posture perfect, if stiff. "Do you remember the questions?"

"Do you?" I asked.

"Of course," he replied, through gritted teeth.

We walked side-by-side up the few steps to the massive front doors. Cam rang the bell while I cast a glance back at my daughter. Taylor had taken her into his arms in a close embrace. *Bless his heart,* I thought, *Taylor knows what to do. That's one very smart man.*

When the doors swung open, I greeted Ms. Warner and introduced her to Cam.

"Everyone's in the great room," she said. "I believe you know where that's located, Ms. Hunter."

"I do, but I'll wait for my daughter and her boyfriend. They're accompanying us."

Ms. Warner nodded and stepped back, allowing Cam and me to enter the imposing foyer. On this occasion it was devoid of flowers, but in their place were several easels displaying unframed paintings.

"Malcolm Stewart's work, I suppose," Cam said, examining a canvas alive with color. It made me think of a gorgeous blooming meadow.

"Yes. Duff and Sharon decided to show off his paintings this evening as part of their reconciliation with him. Malcolm said that was the purpose of this party."

"It's good work," Cam said, somewhat begrudgingly.

"Oh, look, Taylor. Paintings." Bailey sidled up beside me, brushing something off her coat.

"Is it snowing already?" I asked, collecting coats to hang in the closet.

"Just started," Taylor said. He smiled as Bailey excitedly tugged on his hand to pull him closer to the canvases.

"Aren't they fantastic?" She said. "When you sell your book and get disgustingly rich, Taylor, let's buy one."

"Sure. Why not?" Taylor said, his expression betraying doubt over the idea of becoming wealthy off his writing.

"The dinner is apparently being held in a large room in the back," I said after returning from the coat closet. "I've been there before, so just follow me."

I knew I was in the right place when we reached the great room, but it was arranged differently from when I'd attended the gala. A long, linen-draped table filled what had been open space before. *Or several long tables put together,* I thought, as a young woman dressed in a caterer's uniform approached us.

After asking our names she guided us to one side of the table. "Just look for your name on the placeholders," she said, her gaze fixed on Bailey. "Excuse me, but have I seen you on TV?"

"It's possible," Bailey replied, with one of the practiced smiles she shared with fans. "If you want an autograph, come and find me later. I don't want to disrupt your work."

The girl agreed enthusiastically. As she trotted back to the entrance to the great room. Taylor laid a hand on Bailey's arm. "The price of fame," he said, with a sly smile.

"Oh, you." Bailey batted his hand away, but then grabbed it as Taylor lowered his arm to his side. "Let's see. It doesn't look like we're seated together, Mom. Taylor and I are here, but I don't see your name anywhere nearby."

Cam, who'd strolled farther down the table, picked up one of the folded place cards. "Here," he said. "You and I are seated together, Jane."

As Bailey and Taylor sat down, I walked several seats down to join Cam. "Now we just have to see who's next to us to know if we'll have to spend a lot of time circulating later."

Cam pointed to the card on the plate beside mine. "Sharon Stewart. That will be helpful."

"And next to you?"

"Soo Jin Stewart." He pulled out my chair. "It looks like Malcolm must've have a hand in the seating arrangements. He has us flanked by the least combative of his family members."

Sitting down, I looked up and down the table. There were several people I didn't know, but I immediately recognized Roger Easton and Duff and Finn Stewart, who were all seated near each other. "Malcolm must've advised his mother on the arrangements," I said, as Lucas Neri joined the other three on our suspect list. "Now we just have to see who's seated across from us."

That question was answered almost immediately, with the arrival of Malcolm, flaunting his bohemian style in a long-sleeved white T-shirt, black leather vest and black jeans. Lauren appeared beside him, looking more beautiful than ever in a cream body-hugging dress with a bateau neckline that showed off her lovely neck and shoulders.

"Well, this is a pleasant surprise," Malcolm said, his blue eyes dancing with mischief. "Hello, Cam, I hope you're doing well. And hello, Jane. How nice that we'll be able to chat."

Lauren, sitting in the chair Malcolm had pulled out for her, shifted her concerned expression into a faint smile. It was clear that she hadn't been informed she'd be sitting across from Cam.

"Hi," she said, looking down at the table as Malcolm pushed in her chair.

"I'm afraid my dad might be planning on giving a speech," Malcolm said. "I thought I should warn you so you can save some wine for that delightful event."

"Your paintings are interesting." Cam met Malcolm's merry expression with a look of cool detachment.

Malcolm sat down, his grin fading. "Oh dear, *interesting*. The kiss of death for an artist."

"I'm sure Cam means he finds them to be excellent," Lauren said. "The truth is he loves anything he finds interesting."

Cam, placing his linen napkin in his lap, didn't look up at her. "I'm definitely intrigued by things I find hard to understand." Looking up, he fixed Lauren with a gaze that was equal parts disappointment and pain.

"I'm glad to see your family celebrating your artistic success at last," I told Malcolm. It was a futile attempt to dispel the tension.

"Well, my mother has always secretly supported me, haven't you, Mom?"

"It wasn't in secret," Sharon Stewart said as she sat in the chair next to me. "Heavens, Mal, people will think you were cast out into the alley to starve or something."

"Sorry, I was just having a little fun." Malcolm's gaze swept over his mother, me, and Cam. "Honestly, my family may not have loved my choice of career, but I can't say they cut me off. They've been very generous, financially."

Lauren shifted in her chair. "Hello, Ms. Stewart. It's nice to see you again."

His eyes darting from Lauren to Sharon and back again, Cam said, "I didn't realize you'd already met."

"Lauren joined us for dinner at my husband's favorite restaurant not long ago. We had I lovely chat then," Sharon said, offering Cam a smile. "I'm Sharon Stewart, by the way. I've met Ms. Hunter, but haven't had the pleasure of your company before, Mr. Clewe. Welcome."

"Thank you," Cam replied. "I'm surprised you recognize me, Ms. Stewart."

Sharon tipped her head and surveyed him for a second. "You look very much like your mother, who I met not long before she passed away, poor dear."

Cam blinked and turned to face away from us. "You'll have to share your memories of her sometime," he said quietly. "She died when I was so young, I don't remember anything about her."

"I'll be happy to." Sharon glanced over at the head of the table. "It looks like they're about to serve the appetizers now. I hope you all like oysters. It's one of Mal's favorites, and this evening is meant to celebrate him." She beamed at her son.

"Thanks, Mom," Malcolm said, his eyes misty.

Cam, who'd been staring in the direction of the multiple sets of French doors leading to a patio, turned to me with a frown. "I'm afraid Taylor's weather prediction was a bit off," he said. "That's not snow, it's ice."

Chapter Forty

"It concerns me to hear that," Sharon said, casting an anxious gaze at the wall of doors and windows. "I don't want anyone to have to drive home in an ice storm."

I studied her face, trying to discern if she had any particular aversion to ice on the roads, other than a natural fear of poor traction. "It can be quite dangerous," I said. "I'm sure your husband would agree."

Sharon's face expressed bewilderment. "What? Oh yes, he was in an accident involving ice on the road, but that was before we started dating. I honestly don't know much about it, other than the driver, his cousin Lucas, wasn't at fault." She leaned in closer to me. "Please don't bring that up with Duff and Lucas. They don't like to talk about it."

I nodded in what I hope was a sage manner. "I understand."

"Yes, it was just one of those youthful accidents," she said. Although I'd promised her nothing, she appeared relieved. "Oh, here's the food. Please enjoy."

I nudged Cam's foot under the table. He turned to me, eyebrows raised.

"Sharon doesn't seem to know anything," I whispered when he moved closer to me.

"Neither does Soo Jin," he whispered back, inclining his head in her direction. "Very sweet and completely uninvolved in Gabe's death."

I nodded and sat up straighter in my chair as the waiters began setting down small plates of Oysters Rockefeller. Enjoying that, as well as the subsequent dishes, I restricted myself to small talk with Sharon and my other tablemates.

It was after I finished a dessert of meringue and berries that I noticed the light in the room flickering. Looking up, I watched the chandeliers twinkle on and off.

"Oh no." Sharon shoved back her chair and go to her feet. "I'm afraid we might lose power. Excuse me while I check out the situation." She hurried off in the direction of her husband.

"Surely there's a generator," I said.

Malcolm, frowning, shook his head. "Not for the entire house. There's one that will keep the freezers and other kitchen appliances running, so we don't lose the stored food, but that's all. Or at least that's how it was when I lived here." He rose to his feet. "Stay put," he told Lauren. "I'm going to go and look for some flashlights and battery-operated lanterns."

At the far end of the table, Duff Stewart, flanked by Finn and Sharon, hit a glass goblet with a spoon. "Listen up, folks," he said. "It seems we might lose electricity. I deeply apologize for the disruption of tonight's event, but I feel I must encourage everyone to leave as soon as possible. My staff tell me that the roads are still passable now, but ice is accumulating fast, so I'd urge you to get home as soon as possible."

Sharon grabbed his arm and pulled him down where she could speak in his ear. When he straightened, he clinked the goblet again. "If anyone feels unsafe venturing out, we can put you up, but just be aware we may lose light and heat."

The great room erupted in a babble of voices. Most of the guests seemed inclined to depart, with tight clusters of them rushing for the corridor leading to the main entry hall. By the time Cam and I had joined Bailey and Taylor at their seats, the room had almost cleared out.

One person still seated was Lauren, who was apparently waiting for Malcolm to return. Cam, noticing her sitting alone, ran around to the other side of the table and took her by the arm.

"Come with me," he said. "You shouldn't be alone if the lights go out."

She looked up at him, conflicting emotions flitting across her face. Glancing over at Bailey, Taylor, and me, she nodded and acquiesced to Cam's demand, standing and allowing him to guide her back around the table to join us.

"Let's wait till the crowd dies down in the hall, then head for the main entrance," Taylor said. "I'll go outside and assess the situation before we even think about driving anywhere."

"That sounds like a logical plan," Cam said, finally releasing his grip on Lauren's arm. "As long as the rest of us stay together."

"Malcolm was supposed to get flashlights," Lauren said. "Shouldn't we wait for him?"

"Maybe he will and maybe he won't," Cam said. "The other Stewarts have already disappeared, along with Lucas Neri and Roger Easton, so he may have met up with them somewhere. I think it's best for us to head for the front hall now."

"Agreed." Taylor walked over to a spot where he could view the corridor. "It's clear so let's go."

We followed him, Lauren and I having to trot to keep up with Bailey, Cam, and Taylor's longer strides. "Hey, shorter people back here," I called out when the three of them got too far ahead.

The others paused at the entrance to the corridor. Just as we reached them and they turned to forge ahead, the lights went out.

All five of us swore at once, using different words and phrases, which made for an interesting cacophony.

"Who has a cell phone on them? We can use those like flashlights," Bailey said. "Unfortunately, I didn't bring mine because Taylor had one and my purse is so small . . ."

"I left mine in the car," Taylor said.

I frowned, remembering I'd planned to charge my phone before we left but had forgotten that in the rush to get ready. "Mine's in my coat pocket, but it might be dead."

"Mine's in Malcolm's car," Lauren said. "I don't like carrying it into parties. It makes me feel like I'm still at work."

"Well, apparently I left mine at work, or Aircroft, which is the same thing," Cam said.

"Wow, we'd all be kicked out of the Scouts," Taylor said. "So, option two—step sideways until you feel the walls. Then slide your hand along until you reach the end of the hall."

Fingers landed on my arm. "This way," Cam said, forcing me to sidestep until I banged into a chair rail.

"Wall contacted. I can take it from here. Go find the others." I shook off his hand and leaned against the comforting solidity of the wall for a moment. "Where are Lauren and Bailey?"

"Moving forward. Don't worry, Taylor's right next to me," Bailey said from somewhere farther ahead.

"I'm fine," Lauren called out, adding in a softer voice, "I really am. You can stop trying to guide me, Cam."

He muttered something I couldn't understand, but I heard Lauren's sigh and assumed it had been him chastising her for her stubborn independence.

Which is one of the things you like about her, I thought, glad the darkness hid my smile.

It was less pitch black once we reached the end of the corridor and stumbled out into the entry hall. Clerestory windows above the main doors cast a faint trickle of light from above, a blush of moonlight seeping through the storm clouds.

"I'm going to feel my way around to the front doors so I can check the conditions outside," Taylor said.

"You'll need your coat and other winter garb," I said. "Bailey, why don't you go with him and try to find our stuff in the coat closet."

"How will we know if it's ours?" she asked.

"Does it matter?" Cam's shadowy figure appeared next to me. "If we take the wrong things we can always bring them back, but we certainly can't go out without any protection from the weather."

"Good point, good point," Bailey said. "OK, Taylor, let's do this thing."

"What should I do?" Lauren asked as Taylor and Bailey's footsteps moved away from us.

"Stay here. Once Taylor checks out the car situation, we'll know if we can leave or if we have to stay."

Looking past Cam, I noticed another indistinct figure standing close to him. *Very close,* I thought, squinting to see any details. It almost looked like Cam had his arm around Lauren's shoulders, but I couldn't be sure.

A door opening alerted us to the fact that Taylor and Bailey had reached the coat closet. "I think I can figure this out," Bailey said, using her resonating stage voice. "I know what Cam and Mom were wearing, and my own stuff, of course. What does your coat look like, or"—her giggle held a slight tinge of hysteria—"better yet, *feel* like, Lauren?"

"It's long and dark, with a fabric that feels soft to the touch," Lauren called out. "And it has large buttons on the front."

"OK, I think I found it." Another door opened, this one ushering in a blast of cold air. Obviously Taylor was headed outside. "Be careful," Bailey told him.

A couple of minutes passed, then a strange dark form appeared in front of us. It took a second to realize it was Bailey, her arms laden with coats and other winter gear.

"Mom, I think this is yours, and Lauren this is yours," she said, handing over our coats. Fortunately, I'd stuffed a scarf in my coat pocket so at least I had something to cover my head. Pulling my cell phone from the other pocket, I pressed the button to turn it on, but as I'd feared, it was dead.

"Cam, your coat is hanging over my shoulder. Can you grab it?" Bailey asked.

"Just a minute." Cam moved in front of me and whipped the coat off of Bailey so quickly that part of the bottom edge slapped me in the face. "Sorry, Jane," he said.

I sneezed. "No problem. A good slap always wakes me up."

After we finished donning our outerwear, we huddled near the bottom of the grand staircase to wait for Taylor's return.

"We're certainly going to have an interesting story to tell about tonight," Bailey said.

I draped the scarf over my head and tossed the ends around and behind my neck. "You can add it to your collection."

"Absolutely. It will be . . ."

Bailey's words were drowned out by a scream from upstairs.

“That’s a man,” Lauren said. “It might be Malcolm. I need to go check.”

Cam grabbed her arm again. “The hell you will. Not by yourself, anyway.”

“No one can go anywhere without any decent light,” Bailey said. “I mean, you might get up the stairs by following the handrail, but how are you going to search what are probably a gazillion rooms on the upper level?”

“We can’t just stand here,” Lauren said.

“Alright.” Cam’s voice had taken on the robotic flatness that told me he had slipped into pure logic mode. “Lauren and I will make our way up the stairs. Bailey and Jane, wait here for Taylor.”

“OK,” I said.

Cam and Lauren disappeared into the dark shadows blanketing the stairs. As Bailey hummed an indistinguishable melody, I remembered something. “Flashlight,” I said.

“Yeah, what about it?” Bailey said.

“I remember now. When I was here the first time, to collect the books Cam had purchased, I ran into Gabe Neri in the library. He gave me a tote bag that belonged to Sharon, mentioning she liked to stash such useful things everywhere because the house was so big. He also said there was a flashlight placed on the middle bookshelf. If it’s still there, I can take it upstairs to help Cam and Lauren search for the source of that scream.”

“Where’s the library?”

“Off of this main hall. Somewhere over there.” I pointed to my left, even though I wasn’t sure Bailey could see my gesture. “I’m going to follow along the walls like before until I reach that room.

"I'll come with you," Bailey said.

"No, you stay. Someone needs to be here to explain things to Taylor when he gets back."

I started my quest, shimmying along the wall until I reached an opening. *No, that was to another hallway,* I reminded myself as I reconstructed a mental image of the foyer. I crept across the open area, arms out, until I touched a door jamb. More sidestepping with my palm pressed against the wall landed me at another opening.

This had to be the library. I peered inside, almost shrieking when I noticed a dark figure slumped in one of the armchairs.

It looked like Gabe when I'd first met him, but it couldn't be. Gabe was dead. I paused in the doorway for a few moments to slow my racing heart, then walked into the room.

"Who's there?" asked the ghostly figure.

"Jane Hunter," I said. "I came to find a light."

"You probably won't find that here," said Lucas Neri.

Chapter Forty-One

I approached the chair, shuffling my feet so I wouldn't trip on some unseen object.

"Someone told me that Sharon stashed items in the double-sided bookcase that divides this room," I said. "A tote bag, a flashlight, maybe a few other things."

"Was that someone my brother?" Lucas asked.

"Yes." I felt around until my hand landed on a hassock. I sat down, facing Lucas, whose features I could barely make out in the dim room.

"I came looking for the same thing, but couldn't put my hands on it," Lucas said.

"So you decided to sit in the dark?"

Lucas stirred in his chair. "I was going to leave, but the sound of ice hitting the window forced me to drop into the nearest chair, and so here I am."

The pain lacing Lucas's words was palpable. "You were in an accident that involved ice," I said.

"Yes. It wasn't falling at the time, but I still associate ice storms with that night."

I considered my next words carefully. “Are you talking about the night you were driving home from a party and Joseph Carson crossed the center line and hit your car?”

The silence following my question left me wondering if I’d gone too far, too fast.

“That was the official story,” Lucas said at last.

“Is there another?”

More silence, punctuated by a few deep breaths.

“I have a feeling you know the answer to that,” Lucas said. “You and the very inquisitive Mr. Clewe.”

“Why would you think we know anything?”

“Come now, Ms. Hunter,” Lucas said. “Did you honestly believe someone like Duff Stewart or Roger Easton or yes, me, wouldn’t have looked into your previous sleuthing activities when you started snooping around people like Roger and Kaden Ward?”

“Were you the one who sent me warnings? There was some hired thug who stopped me outside a café, and at least one anonymous phone call.”

“No, but I’m not surprised that someone took that route to scare you off.” Lucas chuckled humorlessly. “But you don’t scare easily, do you, Ms. Hunter?”

“I’ve raised a theater-crazed teenager and now I work for Cameron Clewe,” I said.

“Point taken.” Lucas leaned forward, lending more definition to his shadowy form. “What do you think you know? I’m curious.”

I curled my fingers until my nails bit into my palms. “We don’t know for certain. We only suspect. But I believe our theories fit with all the rumors as well as the facts.” I straightened my back and squared my shoulders. “You switched places, didn’t you? You and Duff Stewart. He was drunk and you weren’t, so you thought it was best for the family, and its fortunes, if you became the driver."

Lucas gave me a slow clap. "Bravo. You know, I always thought it should've been obvious, but no one seemed interested in challenging the official report. Except for Joseph Carson, of course, but who was he?"

"A nobody, compared to the heirs to the Stewart and Neri empires?"

"Ah yes, the mighty Stewarts and their lucky lapdogs, the not-quite-as-powerful Neris." Lucas made a disparaging noise. "I believed it back then. Upholding the family honor and all that. It took many years for me to realize how I had been used, and how my brother had been misused."

I inhaled sharply. "Are you saying you want to come clean after all these years?"

"Perhaps. Gabe's death was the final straw. Like Malcolm, I don't believe he overdosed. I think something he ate or drank was laced with the drugs."

"Well, well," said a voice behind me. "How foolish of you, Lucas, tattling our family secrets to Ms. Hunter, who, if I recall correctly, likes to play Nancy Drew."

"I'm a little old for that," I said, rising to my feet. Stretching my arms behind me, I backed slowly, feeling the air for any obstacles.

Duff appeared to be holding a flashlight, but he hadn't turned it on. *Because he wants the cover of darkness.* It wasn't a comforting thought.

"It's a waste of time," he said. "Especially now that Joe Carson is dead. Who's left to care which car crossed the line? I told Gabe, when he came to me whining about feeling guilty after remembering more about that night, that no one would care about his far-too-late confession. Unfortunately, Carson was still alive at that point, and Gabe foolishly tracked him down and tried to convince him to team up."

"So you put a stop to that," I said.

"Let's just say I arranged a little accident." Duff snorted. "He wouldn't shut up. We even offered him money in the past, but that wasn't good enough."

"To be fair," I said, surprising myself with how calm I sounded, "Money couldn't bring back his wife and daughter."

Daughter . . . A chill rushed up the back of my neck. "What did you do with my daughter and her friend? I can't believe they wouldn't be looking for me by now."

"The beautiful young woman and her Swedish-farmer boyfriend?" Duff huffed. "He came back in from his car with his cell phone, so he used that as a flashlight and they both headed upstairs. As they explained it to me, they wanted to help another couple who'd gone up without a light."

"They didn't ask about me? I've been gone for a while."

"Oh, when the girl said you'd gone to the library to search for a flashlight, I told them to go on; that I'd find you and let you know where they were. I guess, unlike you, they weren't particularly suspicious of me."

"I hope you don't plan to silence Ms. Hunter like you did Carson," Lucas said. "Because you'll have to get rid of me too. I'm done covering for your crimes."

"Let's not get carried away. I have no intention of making a preemptive strike," Duff said. "Ms. Hunter is an intelligent person. I'm sure she—and her boss—will realize that sharing their intriguing but hard-to-prove theories with the authorities will only create a serious problem for them, not to mention those they care about."

"The kind of problem Joe Carson faced?" I asked.

"Could be. Why test it? Just keep your thoughts to yourself and everything will be fine. That goes for you too, Lucas."

"Did you kill Gabe?" Lucas asked, his voice rough as sandpaper.

The lamps flickered and then flared on, making all three of us blink against the sudden light. Duff, caught in the glare, looked sweaty and red-faced.

"Did you?" Lucas asked again.

"No. I had nothing to do with that," Duff said, brandishing his flashlight like a baton. "As far as I know, he overdosed."

Lucas stared at his cousin with a stony expression. "What about Kimberly? I know she picked up some clues from Gabe and was looking into our accident, convinced something was wrong, although she didn't have enough evidence to convince the police."

Duff's eyes widened. "No, what do you think I am? I'm no saint, but I draw the line at harming family."

"That's a lie," Lucas said, spitting the words like nails. "You hurt me. I was required to carry a secret all these years, compelled to continue lying to cover your mistake, forced to live with guilt and with the fear of our crime being discovered. How can you say you've never hurt your family? Look what you did to Gabe, always sneering at him for his addiction, something that was partially your fault. And then there's Malcolm, who's never done anything well enough to satisfy you. Don't you realize how your constant put-downs have hurt him?"

"Don't pretend you're a saint," Duff said with a sneer. "You helped me send all those anonymous threats to Kimberly, and you certainly didn't stop Roger from spreading the plagiarism rumors about Kaden. You were around enough to see how much her mental state had deteriorated, yet you did nothing to help her. In fact, like me and Dad, you made sure the police wrote off her suspicions and concerns as the ravings of madwoman."

"I'm not proud of that." Lucas said in a hollow voice. "I thought we could simply drive her into a psych ward, not to suicide."

"Well, let me relieve your mind on that point. We can't definitely say it was a suicide; that's just the story my father concocted to prevent any further investigation. To be honest, I suspect Kimberly was so confused the night she died that she forgot how much medicine she'd taken, and took more. And then became so drugged out that she took more again." Duff lifted his hands. "We'll never know for sure."

Lucas flashed a bitter smile. "That suits you, I suppose. You can pretend it wasn't our fault, just like the car accident."

I moved a little closer to the door. "This is all very illuminating, but may I leave now? I want to join my daughter and friends and make sure everyone is OK."

Duff pointed the flashlight at me. "Just remember what I said. Keep your lips zipped and you won't have any problems. Otherwise . . ."

I gave him a noncommittal bob of my head and hurried over to the door, pausing only when I heard Lucas swear. Looking back, I watched him stand up.

"For heaven's sake, stop talking like some two-bit gangster, Duff. It's disgusting." He walked forward until he and his cousin were face to face. "Am I to believe that Gabe died the same way as Kimberly then?"

"No, I'm afraid another Stewart took up the torch in that case. Both Finn and Ainsley were present when Gabe threatened to team up with Joseph Carson and go to the police. His long-lost memories . . ." Duff cleared his throat. "My children would've realized what a danger those memories posed to the family business and might've acted accordingly. I don't know for sure, and frankly, I don't want to."

"That's convenient, as well as terrifying. Don't you care that one of your older children is a monster? Or they both are?" Lucas took a step closer. "Honestly, I wouldn't blame Ms. Hunter or Mr. Clewe for remaining silent, given the Stewart family's capacity for violence, but I make no such promises. I'm old, unmarried, and childless, and my brother is dead. I have nothing to lose. Prepare yourself, because soon, very soon, I'm going to tell the truth, the whole truth, and nothing but the truth."

I left them facing one another like fighters in the ring and rushed out into the entry hall and up the stairs.

Chapter Forty-Two

"Bailey, Cam, Lauren," I called out as I ran down a white hallway lined with doors. "Taylor? Where the heck are you guys?"

One of the doors flew open and a man stormed out. I prayed it was someone I wanted to see, like Malcolm, but that hope was instantly dashed.

"Another troublemaker." Roger Easton faced me, arms akimbo and his legs spread wide, halting my progress down the hall.

"Where are my daughter and Cam and the others?" I asked. "They rushed up here because we all heard a man's scream. Who and where is he?"

"I'm afraid your daughter and friends interrupted a small family quarrel," Easton said. "They're fine, but we've confined them for their own protection."

I wanted to wipe the smugness from his face with a dirty rag. "What do you mean, confined them? That makes no sense. Take me to them, please."

"Very well, as you wish." Easton gestured toward the open door. "Go in, if you must, but remember, it's your choice."

I stalked past him. The door opened on a small foyer, with closets on either side. Another door, this one closed, was directly in front of me.

Grabbing the doorknob, I turned it and shoved, slamming it back against the inner wall.

I gasped. With their backs pressed against the far wall, Bailey, Taylor, Cam, and Lauren sat on the floor. In front of them, sprawled face down, lay Malcolm. A crimson ribbon of blood trickled from his temple to pool on the plush white rug beneath him.

The scene was incomprehensible until I turned to my right and noticed a woman standing just beyond Malcolm's feet. She was dressed in an elegant purple dress and diamond jewelry and she was holding a gun.

"Ainsley, what in the world . . . ?" When I caught Cam's eye he gave an almost imperceptible shake of his head.

"Jane Hunter," Ainsley said, her lips curling back to show her teeth. "Welcome to the party. Why don't you head over there and join your entourage? Just don't try anything. I'm not opposed to shooting your lovely daughter, although my real target is Malcolm."

I stumbled across the room, careful to keep my distance from Malcolm's head. When I reached the far wall, I allowed gravity to take over and collapsed against the wall next to Cam.

"This is insane," I muttered.

Bailey, her eyes wide as a startled fawn, gazed down the row at me, her finger pressed to her lips. Taylor, sitting beside her, looked like he was battling the urge to leap up and body slam Ainsley.

"You may wonder why everyone is being so compliant," Ainsley said, waving the gun through the air as if it were a conductor's baton. "Well, here's the thing—I've informed them, as I'm telling you, that if anyone tries to take me down, I will shoot Malcolm before they can reach me. Being the bleeding hearts they are, they haven't moved a muscle."

"Why are you doing this?" I asked, keeping my voice as calm as possible.

"Well, you see, my little brother decided he wanted to ruin my life, and I decided he wouldn't." Ainsley stretched out one leg and poked the sole of Malcolm's shoe with the tip of her pointed-toe heels. "Don't worry, he's just knocked out, not dead. Yet. Anyway, Malcolm didn't appreciate how I was willing to do what he, Finn, and Dad wouldn't. Of course, Cousin Lucas wasn't even included in the equation. It all fell on me. And Roger, who isn't as gutless as the rest."

"Ainsley knows how to protect what's important," Easton said, crossing to stand beside her. "Family, heritage, inheritance, and those who've stood by you when you needed them the most."

"You killed Gabe," I said, my stare pinpointing Ainsley. "Your dad admitted you were present when Gabe confessed his plan to team up with Joseph Carson and reveal the truth to the police. He'd finally, clearly, remembered the crash, and realized the official report was all wrong. The lies his brother and Duff told had convicted an innocent man, but the guilt wasn't just on them."

She smirked. "How interesting. I suppose you and Cam figured this out while playing detective?"

"That much and more," Cam said. "I'm sure it became clear to Gabe that the evidence had been tampered with by someone who had access to legal professionals and the police. It wasn't just the Stewarts' money and power that swayed the authorities, it was also the influence of a respected attorney." He turned his intense gaze on the man standing with Ainsley. "Someone like Roger Easton."

"I was simply an advisor." Easton adjusted his tie as if he had not a care in the world.

"Nonsense," I said. "I'm sure you were the mastermind. Do you expect us to believe that Duff Stewart or Lucas Neri, or even Macnamara Stewart, were clever enough to pull off such a feat?"

Cam narrowed his eyes. "You were the one who started that rumor, weren't you? The accusation of plagiarism against Kaden Ward. You had it spread around to smear him, and to control Kimberly, who'd gotten far too interested in the details surrounding the accident."

"She committed suicide," Ainsley said. "Roger had nothing to do with that."

Easton didn't respond, but his smug expression was confirmation enough for me.

"If she did, he drove her to it. Even if not, he and Lucas and your father certainly threatened her to the point where she accidentally overdosed," I said. "Ask him. Maybe he'll tell you, since you're partners in crime. I suppose he was also in on your scheme to kill Gabe by lacing his food or drink with enough drugs to cause an overdose."

"Don't be ridiculous." Ainsley shot Easton a sidelong glance. "Roger helped me afterwards, but I was the one who took the action necessary to save the family."

"Ainsley, there's no point in saying more," Easton said, smacking her left arm. "Discretion is the better part of valor, you know."

"What now?" Lauren asked, earning a sharp look from Cam. "What can you do at this point? Shoot us all and call it what? An unfortunate accident?"

Ainsley aimed the gun at Lauren's forehead. "You shut up. I know your sneaky ways. Going to work for Cam and then trying to seduce him. How's that turning out for you?"

Words I'd never heard him use flew out of Cam's mouth. I reached over and pressed my hand over his clenched fingers. "Lauren has a point. What's your end game? You were clever enough to kill Gabe and make it look like an overdose, but this is different."

"It's insane, is what it is," Bailey muttered. Taylor slid his arm around her shoulders and pulled her close.

"I was only going to deal with Malcolm, who also threatened to inform the authorities about what he knew. Even if it wasn't the whole story, it was likely enough to reopen several cold cases that needed to stay on ice, so I had to put a stop to that. Then you all had to blunder in," Ainsley said, her voice and expression growing increasingly petulant. "Yes, now I have to think about what to do with you, so how about you all sit there quietly while I consider my options." She plopped down on the bed behind her, still holding the gun in her right hand.

Roger Easton watched her, a calculating look in his eyes. I studied him, now convinced he'd been the one behind the threats from the stranger and the anonymous phone call. *That's his method,* I thought. *The puppet master behind the scenes. I've no doubt he encouraged Duff and Lucas in their lies and pushed them to hound Kimberly to death. Not to mention starting a rumor that almost destroyed her husband's career. He uses others, letting them do the dirty work while he pulls the strings.*

I leaned in closer to Cam. "Easton will let Ainsley take the fall," I whispered.

"I know," he said, keeping his voice low. Glancing at Lauren, he must have realized how close she was to crying because he reached out, with only the slightest hint of hesitation, to take her hand.

Startled, she opened her mouth as if to speak, but then simply entwined her fingers with his without saying a word.

Malcolm was still unconscious, which made rage fill my chest. He was Ainsley's brother and yet she was totally unconcerned whether he lived or died. Even if she'd planned to kill him, allowing him to slowly bleed out was incredibly heartless. I stared at her, racking my brains to think of a way to disarm her without endangering Malcolm or anyone else.

I could jump her, falling on the gun. If she shot anyone it would be me, and hopefully my weight would pin her down long enough for the others to take control of the room. Weasel that he was, Easton would probably run rather than fight.

Taking a deep breath, I nudged Cam. "Don't move," I said, leaping to my feet more easily than I'd ever have expected. *God bless adrenaline,* I thought as I barreled toward the bed. I desperately didn't want to die, but for the sake of Bailey, and Cam, and Lauren, and Taylor . . . I flung myself at Ainsley, who shrieked just as a resounding bang rang in my ears.

I didn't feel anything and, looking down, didn't see any blood. Ainsley shoved her palms against my chest and I fell backward, landing on my butt with a thud.

She pushed me with both hands, I thought, totally bemused. *She doesn't have the gun.*

The glint of metal caught my eye. The gun lay on the floor, at the edge or the rug. As I contemplated crawling to grab it, Taylor dove forward and buried it under his body.

Bailey screamed his name and ran to him while Cam rushed over, hand outstretched, to pull me to my feet.

As I'd expected, Roger Easton was attempting to make a hasty exit, but his way was blocked by Lucas and two burly men from the wait staff. The bang I'd heard must have been the door being kicked in.

Lucas grabbed Easton by the collar. "You aren't going anywhere," he told the frantic lawyer. "I've already knocked out Duff with the flashlight he was trying to use on me. Don't worry, he'll live. Sharon and Finn are with him now." Lucas yanked Easton's tie. "So believe me, I'd be more than happy to hold you here while these fine gentlemen throw a few punches at your smarmy face."

Ainsley appeared to be in shock. "What?" she said, casting her gaze wildly around the room. "I don't understand."

"You've been bested," Lucas said. "The police may be a little late due to the weather, but they're on their way, so just sit down and wait for them like a good girl."

"A good girl?" I snorted and glanced over at Bailey, noticing that her normally bright face looked wan and washed out. Realizing how close I'd come to losing her, I ran over with open arms, only to be pulled into a three-way hug by Taylor.

"You were amazingly brave," Bailey whispered in my ear. "Don't ever do anything like that again."

"I'll certainly try not to," I said, my voice cracking like brittle pottery.

With one waiter holding onto Roger Easton and the other clamping his hand around Ainsley's wrist, Lucas took the opportunity to check on Malcolm. "He's awake," he said. "Groggy but awake. No, stay down," he added when Malcolm rolled over and tried to sit up. "Emergency personnel will be here soon. You should stay still until they can look you over."

"Is everyone . . . ?" Malcolm squeezed his eyes shut, as if the light hurt.

"Everyone is OK." I pulled free from Taylor's and Bailey's arms to get closer to him. "Don't worry, just rest."

"Lauren?" Malcolm said.

I turned to check on her so I could make a proper report but, stunned by the vision of Cam and Lauren locked in a close embrace, I immediately looked away, focusing on Malcolm again.

"She's fine," I said. "Absolutely, perfectly fine."

Chapter Forty-Three

A week after the events at the Stewart home, forever known in Bailey's collection of disaster stories as the *Ice Storm Extravaganza*, Cam hosted a much more peaceful, and successful, dinner party.

When the meal was over, he invited us to gather in the music room. "I'll put on some of Al's cherished records, and we can chat and listen to recorded music the way it's supposed to be heard, on vinyl."

Additional chairs had been set up in the room, most of them harder than I liked. But I knew the two comfortable armchairs were reserved for Lily and Gordy and chose my seat accordingly.

"I loved your story in the paper, Vince, I'm glad they let you write it even though you're retired." Bailey, sitting cross-legged on the floor next to Taylor, gave Vince a thumb's up.

"Someone had to provide justice for Joseph Carson," Vince said. "I simply wrote the truth. With help from Lucas Neri, I might add."

Donna scooted her chair closer to his and patted his knee. "Bailey's right, your article was honest and thought provoking.

It was the best way I can think of to right the wrongs done to that poor man."

"His criminal conviction will be overturned, too." Cam leaned back against the needlepoint cushions of the Victorian settee moved in from a guest bedroom. "I asked one of the lawyers I keep on retainer to handle the case."

Lauren, sitting beside him, smiled at him with a look blending approval and pride. "It's the least we can do. He didn't deserve to have his reputation tarnished."

"He lost his wife and child and then had to suffer at the hands of the legal system." Lily's eyes grew misty. "Whenever I think I've had a difficult life, I remember others dealing with much worse. At least I still have family." Her gaze shifted from Gordy to Cam. "I dearly appreciate that blessing."

Taylor looked up, Lily's words obviously raising a question in his mind. "Is there any news about your father, Cam? Bailey's filled me in on that scammer, Vanessa Gale, but I haven't heard anything more beyond that."

Cam shook his head. "Nothing yet. Vanessa is back in Peru, but she hasn't provided any solid leads yet."

"She probably won't," Gordy said, with a huff. "She's the kind who'll take your money and run."

Cam lifted his hands. "What can I do? I know I'm playing the odds. But don't worry, I'm not pinning all my hopes on Vanessa Gale. Now that I know my father's attempts to do the right thing may have entangled him in a ring of thieves and smugglers, I've directed a couple of private investigators to pursue that angle. They're touching base with Peruvian law enforcement agencies as well as hunting down any leads on their own. I have hopes"—he cast Lily a determined smile—"we'll be able to bring Rafe home soon."

"What's going to happen to that Neri fellow?' Gordy asked. "Lucas, isn't it?"

"Malcolm, who's improving daily, thank goodness, told me the authorities don't have any plans to charge Lucas," I said. "The accident happened so long ago, and while he lied back then to cover for Duff, it's Duff who caused the crash by driving under the influence. Not to mention, Lucas is willing to be a witness for the prosecution."

"You mean he'll testify against Duff?" Bailey yawned and laid her head on Taylor's shoulder. "Sorry, that delicious meal made me sleepy."

"Lucas will probably also have to provide evidence against Ainsley and Roger Easton," Cam said, in a grim tone. "My police contact told me it's like roaches in a bucket right now. Duff, Ainsley, and Roger Easton are scrambling to get out of the hole they're in by climbing over each other. Everyone's looking to cut a deal, but I don't think anyone but Lucas will be granted immunity."

"Do you think the DA can make anything stick to Roger Easton?" Taylor frowned. "I know guys like him are slippery as eels."

"Yeah, he claimed he was simply an advisor," Bailey said. "And I suppose it's true he didn't actually kill Kimberly Ward, even though he probably did orchestrate a smear campaign against her husband."

"Even that will be difficult to prove at this late date," Cam said. "Easton is clever. He may have wanted Gabe dead, but he didn't give him the overdose, so unless Ainsley can prove he was in on that murder, he's likely to get off on reasonable doubt."

"Especially since it was Duff who hired someone to hit Joe Carson. Easton may have advised him to do so, but he didn't set that up." I sighed. "It's possible Ainsley or Duff may have kept texts or emails or other evidence of Roger Easton's involvement in their crimes, but we won't know that until the trial."

"Trials," Bailey said, rolling her eyes. "And people claim it isn't safe to live in New York. I think this place is worse."

I pointed my forefinger at her. "Watch it. This is my home you're talking about."

"Mine too," Taylor said, bumping her with his elbow.

Vince's serious expression put a damper on the lighter mood. "As far as Easton is concerned, there are no guarantees he'll get what he deserves, but at least his political career is dead in the water."

"Not just dead; probably dead and sunk to the bottom of the Marianus Trench." Donna pinched her nose and imitated an old dance move.

"I hope so. He's done a lot of damage. The Stewart family is shattered, and he's one major reason why." Lauren's voice overflowed with sympathy. "I feel sorry for Sharon and Finn, as well as Finn's wife and daughter. All this is going to haunt them for a long time."

"Forever, I expect," Lily said, sorrow dimming her eyes.

She's remembering her own loss, I thought. *The violent death of the man she loved must still bring her pain.*

Gordy crossed his arms over his chest. "I suppose the older son will manage the family's business concerns now. I'm not sure that Neri fellow will be allowed to be involved. The stock holders will probably put the kibosh on that."

"Yes, now Finn has to take over and clean up the mess." Cam shook his head. "I don't envy him."

"At least, like Malcolm, he wasn't involved in any criminal activity," Lauren said.

"That we know of, anyway." Cam took her hand in his. The fire in his eyes as he gazed at her made even a nonromantic like me experience a hot flush.

"There you go." Donna grinned. "Already looking for another case to solve."

"Don't say that." Bailey sat up and playfully made the sign against the evil eye. "Don't give them any ideas."

"I daresay no one needs to give Cam or Jane ideas," Lily said, the lilt in her voice betraying her amusement.

"Very true." I shared a wry smile with Cam. "These cases just seem to find us. We don't go looking for them, we simply turn around and there they are."

Bailey exhaled a dramatic sigh. "Just like stray kittens and puppies. And like people who take in every stray, Mom and Cam can't seem to say no."

I shrugged. "At least it keeps us out of trouble. No, wait . . ."

The resulting laughter drowned out Cam's carefully curated background music.

Acknowledgments

My sincere thanks go out to all those individuals whose skills, talent, and dedication have helped A Deadly Clue become a published book . . .

As well as all who have supported me on my writing journey:

My agent, Frances Black of Literary Counsel.

The Crooked Lane Books team, especially my editor, Faith Black Ross.

Cover designer Alan Ayers – thanks for the gorgeous artwork gracing all of the Hunter and Clewe covers!

My friends and family, especially my husband, Kevin, and my son, Thomas.

My fellow authors, many of whom have become friends as well as colleagues.

Bookstores and libraries – who not only support my work, but also provide me with wonderful reading materials.

The bloggers, podcasters, Youtubers, and other reviewers who have mentioned, reviewed, and promoted my books.

And, as always, my lovely readers!